AF176801
PART ONE

The One Who Rocked Away

SERENE STONE

one

UNEXPECTED PREGNANCY & UNWANTED PERFECTION

Behind the cameras and in the shadows, Serene Stone tried to tone down her goofy smile when Nolan's gaze swept the studio, only stopping when his brown eyes landed on her. He rubbed the scruff on his jaw and winked at her. Of the many talents and skills her husband had, one of them was still his ability to take her breath away. Her chest puffed with the knowledge that he was hers and she was his, just as the first interviewer climbed the square platform and sat on the leather chair across Nolan.

Serene pointed at the young woman in a checkered pencil skirt and a black tucked-in blouse. Returning Serene to the shadows so he could step into the spotlight, Nolan stood up and extended his hand to the young journalist sharing the platform with him — the platform, but not the spotlight. All the bright lights casted a glow on Nolan and him alone.

What was new?

The wide-eyed glimmer in the interviewer's eyes wasn't new to Serene either; it was one familiar to her after having recognized it in the faces of multiple die-hard fans graced by Nolan's presence. In most cases, it would take them a few seconds simmering in disbelief that he was right there with them before they could respond to the most mundane of interactions with him. This situation wasn't an exception, as the young woman's lips quivered when Nolan let go of her hand.

"It's such a pleasure to meet you, Mr. Stone," she said, her tone high-pitched enough for Serene to wonder if that was her normal voice. "I am such a huge fan."

"Yeah?" Nolan placed his palm against his chest. "Thank you for supporting my music."

"Your song, *Broken Wings*, is the theme song of my recent break-up. I wouldn't have survived the heart-break without your music."

"It's been a while since I sang that song." Nolan returned to his seat, but cast a glance at Serene. "It's been a long time since I've experienced heart-break, not that I'm complaining. I'm glad the song helped you out. But—" he clasped his hands together "—we're here about the movie."

"Yes!" The interviewer jolted to attention, perhaps remembering that she had limited time to do her job, because there were other reporters waiting. "Is it time to start?" She looked at the cameraman nearest Serene. "Are we rolling?"

He gave her the thumbs up.

The interview began, and the press junket for *Staged* was officially underway. Nolan's role in the film was, in fact, a minor one; he had only one musical number with the lead actress. They had asked him to join as more of a publicity stunt, but after initial viewings conducted for critics and the press, early reviews had raved about his performance.

Once again, like he had done many times in his life, Nolan Stone had stolen the show.

Serene yawned as she sat in the director's chair they had provided for her. This was going to be a long day, and if Nolan hadn't asked her to be there, she would have preferred to be anywhere else. This was his scene, not hers, and yet, despite how at ease he appeared to be, interviews like this still made him nervous. Not necessarily because he didn't know what to do or how to respond — that part came naturally to him — but because of experiences with female fans who mistook the smolder in his eyes and the easy smile on his face as a sign of interest. With his wife around, it was easier for him to deflect and remind anyone interested that he was spoken for.

It wasn't like Serene could blame them. She had married a handsome, charismatic, and talented man, who had laid claim of her heart as early as six years old. His relaxed posture and his friendly nature were an intoxicating contrast to his brooding ballads and intense stage presence. After over a decade taking the musical industry by storm, Nolan Stone was still breaking barriers and showing everyone he was capable of so much more than they had already seen.

"One last question, since I'm almost out of time." The interviewer was giddy as she shifted in her chair. "What's it like to have everything in your life be so perfect? Perfect career, perfect wife, perfect daughter — a perfect life. It must be such a dream-come-true to be living your life."

Serene winced. Perfect? The word stung her ears and hit her chest. Why did this stranger's line of questioning feel like such an affront to her? What was wrong with being perceived as perfect? Serene held back a scoff. The fact that it wasn't true, for one. They were far from perfect — most especially her.

What Nolan said in response made her flinch in her seat. "Perfect, huh?" He snickered and brushed a hand against his dark hair as he slouched in his seat. "I wouldn't say perfect, especially as far as my career goes. I've had my share of ups and downs, but I have an amazing life that I wouldn't exchange for anything. Playing a part in Staged, for example, is one of those things that is unexpected and enjoyable for me, but I'm nowhere near perfect in this movie. Just ask my co-stars."

"Most of us think you're perfect for the role you played, and we're dying for more."

"You're too kind." Nolan smiled. "Let's just say that for me, my wife and daughter are as close to perfect as it gets. Everything else is a bonus."

The scoff she had withheld earlier escaped Serene's lips. After everything that had happened over the past year, how could anyone refer to her as perfect? Even Nolan. Serene recoiled at the movie reel of her failures playing scene-by-scene through her mind. Losing control of the company she had founded. The media firestorm over her most recent art exhibit, which had been inspired by her two miscarriages. The constant sense of not measuring up to expectations placed upon her as wife, mother, and daughter.

Perfect.

Serene flinched. Her husband was being kind. As close to perfect as it gets? Maybe that could be true of their daughter, but certainly not of Serene.

The next reporter awaiting her turn stood a few feet away from where Serene was sitting. Serene bristled when the woman raised a brow at her. When the first interviewer left and this new one took her place, the first question thrown at Nolan was, "Mr. Stone, are you and your wife having any trouble at home? Is there any reason your life, wife, or daughter may be less than perfect? Is the version of perfection you portray more than a little *staged*? And did that have something to do with why you did so great in a role for a film called *Staged*?"

Serene's mouth dropped open. Where were these questions coming from? Had Serene placed her husband in the hot seat when all she had done was mindlessly scoff at the word, *perfect*?

The hum of the engine masked the sound of Serene hurling out her lunch on the cramped toilet of her husband's tour bus. Interview questions from her husband's press junket were haunting her as she rose to her feet, put the toilet cover in place, and wiped her mouth. She stared at her reflection in the mirror as she gripped the platinum-plated sink. On the edge of it was yet another thing mocking her for being anything but "the closest thing to perfect".

A pregnancy test.

The device was taking its precious time to inform her of a result she wasn't certain she wanted to see. The bus slowed down and went over a hump. With one hand, she held on to the wall of the cramped bathroom to steady herself. With the other, she pressed two fingers on the pregnancy test to keep it from falling over and going down the drain, which was exactly what Serene felt was going on inside her — like she was spiraling down a proverbial drain of disappointment and failure.

And it was all because of that word.

Perfect.

The word made bile rise to her mouth, spreading bitterness on her tongue.

Over the years, Nolan had done everything in his power to protect Serene from the media and keep their marriage and family life private, but these past months, Serene could sense it coming — the scenario she had dreaded since marrying Nolan. Time would come when the world would figure out that Nolan had married a failure.

Bitterness consumed her. Was she jealous of her own husband? What a ridiculous idea, and yet, there it remained, accusing her of vanity, selfishness, and shallowness — so much so, she could almost believe it to be true. Her life was evidence enough.

While her wonderfully talented and passionate husband continued to skyrocket to legend status in the music industry and was now dipping his toes into the film industry, everything Serene had built continued to fall apart. She had lost control of her creative incubator, *Thrive*. People she had nurtured and trusted had betrayed her and edged her out of the company she had built from the ground up. The worst part was she had let them, because she couldn't take the pressure any longer. From the stress of losing her company, she had suffered her second miscarriage after Lily Red's birth.

Heart-broken by the miscarriage, she had poured her heart into paintings featuring the sanctity of life in a mother's womb. When she launched her first art exhibit in years — *Live.* — the social backlash had blown her away. Multiple art reviews criticized her exhibit as a scathing commentary against a woman's right to choose what to do with her own body. She had been confused at first, but eventually realized that people had taken her art as a stance against abortion. When asked point-blank about her views, Serene couldn't lie. She had explained that her paintings were reflections of her personal experiences with her two miscarriages, which only fueled her convictions against taking the life of children in the womb. Her response wasn't met with welcome arms, and the art circles that had once embraced her "artistic genius" had turned on her and labeled her a bigot.

Serene could have dealt with the blows had things been going well back home, but the church her father was pastoring — the one she had grown up attending — was falling apart.

And now, this.

Serene covered the result of the pregnancy test with her finger as she sat on the covered toilet seat in hopes of avoiding having to tell her husband and daughter. She didn't need to see what the pregnancy test was saying, because she already knew. She would have to go through all of it again. The morning sickness, the anticipation surrounding the pregnancy, and the gnawing fear that again, it might not turn out well. How would she deal with once again seeing the pain and disappointment in Nolan's eyes?

Serene gripped the edge of the sink to brace herself for the inevitable. The symbol on the pregnancy test reflected a positive result. Serene tightened her hold on the sink as a whirlwind of conflicting emotions rushed through her — none of it anywhere close to the joyous expectation that should accompany news of life forming in her womb. Tears rushed down Serene's cheeks as she opened her mouth wide to let out an inaudible yell as a means to release the pressure building up within her.

The walls of the trailer were too thin. Nolan's and Lily Red's laughter as they played together was a mocking juxtaposition to the waves of fear and grief crashing over Serene inside her temporary cocoon — the bathroom stall of her husband's luxury tour bus, which was yet another status symbol of her husband's burgeoning success.

As she listened to her family's joy, Serene gritted her teeth. She needed to get a grip, so she allowed herself a few more seconds of authentic pain and grief and counted down from ten to one before squaring her shoulders and rising to her feet. She clutched the pregnancy test in her hand and wiped her tears away before practicing her smile in the mirror.

"You're knocked down, not broken," she said to her reflection. "Nolan will be fine. You didn't ruin his career by scoffing. Stop overthinking." Her hand tightened around the pregnancy test. "This is a good thing. This is hope."

"Serene? You okay in there?"

The concern in her husband's voice transformed her practiced smile into something more genuine. Despite everything she was going through, she accessed her gratitude over all the blessings God had given her. Her hardened fist gripped the pregnancy test as she stood to her full height, nodded at her reflection, and slid the door open to walk out of the stall with an image as close to perfection as she could pull off.

"Mom!" Lily Red's raven ponytail bounced as she waved a piece of paper in the air. Her green eyes sparkled as she coaxed her mother to approach her. "I wrote a song."

"You did?!" Serene tried to sound excited as she slid herself into the booth across from her husband and daughter. She laid her fist on top of her lap, the test still enclosed within.

"Dad helped too, but I made up all the words." She held her glittery pink pen and started scribbling something on her paper. Seven years old, and she was already showing as much talent and potential as her father.

"That's amazing, poppy." Serene's eye twitched, her heart overwhelmed by the addition of the pride she felt over her daughter.

"You okay?" Nolan mouthed at her.

She nodded at him. His smile made her draw a breath. The ache in her chest grew. What was happening to her? How could she feel this way when she had these two amazing people in her life? When had she become so ungrateful?

"Do you want to listen to the song, Mom?" Lily Red's wide, gap-toothed grin could have made the most hardened, humorless cynic grin right back.

"I would love to." Serene exaggerated her nods. "Go ahead. Sing the song for me."

"These are the lyrics." Lily Red slid the sheet of paper across the table. "You can sing along, too."

Serene's smile was starting to make her cheeks ache. Nolan's intense stare made her bristle. She forced a wider smile. "Nolan, what?"

His dark brow rose as he set his guitar aside. "What's going on, love?"

Serene blushed. Was she so transparent, or did he just know her that well? "What do you mean? You and Lily are singing for me."

"Why'd you put the guitar away, Daddy?" Lily Red asked. "We're singing our song now."

Nolan narrowed his eyes at Serene before brushing his hand against their daughter's head. "Give us a minute, poppy. Daddy just wants to know what's going on with your mom."

Serene's grip on the pregnancy test tightened. She swallowed hard and bit her lip. There was no escaping this. Not with that fierce stare in Nolan's eyes. She huffed. "Fine." She placed the pregnancy test on top of the table and pushed it toward Nolan.

It took a second for what the test meant to register. The delight on his face upon realizing what it meant boggled her. How did Nolan have as much excitement about this pregnancy as the day they had found out about her first? Not a hint of apprehension or doubt was on his face. Just this pure, unabashed joy Serene so desperately wanted a taste of.

As if attempting to grant her unspoken wish, Nolan slid out of the booth, gathered her in his arms, and twirled her around. "Serene, this is amazing! The timing couldn't be more perfect!" His lips searched hers.

Perfect? What? Why?

"What's happening?" Lily Red asked. "Why is Daddy so happy?"

That was Serene's question, too. How could the timing be perfect? What did he mean by that?

Nolan set her back on the ground before pulling his lips away from hers. He cupped her face between his palms, his guitar-calloused fingers brushing her bristling cheeks. "This is great. God works everything for good, Serene. With all the free time you have, you can be at rest, there's less stress. There's a greater chance our baby will make it this time." His mouth was on hers again.

Meanwhile, Serene stood there, responding to her husband's kiss as best she could while her mind reeled to process his words. All the free time she had? Why? Because she had obliterated her art career and her company? Was Nolan subconsciously blaming her for the past miscarriages? The notion hit her heart like a lightning bolt, electrifying her veins, so it could carry her indignation through her bloodstream, firing up her nerves.

Nolan held her hands and squeezed tight. "This is perfect, Serene. Praise God for this."

There was that word again. Nothing was perfect. Especially her. Hurt gripping her heart, Serene sat back in the booth and tried to pay attention to her daughter's song, but as she clutched her stomach, she prayed quietly. For healing and hope. For herself and her child to survive this dark night of her soul, so they could both make it to the Light.

Until then, she would have to grapple with the shame and the blame, the regret and the pain, and grit her teeth every time someone uttered the word, *perfect.*

two

ENDURING **I**MAGERY & **E**XPOSING **I**MPOSTERS

The bus passed through the electronic gate and entered the winding driveway leading to the modern mansion that had been Serene's home since marrying Nolan. The house came into view, and no matter how many times she had seen it, Serene still wasn't used to the glass paneling and the white stucco exterior with black detailing, which gave their house an almost industrial edge to it. Lilies and rose bushes beautified the front yard — Serene's touch — but she gritted her teeth at the notion that even to this day, the house looked to her like a blank canvas.

Now that she had all this "free time", she could make it her own. After all, she had been married to Nolan for almost a decade now. Why hadn't she yet done anything to put a little splash of her personality and art into her own home? Multiple conflicting answers to her questions flooded into her mind — none of which made her feel better about herself, so she shoved the thoughts away. She had no time to process, anyway. She had to get out of the bus.

Serene took Lily Red's hand while heaving as many bags as she could carry over her shoulder. She alighted their moving home. Once her feet hit the pavement, she breathed in, the fresh air filling her lungs. She couldn't wait to get inside their home, but Lily Red seemed to have other ideas, because she wriggled her hand away from Serene's and ran to Nolan's roadies to give them each a hug.

Serene waited for her daughter to finish saying goodbye to their friends while Nolan helped unload Serene's and Lily Red's luggage from their "rooms" inside the bus. Serene winced upon noticing Nolan's bags weren't included, a reminder that they would only have him for a few days before he had to go back on tour again. This would be their life for the next two months until his cross-country tour was complete. Meanwhile, Serene got to stay at home, with all her "free time", as Nolan put it, nurturing her unborn child.

The root of bitterness grew within her, spreading its hold in her heart, deeper and deeper. How could Nolan have been so callous as to call this hollowness left by her failing career "free time"? She shook her head and yanked out the bitter root. This melancholy and self-pity would take her nowhere. This was the way of things right now. She had to make the best of it.

"Lily Red!" Serene called out as she extended her hand toward her daughter.

Lily Red skipped toward her. When Nolan noticed all the bags Serene was carrying, he shook his head and rushed by her side. "Let me get those for you." He reached for her bags.

"I'm fine. Go help your friends." The words came out sharper than Serene had intended as she withheld the bags from him. "I'm not useless yet."

Nolan's brows creased in confusion. "You're never useless, love." He brushed his thumb against her cheekbone and kissed the corner of her lips before running back to his crew, some of whom were already lugging their bags inside their home — a mansion to most, one afforded to her by her husband's fame and wealth, one that had always been far too extravagant, too grand for her taste.

Serene held her daughter's hand as they made their way up the stairs leading to their front door. Nolan's roadies were already hurrying out to get back to the bus. At the foyer, their suitcases were stacked taller than Lily Red, who once again wriggled her hand away from her mother's and threw her arms in the air. "We're home!" she exclaimed before twirling round and round until she bumped into the suitcases, too loaded to topple over. Lily Red grabbed her arm and whispered, "Ow."

"Be careful, poppy." Serene huffed as she took in the sight of the grand staircase leading down to their foyer, which had a lounging area of its own. There were times when she felt like she could still get lost in her own home, considering how spacious it was. She caught herself. Was she really complaining to herself about how big her house was? How had she gotten so rottenly spoiled?

Nolan stepped in, shut the door behind him, and immediately wrapped his arms around Serene's waist. His lips grazed her jaw.

Ah, yes. This man was how.

"Finally. We're alone," Nolan said, rocking her from side-to-side. "Just you, me, our daughter, and our baby." His hands caressed her stomach. "I can't wait."

Serene tried to bite her tongue, but the edged response rushed out of her lips. "Can't wait? Nolan, how are you okay with this?" She pushed his arms away and spun around to face him. "This is terrifying to me. How is it not to you?"

Nolan's face went blank. "Because—" He narrowed his eyes. "Serene?"

Lily Red held her father's hand and frowned at Serene. "Why are you scared, Mom? Grandpa told me not to be afraid, because Jesus will look after us all the time."

"Great." Serene threw her arms in the air. Now, she was an awful example to her daughter, but was it wrong for her to feel this way?

Nolan lifted Lily Red in his arms. "Your mom is just going through a lot, poppy. Let's put away the stuff in your suitcase while Mom gets a bit of rest, okay?"

Lily Red dropped her head to her shoulder. "I'm tired, too."

Nolan laughed. "Not tired enough, I think." He tickled her stomach. "Come on. It'll be fun." He put her on the ground. "Now, go to your room. I'll be with you soon. Mom and I need to have a short chat for now, okay?"

Lily Red scrunched her face. She took a semi-turn on her heel before facing them again and throwing her arms around Serene's waist. "It'll be okay, Mom. The baby will live this time."

The last statement caused daggers flying right to Serene's heart, as she mourned the loss of her unborn children while praying for the life of the one in her womb. She held her daughter's arm, squeezed, shut her eyes, and nodded. "Thank you, poppy."

Satisfied she had done her part, Lily Red rushed up the grand staircase to her forest-themed bedroom.

The moment their daughter reached the top of the staircase, Nolan gripped Serene's arms and made her face him. Because she had her eyes downcast, he had to bend his head so he could look her in the eye. "I feel like I'm missing something, Serene, and I want to figure out what that something is, so we'll talk about this, okay? I'm here, and I want to hear you."

He was trying to be thoughtful and nice, and it was only making Serene feel worse. "I'll be fine, Nolan," she said. "I probably just need rest or a few minutes alone to gather my thoughts."

Hurt darkened his brown eyes, but he nodded slowly and held her hands in his. "It won't be the same as before. I promise."

"There's no way you can be sure of that."

"I have faith." He grinned as he twirled strands of her hair on his finger. "Remember when you had that, as well? You taught me to have faith, Serene, but I understand how tough this season has been for you, so let me have enough faith for both of us right now and let that pretty red head of yours rest easy that God's got us."

Despite herself, Serene had to smile. Why was he being so perfect today?

"Look. I'll give you space, for now. I'll be with our little poppy and try to convince her to go on a nap or something, so we can discuss this further, okay?"

Serene nodded to get him off her back. "I doubt you'll get her to sleep, but you can try. I'll get dinner ready."

"Don't." Nolan shook his head. "Rest. As much as I miss your cooking, it's been a long day. Let's get something delivered tonight." A sneaky smile appeared on his lips. "Let's also find someone to look after Lily Red one of these days, so we can go out — just you and me — before I head back on tour." He held her face in his hands and pressed his forehead against hers. "I love you."

"I love you, too." Serene meant it. Somehow, saying it out loud was enough to remind her of what mattered. She pressed her lips against her husband's — a hard kiss to let him know she meant it despite whatever it was she was going through — something she herself didn't fully understand.

Nolan brushed a finger against her red hair, tucking strands behind her ear.

"Daddy!" Lily Red called out from the top of the stairs. "Where are you?!"

Serene grinned. "You have been summoned."

"I'll find you later. Daddy duty calls." He flicked his brows at Serene, grabbed Lily Red's zebra-print suitcases from the pile, and jogged up the stairs. "Coming, poppy!"

Left alone, Serene stared at the smaller pile of suitcases left behind before giving the staircase a lingering gaze. In nine months, they would celebrate a decade of marriage. When around him, she no longer felt as giddy as when they had started dating as teenagers, but what they shared as a married couple was something that ran deeper. The trust and love developed over the years of growing up as best friends, becoming a couple, breaking up, and getting back together again had built a solid foundation for their marriage. Of that, Serene was certain. She had married her best friend, and they had a wonderful life together. Why then was this inexplicable heaviness still in her chest, and it only got heavier the more she thought of all the reasons she should be thankful, but somehow wasn't? What was wrong with her?

Serene shook her head. She needed to snap out of this and find something to distract herself. She wasn't willing to tackle her luggage yet, so she ambled into the living room, kicked off her leather boots, and dropped her entire weight on the suede sofa. The stark contrast of the red couch with the crisp white walls — like blood and purity — was somehow comforting to her. Serene brought out her phone. Her screen was flooding with messages. She had multiple missed calls.

Panic rushed through her.

Serene opened a message from Nolan's older sister, Nova. It had been a while since they had talked. Serene made a mental note to have a coffee date or a visit with her. Lily Red would love to see her cousins, too. Nova would know how to comfort Serene; her message, however, brought more conflict within Serene than comfort.

Nova: Serene, are you back from the trip? If you ever need someone to talk to, let me know, okay? Remember, it's only what God says about you that matters. Caleb and I are praying for you and Nolan!

Serene froze. Huh? Why was Nova saying these things? She opened the next messages. One after another, each message expressed some sort of comfort or consolation — over what, she could only guess. Finally, she reached the last message. It was from her brother, Jeremy, who was halfway across the world in China.

Jeremy: Rachel and I are waiting for our flight home. Can't wait to see you guys! Don't let them get to you, okay? You are an amazing artist and a creative entrepreneur who has impacted countless lives through your work. Don't ever forget that.

What was going on? Upon noticing her brother was online, Serene launched into a chat with him to figure out what on earth everyone was talking about.

Serene: Praying for a safe flight for you and Rachel. Thank you for the reminder, but... why?

Jeremy: You haven't seen?

A link to an article followed his message. The headline read, *Why Nolan Stone is Less than Perfect: Serene Stone.*

Serene's heart dropped. The day she had always feared had arrived. The rest of the world had caught up and figured out what she was: an imposter who had no success apart from her husband.

What would happen if Nolan ever realized he had married a complete failure? Serene shuddered, because she knew the answer: he would still love her.

If only she could also learn to love herself the same way.

three

RUDE PAPARAZZI & RUINING PICTURES

Over and over again, Serene read the article, her heart sinking further into despair with every single line absorbed. Had she somehow triggered this scrutiny by simply scoffing at Nolan's statement that she was as close to perfect as it gets? The reporter had dug deep into her past, her rise to fame with Nolan as *Red & Ice*, their fall-out as a young couple, and how they had gotten back together and eventually gotten married. However, the write-up — a hit piece by all intents and purposes — insinuated that she had somehow used her art and her company to get Nolan back after he had become far more successful than he had been while "saddled" with her as *Red & Ice.*

The entire article painted her as dumb, at best, an exploitative huckster, at worst. It downplayed all of her accomplishments by saying her art never would have gotten the attention it had gotten if not for her connection to Nolan, and her company had only profited because of Nolan's support and the raw talent of the people who had joined *Thrive*, her creative incubator. It blew up the idea that even the people she had purported to help had turned against her by throwing her out of her own company.

The worst part about reading the piece was Serene couldn't come up with a defense against any of it. The article called her "a gifted rock star's glorified housewife, who convinced herself she's talented because her husband says so".

In the middle of her third read, the tears threatened to come out, but just as it was about to, Nolan entered the room, gyrating his hips and pointing his fist to his mouth like it was a microphone. He sang the lyrics of his latest hit as he approached her. His warm, soothing voice, which millions of people around the world would pay to hear, did little to give her wounded soul some balm.

After crooning out a few lines, Nolan bounced onto the empty space on the couch beside her. "It's a miracle. She fell asleep as soon as we finished putting away her stuff." He laid his head on Serene's lap and lifted his left leg on top of the backrest of the couch, resting his right ankle on its arm.

Serene quickly turned her phone off. Had Nolan already read the article? Did she want him to read it? She stroked his forehead, her fingers brushing his dark hair. "Lily Red is probably far more tired than she's trying to let on. The schedule on this one trip was a lot more hectic than the past ones."

"Yeah, which is why it's best for both of you to stay home for now. It'll get even more hectic in the next few weeks. Thanks for coming, though." He lifted his arm and felt for her face, his palm covering her mouth.

"What are you doing?" Her words came out muffled because of how his hand was groping her face.

"I'm trying to caress your cheek." He snickered.

"It's not working!" She put his hand away, laughing. The momentary distraction wasn't enough to completely turn her mind away from what he had just said. Why was Nolan always talking about her staying home? He usually loved having them on tour with him. Was he trying to do damage control from the article by hiding her for a while?

Serene winced. Perhaps it was for the best. After this article, the press would scrutinize her under a microscope. They would most likely try to interpret her every action and reaction, putting their own spin to it to come up with whatever story would sell.

"What's on your mind, love?" Nolan's tone went from mirthful to pensive. "I'm sorry if I'm not being sensitive enough to what you're going through. It's been a tough year, I know. For the record, I'm excited about the pregnancy, because we've prayed about this, Serene. We want another child, and this is another opportunity to get what we have been praying for. That doesn't mean part of me isn't terrified of going through what we had gone through after the last two. I'm just trying not to dwell on that. I'd rather hope and believe that we will experience again what it felt to hold Lily Red in our arms for the first time."

Even her sour mood couldn't keep her from smiling at that particular memory. "That was amazing, wasn't it?"

"The best! But enough about me. What is happening to you, wife? You've been putting on that pretty smile of yours, but I won't let history repeat itself and let you get away with not telling me what's on your mind."

She rolled her eyes at the mention of how their break-up had happened, of how she had kept silent for years, all because she had wanted to support him. Yes. He was right. She shouldn't keep what she was going through to herself. He was her husband, and he deserved to know. She blew out a long sigh, before recalibrating her brain to focus on processing this pregnancy instead of how a hit piece was wrecking her soul. "I don't know what's on my mind, Nolan. My brain is full, my heart is overwhelmed. It's only been a few months since I lost control of *Thrive*. After the disaster that was my latest exhibit, I'm barely able to create art, and to top it all off—" she held her tongue from talking about the article and scrambled for another issue she had to wrestle with "—there's all this drama happening at church, so it's almost impossible to get support from the usual people I run to for prayer. Everyone's going through something."

"I'd forgotten about that. Have you talked to your dad?"

"I called him while we were on the tour bus to ask him if he wanted to spend the night with us. He said he'll see us tomorrow, because he has a meeting with the board tonight. Max and Jenna will be there as well."

Nolan wrinkled his nose. "I still can't imagine Max Owens being the pastor of our church. Remember when your brother and him used to follow us everywhere whenever we were at church?"

Serene laughed. "Yes. You were always so annoyed, but they were star-struck by you, even then."

"I was always suspicious Max might have had a crush on you."

"He was a kid!" She lightly slapped his shoulder. "Besides, you always had this idea that boys who never even talk to me might have a crush on me."

"I saw the way they looked at you, love, and the only reason they didn't bother to talk to you is because I was already with you."

Serene bristled. Was that true, though? Or was that just Nolan's perception because of how much he loved her? How had he fallen in love with her to begin with? It was hard for her to pinpoint when and how, because of how close they had been since they had met each other at five years old. She gritted her teeth. Enough of this. She had to think of something else. "Dad is asking if we want to go pick up Jeremy and Rachel at the airport tomorrow."

"Will Rachel's parents be there?"

"Most likely. They'll pick their daughter up."

"Do they know Jeremy and Rachel are engaged — well, kind of?"

"I'm assuming they do. I doubt Jeremy would ask Rachel to marry him without her parents knowing. And they're not kind of engaged. They're engaged."

"They haven't even dated yet. Weren't they just barely friends before going on this trip? That was what? A month ago?"

"Almost two months," Serene said, defensive of her little brother.

"A month and a half, at best."

"I guess sparks flew? Funny that it happened while all this drama is going on at church with Rachel's parents splitting away."

"Still can't believe Mr. and Mrs. P are going through with this. I mean, I was surprised when your dad announced that he would soon retire and he would train Max to take his place, but still, to divide the church like that?" Nolan shook his head. "Makes it all the more weird that their daughter is now engaged to your brother."

"So, are we going to the airport? Max and Jenna are going as well."

"I want to go if only to support Dad," Nolan said. "If Mr. and Mrs. P will be there, he will need all the support he can get."

Serene sighed. "It will be interesting to see how it will all play out. I haven't seen Rachel's parents since Max and Jenna's wedding. It's kind of awkward to think of making nice with them."

"And we think the music industry is dramatic and controversial." Nolan let out a whistle. "The church can be as full of drama and intrigue, and no matter how many times I've encountered controversy at church, it still shocks me."

The mention of the music industry reminded Serene of all the shade it was throwing at her at the moment, and she spoke out loud the words she wished someone would say to her. "We're all still works-in-progress. The church, its people, us—" she sighed "—me. None of us are perfect just yet."

Nolan sat up. He smirked at her. "I think you are." He stroked her cheekbone with his fingers. Suddenly, he pulled her onto his lap, making her yelp. He took a second to look at her before a naughty grin appeared on his face. "Our girl is taking a nap. We have about half an hour." He flicked his brows at her.

Serene welcomed the escape and leaned over to capture her husband's lips with hers, thankful for the temporary reprieve from circumstances beyond her control. She lost herself with him in that moment. Maybe it would help distract him from what the rest of the world was saying about her and about how she was nowhere near the perfect wife for him.

Here she was again, diving into Nolan's world, so she could avoid dealing with all the unspoken fears and doubts ravaging her chaotic soul.

Serene's grip on Nolan's hand tightened as they walked from their car to the airport's arrival area. In the midst of all the drama surrounding her younger brother's return, she had another concern simmering in her mind: the unlikelihood that no one would recognize her husband. The last thing she wanted was for a bunch of paparazzi to snap pictures of a private family gathering that was already precarious to begin with.

When the door to the arrival area came into view, her fears materialized when a man rushed toward them and started snapping pictures with his camera. "Mr. Stone! What can you say about all the rumors surrounding your wife?"

"No comment."

If the question surprised Nolan, there was no hint of it in his demeanor other than his tightening grip on Serene before he let go of her hand and laid his arm on her shoulder to gently nudge her ahead of him — an attempt to protect her from the unwelcome camera the reporter was shoving in their faces. Nolan shifted to her other side, so that he was in front of the man, shielding her. He lifted his hand to cover himself with his palm.

"Where is your daughter?"

He let out a smile. "This is your business because?"

"Where are you flying off to?"

Nolan snickered. "We're at the arrival area."

"Oh, right. So, who are you picking up?"

"None of your business."

Serene winced upon remembering her brother had his own claim to fame, with his social media following having shot to the millions after his latest video uploads. Would the airport security actually let these guys inside?

The paparazzi tried to get past Nolan to snap a photo of her. "Are you a gold-digger, Serene? Are you only using your husband to further your floundering career and failed business endeavors?"

She tensed up. Even Nolan's hand on the small of her back stiffened. "What kind of questions are those?" This time, he couldn't hide the edge in his voice, the attempt at being cordial completely obliterated. "We've been a couple since we were teenagers when I was dirt poor and had nothing to offer her."

"Didn't she leave you when she thought you weren't going to become the star that you are? What do you see in her, Mr. Stone? You can do so much better."

"Enough." Nolan's hands quickly turned into fists. Few things riled her husband up, but the words coming out of this stranger's mouth were undoubtedly getting under his skin.

Aware of what would happen should Nolan get aggressive, Serene stood in between him and the paparazzi. She embraced his waist and held on to him when he poised himself to lunge for the cameraman. "He's provoking you, Nolan. Let it go," she whispered into his ear. "We're almost inside. Let it go. Don't let him win. Think of all the repercussions, all the needless stress it would cause."

Nolan's body was still tense and braced for attack, but he allowed her to nudge him toward the door leading to the airport. Before they could get through, he still managed to point at the paparazzi and yell, "Don't ever talk about my wife that way again!"

Whatever the stranger's response was, she no longer cared. All she could think about was how to get her husband out of a situation he might regret. "Let it go, Nolan. Let's just get in."

To her relief, to avoid further altercation, airport security held the paparazzi back, but the commotion had already led to a lot of attention directed their way. When Serene noticed a fan trying to approach for an autograph, she let go of Nolan, who was still seething, and pressed her palms together to plead with the fan. "Not now, please," she mouthed.

The disappointment on the fan's face made Serene feel horrible, but Nolan was human. One would think this woman would be able to tell that he was not in the proper state of mind to sign her piece of paper and take a picture with her. To her relief, the fan backed off, and everyone seemed to get the message that they weren't open to entertaining anyone right now.

Situations like this one had been among the many things that had turned her off from the life of fame her husband was leading. For many years, she had gotten away with the press not hounding her too much, with Nolan constantly emphasizing how much she valued her privacy, but this article had opened up a whole new interest not only in Nolan, but in her. What would this mean for them in the coming months?

Serene stroked his back. "Calm down," she said. "It's over. They're leaving us alone."

"What was that idiot going on about?" Nolan muttered under his breath, his tone sharp, and his teeth gritted. His hooded gaze told Serene everything she needed to know about what was going through his mind. Her husband's warmth, when flared, could quickly turn into a wildfire, burning from his consciousness all that surrounded him, making him zone in on whatever it was that had sparked his blaze. It often took long periods of solitude, creating music, for him to get to a place of peace, kindling the fire that had broken out within him. "Can you believe the gall of that man to talk about you that way? And right in front of me! This is madness. Why was he going after you? Ramona needs to deal with this." He patted his jacket pockets for his phone. His manager was about to get an earful from her most successful client, but not right now, if Serene could do anything about it.

"I have your phone in my purse," she said. "You gave it to me after we got out of the car. You can call Ramona when we get home. Calm down first."

The pace of his walking slowed as he took several deep breaths. She clasped her hands with his, aware of how much effort it was taking him to reel in his temper.

"We're together. We're fine," she said as she nuzzled her cheek against his shoulder. "They don't matter." She smiled and waved upon seeing her father standing at the arrival area with Max and Jenna from church. "They're here, Nolan. You calm?"

He stopped walking altogether to face her. He gathered her in his arms. "I'm sorry, Red."

The nickname shook her. It had been so long since he had called her that. For some reason, it made her feel vulnerable — like she had once did when she was a young woman, carried away by the rising star of the man she loved. She buried her face in his chest because, despite her attempt to hold it back, a sob broke through her.

Nolan's hug tightened. "I'm so sorry. You don't deserve to deal with that. Whatever caused them to insult you that way, I will fix it. I won't let them get away with this." He continued to whisper comfort and encouragement to her, his words sweet and loving, but none of it stopped her growing sense of weakness and ineptitude.

"Pull yourself together, Serene," she whispered to herself before swallowing the tears back. She couldn't prolong this and give anyone else more reason to pay attention to them. She gathered her composure and pulled away from her husband's embrace.

He wiped her tears away with his thumbs, his hands cupping her cheeks. "You'll never cease to take my breath away."

Her brain in a fog, she couldn't tell if he meant it or if he was just trying to be kind.

"You okay?" he asked.

She grinned. "Are you?"

"I still want to hit something, but I won't." He clenched his jaw. "Thanks for holding me down. That could've gone a million different wrong ways."

Serene bit her lip. "Can we pretend none of it happened and just welcome my brother home?"

"Ramona will still hear from me one of these days, but for today, consider it done." He clasped her hand in his and led her to where Dad, Max, and Jenna stood, waiting for Jeremy and Rachel to arrive.

Upon closer look at her, Dad creased his brows. "Serene, are you all right?"

"I'm fine, Dad. A little shaken, but fine." She hugged her father while Nolan caught up with the newlyweds. "We had a run-in with some paparazzi, but it's all sorted out now."

Dad's stare lingered on her, but he let it go, thankfully. "Where's my granddaughter?"

"We dropped her off at Nova's to hang out with her cousins."

"It was a good call, because I would have hated having her exposed to all the nasty things that idiot said." Nolan once again seethed at the memory, but quickly collected himself so he could hug his father-in-law. "Dad."

"Son." Dad hugged him back. "What happened?"

"It's nothing," Serene was quick to say, widening her eyes at her husband. "Let's not give the incident more attention than it deserves."

Nolan got her drift and flashed the relaxed, charismatic smile that never failed to make people around him feel like he had everything under control. "Serene's right. We're just excited to have Jeremy back."

"Before I forget—" Dad clapped Nolan's shoulder "—congratulations on that award you received for that new song of yours. Platinum, is it?"

Nolan nodded and pointed upwards. "The Lord continues to be good to us."

Serene backed away from the conversation and turned to their friends. "You both look amazing!"

she gushed as she hugged Jenna and then Max. "How was your honeymoon?"

"Great!" Jenna exclaimed, but a slight quiver in her voice made her sound less than enthused.

Serene was about to ask the couple about how they were dealing with what was happening at their church, when an all-too-familiar voice interrupted their reunion.

"How nice." A sharp female voice triggered a violent gut reaction.

Serene turned to find Mr. and Mrs. Petersen giving them guarded smiles.

As if to rescue them all from the awkwardness of not knowing how to interact with one another, Mr. Petersen waved to someone behind Serene. "There she is!" he exclaimed.

Jeremy and Rachel had just stepped into the arrival area, and upon seeing them all together, the first thing Serene's brother did was lift his camera to snap a photo. Serene let out the best smile she could muster, only to groan when Jeremy took the shot and exclaimed, "Perfect!"

four

PAINFUL PRAYERS & LOOMING LAIRS

A convoy of three cars rolled along the highway from the airport to the Petersen Residence — the Sinclairs in Serene's car; the Petersens in Mrs. P's car; Max and Jenna in their own vehicle. Serene relaxed as soon as the airport was out of sight. She patted her brother's knee as she shifted to make herself comfortable in the back seat. Up front, Nolan was driving and exchanging small talk with Dad.

Jeremy rubbed his palms together and flashed a grin at her. "We're all headed for the enemy's lair. What secrets will we find at the pink, floral abode of the legendary Rhoda Petersen? Will we discover treasure hidden in the depths of her heart or will she once again materialize as the dragon lady, breathing fire on all who dare cross her?"

Serene gave him a long, pointed look, keeping an air of stoicism while her lips quivered to hide a smile. "Can't believe Rachel agreed to marry you."

"She didn't have much of a choice." Jeremy shrugged. "God told her to. Can't argue with God."

"Fact." Serene had already tried. Arguments with God were unwinnable. She smiled. Her heart had lifted after the exchange with her brother. Jeremy had such a way of making heavy and awkward situations feel a lot lighter, more bearable. Serene's hypothesis was that he had formed this carefree attitude as a defense mechanism to all the trouble he had gotten himself into when he was younger. Back at the airport, Serene had thanked God for his ability to diffuse the tension building between the Petersens and their family.

"Did you know the Petersens would invite us to eat with them?" Jeremy made it sound like the most ridiculous idea ever conceived. "Is that why you didn't bring my niece with you?"

"Lily Red is at Nova's," Serene said. Not wanting to explain the fallout of the article her husband still didn't know about, she changed the subject quickly. "How was your trip? Care to elaborate on how you went there, single, and returned here, engaged?"

"You already know most of the story," Jeremy said. "I started developing feelings beyond just my physical attraction for her. I witnessed it with my own eyes, how she thrived throughout her trip. Somewhere along the way, as she reached full bloom, for the first time since we were kids, I could imagine a future with her. I wanted to make sure it was the right move to pursue her, so I fasted about it and got this confidence from the Lord. When I told her about it — announced it to our team, actually — she prayed and fasted, too. After her three-day fast, we told her dad, and miraculously, he gave us his blessing."

"How did Rhoda react?" Dad asked. "I can't imagine she's too happy about marrying her daughter off to a Sinclair."

Jeremy winced. "That part, I'm not sure about yet. Rachel hasn't been willing to talk about it with me. Mr. P did say he would be responsible for telling Mrs. P, but there's no way for me to find out what she thinks about it now. I'm kind of worried about Rachel being there alone with them."

"Rachel can stand her ground." Serene sighed. "It's just strange timing, Jeremy. What do you reckon you will do with everything going on at Connect? Plan a wedding with the daughter of the couple who has just divided our church?"

"Well, yeah. Why not? Seems like the logical destination, if Rachel and I are sure we want to get married, but before you freak out on me, it's not like we're rushing to have the wedding," Jeremy said. "We want to date first. We got engaged before we even started dating, so it's all kind of topsy-turvy, but we still want to experience that phase. We need to, so we could at least be more intentional about getting to know each other and be able to discuss our hopes and expectations about this marriage."

"That's great," Serene said, "because honestly, I think a lot of us are overwhelmed by what's happening at church, not to mention our personal lives, so I personally can't even get into the proper headspace of planning and preparing for a wedding."

"Everything in God's perfect timing," Dad said. "It all depends on how the Lord leads. If we feel it would be better for you two to get married sooner rather than later, then I bless you in your choice to do that. What's happening between the Petersens and our church shouldn't prevent you and Rachel from starting a life together — especially since you have the blessing of both families. As you said, that was a miracle in and of itself."

Serene huffed and shrugged at her brother. "What Dad said."

Jeremy snickered and poked Serene's shoulders. "How are you holding up? I imagine it's been a tough twenty-four hours."

Serene widened her eyes at her brother. Through the rear-view mirror, Nolan cast a quizzical glance at her. "I could be better, but still blessed—" she grappled for words before remembering something that could distract them from that stupid article "—I'm pregnant again."

The way Jeremy's face lit up made her feel better, but from the way Nolan's jaw twitched, she could tell she would have some explaining to do later. After all, she had made such a fuss about her doubts and fears when it came to this pregnancy, and now, she was blurting it out and announcing it to her family before she and Nolan could have the opportunity to discuss all her issues about it.

"That's amazing!" Jeremy exclaimed.

Dad patted Nolan's arm. "I'm glad to hear that. We'll take care of this baby in prayer. I'm grateful you told us as soon as now."

"Congratulations, Nolan." Jeremy reached forward and tapped Nolan's shoulder. "This is great news. We'll back you both up in prayer, for sure."

"Thanks. We definitely need it," Nolan said. "It'll be a challenging season ahead. I have to go back on tour next week, so it'll only be Serene and Lily Red at home. While it's a good thing because at least she can rest a bit, being apart for so long will be a real challenge for us. My tour will go on for quite a number of months. Ma and Nova promised to check on Serene once in a while, though, so at least there's that."

"Can I stay there once in a while?" Jeremy asked. "I'd like to take turns staying at Dad's place and yours. A few nights here, a few nights there. I can fend off the paparazzi when I'm there. Also, I'm sure Rachel and Jenna won't mind stopping by to make sure you get all the help you need."

"You're welcome to stay with us any time, Jeremy," Serene said, "and don't worry. It's only my first trimester. I've been here before. No need to fuss."

"I counsel you to accept all the help offered, Serene," Dad said. "Especially knowing how delicate your pregnancies are."

Serene and Nolan exchanged glances via the rear-view mirror. "We'll arrange something before I leave, Dad," Nolan said. "I'll make sure she and Lily Red are well taken care of."

"No doubts on my part that you'll do everything to watch over your household, Nolan. Just remember that even if our church is encountering upheaval at this time, you still have a community behind you. That goes for Serene's pregnancy and Jeremy's wedding." Dad paused. Suddenly, his laughter echoed inside the car. "Can you believe what I just said? My daughter is having another child, and my son is getting married. Despite what is happening at church, Aida would have loved this season."

The mention of her mother formed a lump in Serene's throat. "You're right, Dad. She would have been thrilled."

"If only she was here." Jeremy's voice cracked. "Everything would be a lot easier with her around."

As he said the words, they pulled over in front of the house of the one woman who had nothing but negative things to say about their late mother. Serene gritted her teeth. They were now at the Petersens' colonial townhouse. An awkward silence filled the car before Jeremy broke the tension by snickering. "So, guys, ready to enter the enemy's lair?"

five

PITY PARTIES & PETTY PETERSENS

The white, lime-washed colonial townhouse didn't appear like much of an enemy's lair. The rose bushes lining the front yard were breath-taking and the house itself had a welcoming, homey feel to it, even if it did seem like it was too big for a family of three. Nolan squeezed Serene's hand as they made their way through the pathway leading up to the front porch.

"I've never been here before," Nolan said. "Have you?"

Serene's nose wrinkled as her red hair cascaded down her left shoulder when she tilted her head. "Come to think of it, I haven't either. Jeremy has, though."

"Shouldn't come as a surprise that we both haven't been here. Remember how much we avoided Mrs. P like the plague when we were kids?"

"Heh." A wave of nostalgia hit Serene. "Only because we were trying to hide our relationship from her."

"She was never our biggest fan, was she?" Nolan pulled her close and brushed the tip of his nose against her cheek.

"Definitely not yours." Serene chuckled. "You and your heathen music."

"Mmm... Heathen, is it? Whatever. All I know is there's no need to hide now." Before she could climb the steps leading to the front porch, her husband claimed her lips, his grip firm on her waist. She gave in, only because making out with her husband in Mrs. P's yard was the closest thing she could get to revenge after a lifetime of criticism from this woman.

Dad cleared his throat. Jeremy snickered. Heat rushed to her cheeks as Serene stopped kissing her husband. The mischievous expression on Nolan's face reminded her yet again of how daring he had always been, even when they were children. He had always been able to sweep her off her feet; this time was no different. She gave her dad and brother a sheepish grin as she tried to catch her breath.

Before anyone could comment on their PDA, Max and Jenna joined the party.

"What's happening here?" Max asked.

Jeremy shrugged. "Nothing new. Just Nolan and Serene making out in some random public place."

"Yeah?" Max snickered. "Some things never change."

"Come on now." Dad clapped Nolan's back and led him inside the house. "Let's announce our presence to our hosts."

Jenna linked arms with Serene, and they both trailed behind the men, who entered the house like they owned it. Mr. P was already in the foyer to welcome them.

"Serene, Jenna," Mr. P said. "Rachel will be here shortly to instruct you on what to do."

"Okay, Mr. P." Jenna's voice had a slight tremble to it.

Mr. P gave the men a curt nod. "Gentlemen, if you could follow me to the kitchen, the ladies are requesting help to carry a few things to the backyard."

With just the two of them left behind in the fancy entryway, Serene felt like the pink floral pattern of the wallpaper might swallow her up any time. She had no clue how to move or where to go.

"I was a kid the last time I was here," Jenna said. "It hasn't changed much."

"I've never been here before." Serene brushed her hand against Jenna's arm, almost as a way to comfort herself. "Nolan and I never had much reason to interact with the Petersens."

"I can't believe they left you here." Rachel rushed out of the kitchen. Ever the perfect host, she laid her hands on each of their backs and prodded them toward the direction she wanted them to go: the backyard, where a covered patio led to a gorgeous garden, perfect for parties and hosting people.

Serene drew a breath at the gushing of water on the fountain in the middle of the garden. The grass was bright green and freshly cut. A hummingbird's wings fluttered as it circled a bird feeder hanging from the branch of a pecan tree. An assortment of flowers — roses, hydrangeas, lilies — provided splashes of color to the thoughtfully designed landscape.

"Please make yourselves comfortable." Rachel gestured toward wooden tables and cushioned benches covered by a canopy with artisan light bulbs hanging from it. "Lunch will be ready soon."

Serene snapped out of admiring the landscaping and took hold of Rachel's wrist. "Rach, you just got out of a fourteen-hour flight. You sure we can't help cook or set food on the table?"

Rachel flashed them that brilliant smile she had always been known for. Her soft blonde hair caressed her face as she shook her head. "I had plenty of rest during the flight. Slept through most of it. You're our guests, so just relax. Jeremy and I are on it."

Serene chuckled. "You sure you want to trust my brother in the kitchen?"

At the mention of Jeremy, Rachel's countenance shifted. Her wide smile softened, and her cheeks took on a pink blush. "Jeremy is honestly a great cook," she said, her lashes fluttering into a hooded, dreamy gaze. "I didn't know that about him until this trip."

Neither did Serene. She wasn't even sure if she had already tasted Jeremy's cooking. She should get him to cook for her one of these days. Then again, was he really great at cooking, or was Rachel just in love? "I'm glad he has your vote of confidence," she said to her brother's fiancée. It was still hard to wrap her mind around the idea that Jeremy was marrying Rachel. How had love blossomed between these two? Especially considering all the tension brewing between the Sinclairs and Petersens.

As if reading her mind and seeking to assure her, Rachel took hold of Serene's hand. "I love him. It's weird to say that out loud, but I do."

"For all it's worth, I'm glad it's you, Rachel." Serene meant it. The more she thought about it, the more she could see why they would make a perfect match. Rachel would be the sensibility and the order to Jeremy's method in madness. "God is the most creative of matchmakers, isn't He?"

At that, Rachel teared up. "He is." She nodded, affection softening her lovely face. "I'm so grateful you're on board with this, Serene. It means the world to me."

That's when it hit her. She had to stop thinking about this place as the enemy's lair. This was Rachel's home, and Rachel was about to marry Jeremy. The Petersens would soon become family. That was the reality of this union, no matter what was going on in their church. Serene brushed Rachel's hair. "I can't wait to call you my sister." Serene looked over Rachel's shoulder and found Mrs. P inside the house, glaring at Rachel through the screen door. "Now, go help your mother. Jenna and I will be here, and please. Let us know if there's anything we can do to help."

Rachel pressed her thumb against the corners of her eyes to prevent her tears from falling. She squeezed Jenna's hand before rushing back in, leaving Serene and Jenna on the patio. The laughter of the men boomed from inside the house — a stark contrast from the scowl Mrs. P was giving Rachel as she made her way back inside. They sat together on one of the sturdy benches made of fine wood and cast iron swirling in elegant designs, akin to something one would see in the streets of Paris or Rome.

Jenna, seated against a wall, twisted her torso to peek through the window to find out what was happening inside. "They're interacting like pals. Pastor Sam and Mr. P are carrying trays of meat somewhere. I'm guessing we'll have barbecue. Nolan and Max are on their trail. Can't see Jeremy, but he's probably helping Mrs. P and Rachel. May God preserve him." Jenna sighed and slumped her shoulders. "I guess we're the only ones who weren't given a task."

Serene stared at the flow of water on the white marble fountain. "I won't pretend to care about whatever is going on in Mrs. P's head. I'm just here to lend support to my father, so he doesn't have to go through this alone. If Mrs. P wants me to sit here the entire time, I'll find a way to make the best of it." She pried her eyes away from the fountain and directed it at Jenna. She squared her shoulders and paid more attention to the young woman in front of her. "We've never really spent time together, have we? I don't think I've ever had a conversation with you."

A soft smile appeared on Jenna's lips as she twirled her dark hair with her finger. "No, I don't think we've ever had a one-on-one conversation. We've interacted, but not in an intimate, getting-to-know each other way."

"We should fix that. After all, you're the wife of the man who is about to become my pastor."

"Heh." Jenna's eyes lowered. "I don't know about that. It's all still so strange to me." She let out a wry chuckle. "Can't complain, though. When I agreed to marry Max, this was what I signed up for."

"That doesn't mean you can't let him know when things are becoming too much for you to handle. I hope you're aware of that." Serene fidgeted in her seat. Was she telling Jenna or herself?

Jenna nodded. "I am. So far, we've been communicating openly about the challenges we've been facing." A fond smile appeared on her face as she fidgeted with the hem of her skirt. "I love that about Max. He made sure I would walk into this with open eyes. He made it a point to inform me what I was in for by marrying him, but neither of us expected things to turn out as it did. Despite all the assurance, support, and encouragement Pastor Sam and the church board have given us, it's still easy to believe it is somehow our fault."

"Don't let the enemy get to you that way. All of this is happening for a reason." The disconnect between the wisdom she was doling out and what she was feeling wasn't lost on Serene. How could she say something like that to Jenna when she herself was letting the devil's obvious machinations get to her?

"I believe that." Jenna giggled before standing up and shuffling on her feet. "It's just funny, because Max and I sometimes joke with each other that we think we should back up Mrs. P and convince everyone to make Mr. P pastor instead. After all, neither Max nor I have a stellar record as far as righteousness goes. We're both prodigals." At this point, Jenna was performing hip-hop footwork in front of Serene. "We don't have a perfect record like Mr. P and Mrs. P, or even Rachel, do. I don't know what the Petersens put in their food, but it's like P is for perfect."

Despite her amusement at Jenna's constant motion, Serene still had to scoff at that statement. There was that word again. "I wouldn't call Mr. P and Mrs. P perfect. More like P is for petty, honestly. They pinpoint everyone's flaws while being completely unwilling to recognize their own." It took a second or two before her consciousness caught up with what her mouth had just released. She bit her lip. "Sorry. I shouldn't speak negatively about them. We're guests at their home. It's not right, no matter the circumstance or justification. After all these years, I'm still a work-in-progress. So much for being an example to others, huh?"

Jenna stopped her dancing, crossed her arms over her chest, and leaned against one of the iron poles holding up the patio's awning. "For all it's worth, Serene, in all our interactions, you've always been kind to me. I looked up to you as a kid. Even as an adult, it inspired me how you followed your convictions and left *Red & Ice* even if it meant you might lose Nolan, which is why—" she threw her arms in the air "—I don't understand why the press is going after you! Are they stupid? What they wrote about you was horrible, Serene, and I hope you're aware that those who know you, the ones who have been impacted by your life, we know that the nonsense they're spouting is nowhere near the truth of your past and your relationship with Nolan."

Serene winced. Jenna was saying such kind words of support, but it still bothered Serene that Jenna even knew about the article at all. Then again, why would she be surprised? Everyone always had their faces glued to a screen. There was no way Serene could hide the smear campaign the media had launched against her. "They'll get tired of talking about me eventually," she said to appease herself, hoping her words would come true. "The novelty of it all will wear off, and they won't even remember my name once all is said and done. I just have to ride it out. Lily Red and I will be at home while Nolan goes back on tour, so we won't be exposed to it too much. Nolan will know how to wade his way through the questions the press will throw at him. It'll all blow over. Hopefully, sooner rather than later."

"Yes! I agree, because it's all so ridiculous to begin with."

Delighted by Jenna's carefree character and curious about what kind of pastor's wife she would make, Serene extended an invitation. "You should come visit Lily Red and me one of these days. Spend an afternoon with us. My daughter adores you."

"And I adore your daughter!" Jenna held on to the iron pole and twirled around on it. "She is so sweet and adorable and not at all spoiled, which is probably what most people would expect her to be, considering her father is Nolan Stone. But, she's so kind and down-to-earth. You're an amazing mother, Serene."

Serene leaned back in her seat in amusement, not because of the compliments Jenna was giving her and her daughter, but because right in front of her, Jenna was choreographing an entire dance with her every word. She was making something beautiful out of her nervous energy. Serene could immediately tell why Max had fallen in love with Jenna when she played the angel hanging from an aerial hoop at a church play they had performed over a year ago. Those had been better days for their church. Nolan had composed the music for the play, while Nova had written the script. *Prodigal Once*, it was called. It had been a moderate success, but now, most of the people at Connect Church remembered it as the play that opened Max's eyes to the possibility of Jenna being "the one" for him.

Now, here she was, his wife, performing a dance for Serene. "Are you always like this?"

"Like what?"

"Dancing?"

"It's what I hope to be," Jenna said. "Always dancing." She smiled. "It helps me stay connected to Jesus. Especially when I'm anxious."

"No wonder God opened Max's eyes and heart to fall in love with you while you were dancing."

Jenna grinned as she continued to move. "Ah, yes. The play. I wish we could pull a production like that again. We were so united when we put up that play, and now we're struggling to even look one another in the eye. All because Mrs. P can't stand to call Max a pastor."

"Excuse me?" The door to the patio swung wide open and out of it emerged Rhoda Petersen. The stern look she was casting at Jenna made even Serene shrink back in discomfort.

To Serene's relief, Jenna didn't respond. However, based on her flaring nostrils and the tension in her frame, all signs pointed to the poor girl soon being on the receiving end of one of Mrs. P's cutting diatribes.

Pure mercy from above, it was then that the men stepped onto the patio, the saucy aroma of grilled barbecue doing little to diffuse the brewing tension. Max went straight to his wife, whose cheeks were turning beet red as she squirmed at the way Mrs. P kept sending her cold glares.

Nolan slid on the bench next to Serene, his shoulder pressed against hers. "I'm not sure what's happening," he said. "The quiet is thick, and the vibe is weird, but Serene—" he looked her straight in the eye "—did you know about that hit piece?"

She winced. "Who told you?"

"Max." Nolan's jaw tightened. He laid his palm on Serene's knee. "I should've found out from you, Serene. Didn't we agree we would be open with each other about these types of things?"

To that, Serene couldn't come up with a defense. He was right. They had promised each other that. She bowed her head and bit her lip. "I'm sorry," was all she could come up with to say.

Nolan shook his head. "No, I'm sorry, Serene. You shouldn't have to deal with stuff like this just because of what I do for a living. That article was—"

Serene grabbed hold of his hand. "This isn't the right place to talk about this, Nolan." She sent a glance toward Max and Jenna, who were in a corner having a hushed conversation.

Nolan followed the direction of her gaze. His lip twitched. The veins in his neck protruded like he was straining himself with something. To Serene's relief, he relaxed and nodded. "Okay." He kissed the back of her hand. "This conversation isn't over, though. And I promise you I'll have a talk with Ramona, and we'll figure out a way to steer this narrative in your favor."

Serene wasn't sure if that would work this time around. Most likely, the press would just spin it as Nolan covering up for his wife's failures yet again, but she let it go. There was no point in tackling this with him right now.

Jeremy stepped out of the house, with Rachel right behind him. They both paused and took a moment to process the scene. Max and Jenna were in their corner. Dad and Mr. P were trying to appease an upset Mrs. P.

Jeremy held Rachel's hand before making his way to Serene. "What happened?"

Serene tried to smile. "Come on. You didn't expect this lunch to proceed without a hitch, did you?"

"Can I announce that you're pregnant?" he asked.

Rachel gasped, her jaw dropping open as she tried to withhold a squeal. "Really?" she mouthed at Serene.

Nolan and Serene exchanged looks. Her husband grinned and shrugged. "Up to you," he said.

"Why, though?" Serene asked her brother.

"It's something everyone can be excited about." Jeremy shrugged. "I mean, just look at this one—" he pointed at his fiancée "—she's about to lose it."

"What?!" Rachel seized his arm and squeezed. "Lily Red is such an amazing kid, and she's cute as a button, and I'm sure I'm not the only one who wants another Nolan-Serene baby! Their genes are too good for them not to share it with the world by having another baby!" The volume of Rachel's voice escalated with every word she spoke out, until finally, she exclaimed, "This is amazing news!"

At that last exclamation, heads turned toward her.

"What's going on?" Max asked.

Jeremy answered, "Serene is p—"

"I'm thinking of putting up money to hold another performance of *Prodigal Once*," Serene said. "It was such a hit when we put it on the first time, and I think we can all use a reminder of God's grace and how it is His work to carry us all through into perfection."

As she said the words, even if she had only used this as a way to deflect attention from her pregnancy and the surrounding tension, the idea formed in Serene's heart as something she actually wanted to do. "What do you guys think? Let's put on a play?"

six

HIT PIECES & HEROIC PAIN

During the rest of the gathering, Mrs. P completely shut down. Everyone else made an effort to lighten the mood and enjoy the situation they were all in, but having Mrs. P's sullen presence was a stormy cloud looming over all of them. When time came for them to politely excuse themselves and leave, the distinct sense of mutual relief on both sides spoke volumes about how fractured their relationship with Mrs. P was, so much so that Serene could hardly believe they had once been a part of one church.

Rachel walked them back to the driveway, where their cars were parked. "Thanks for coming, guys." She hugged everyone one-by-one. "I appreciate you being willing to spend time with us."

Dad smiled. "Always precious to me being able to sit down and have a meal with you and your family, Rachel. It brought back a lot of memories."

Nolan smirked at Serene. That was true enough, but whether the memories were positive or negative was still up for debate.

Jeremy approached them. "I'm staying behind with Rachel," he said. "Max and Jenna volunteered to take Dad home, in case you two have other plans."

Serene looked to her husband. She wanted to bring her father home with them, because she was so aware of how much Nolan wanted to discuss the article with her and what to do about it, but from the steely look Nolan was directing at her, it was clear he would rather they be alone. "We need to pick up Lily Red at Nova's house. Dad, do you want to sleep over at our place?"

Dad shook his head. He wasn't one to ever want to stay anywhere else other than his own home unless necessary. "No. I'm fine with going home. Jeremy will be there tonight."

"Speaking of which," Jeremy said, "I need to move my luggage to Max's car."

"Let's go." Nolan followed Jeremy to Serene's car to remove Jeremy's stuff from there.

Serene hugged her father. "That wasn't easy to get through."

A smile appeared on Dad's face. "It wasn't, but we still made it through by God's grace. Hopefully, there'll be more gatherings like this, as awkward as it was at times. It will help build bridges between them and us."

"It's just sad that there's a them and us, when once upon a time, we were all just us."

"I'm still believing God will make all things beautiful in its time. He will show us what this was all for in due time."

Serene's admiration for her father and his willingness to trust in the Lord grew, even if it wasn't lost on her how much older he looked, like all the stress of what had been going on had taken its toll on him and the way he looked. This wasn't the retirement he deserved after serving this church for far longer than Serene had even been alive.

"We will drop by the house at some point, Dad. Lily Red keeps asking about when she will get to visit her grandfather."

"You're always welcome to come over. Just tell me when." Dad then pressed his palm against her stomach. "Don't be afraid, Serene. God has you in the palm of His hands. Keep hoping."

"Thanks, Dad." Serene nodded. "I will."

"Serene?" Nolan placed his arm on Serene's shoulder. "Dad." He gave her father a curt nod.

"Nolan. Make sure you all come visit. Your mother would also love a visit from you, I'm sure."

"Of course." Nolan smiled. "We'll just get settled in the next few days, and then we'll be out and about making visits. Serene already has a play in the works, so I can only imagine how full of activity the next few weeks will be for her."

Dad nodded as he gave Serene a hopeful glance. "I hope it pans out, Serene. If there's anyone who could pull it off, it would be you. We certainly need something to bring us together instead of push us apart."

"Let's pray it works out."

Max's SUV rumbled to life. Jenna sat in the back, so Dad could ride shotgun.

After Nolan and Serene waved their father goodbye, they exchanged hugs with Jeremy and Rachel before finally getting in their car. The moment they were alone, Serene bristled, knowing Nolan would eventually bring up the one thing he wanted to talk about: the hit piece.

As they pulled out of the Petersens' driveway and steered the car into the street, Nolan said, "Talk to me, Serene."

She sighed. "That was something, wasn't it?"

He side-eyed her. "It was, but that's not what I'm talking about, and you know it."

She winced. How was she going to get herself out of this conversation? She looked straight ahead as she tried to collect her thoughts about why she even had such a resistance to discussing the issue with her husband.

"Serene, you know I don't agree with anything they said in that article, right? How can anyone? None of it holds any water."

"It's my fault, Nolan."

"What? How is any of this your fault?"

"When you were having that press junket for the movie, there was one interview where you said that Lily Red and I are as close to perfect as it gets for you. It was sweet, but when I heard you say it, my first instinct was to scoff. The reporter who was next in line to interview you noticed me. She's the person who wrote the article."

Nolan didn't say anything immediately. He focused on the road ahead, staying quiet long enough for Serene to assume he wouldn't push the matter, but just as they took a turn leading them to his older sister's neighborhood, he asked, "Why did you scoff, though?"

Taken aback by the question, Serene huffed and shook her head. "No. I can't do this, Nolan."

The car slowed down as Nova's house came into view.

"Can't do what, Serene?" Nolan asked.

"This has been an exhausting afternoon, emotionally and mentally. Can we maybe put a pin on this for now? Honestly, I'm trying my hardest not to think about the article right now. With everything going on with my brother and the Petersens, not to mention our church, and then this pregnancy, a bunch of written lies is the last thing I want to think about."

"I understand that, Serene," Nolan said. "I do, but you can't keep putting this off. We know how media works. This will have repercussions, especially when it comes to—"

"Nolan." Serene tried to sound stern. "Please."

He tightened his jaw. "You're doing it again."

"Doing what?"

"You're shutting me out."

"From what?" Serene asked. Why couldn't he just let this go?

"For one thing, why wouldn't you have gone to me with this immediately? Why wasn't your first instinct to come to me for comfort, especially since the reason they are attacking you is me? Why did I have to learn about this from someone else?"

"Because I knew you would react this way, Nolan. You would turn it into this huge thing. The truth is as much as you pretend there's something you can do about this, there's nothing either of us can do. They will believe what they want to believe. Stop trying to save me, Nolan. You're not some sort of hero." Her mind raced to process all the words that had just come out of her mouth and cringed at the wounded look on her husband's face. "Nolan—"

He tensed, his entire body going on full alert. "You're right." He pointed outside the window. The front door opened and Nova emerged from inside. She gestured for them to come in. "We should talk about this some other time."

"Nolan..." Serene tried to reach for him, but he had already made his way out of the car to go hug his older sister. She leaned her head back in her seat and closed her eyes to try to get some peace. There it was. She had said it out loud. The truth behind her hesitation. She didn't want her husband to be her hero, because based on their history, whenever she let him rescue her, somehow, Serene always ended up with a gnawing feeling that she was giving up a part of herself.

seven

HEARTFELT PRAYERS & HOPE-FILLED PLAYS

Acoustic music flowed out of Nolan's personal home studio as he switched from guitar to piano to beatbox — noise in the process of becoming music. While Nolan had made sure to soundproof the studio, unless his bandmates, producers, or industry friends were around to jam with him, he never could remember to close the door. So, his "process" could be heard all the way up the second floor inside their daughter's bedroom, situated right above it.

Lily Red giggled as she dabbed paint onto her canvas with her fingers. The blobbed mixture of colors was nowhere near taking any semblance of form. In fact, there was probably more paint on her face, arms, hands, and T-shirt than there was on her canvas, set on an easel perfect for her height. Even then, at least she had some paint on the canvas. Serene's was still blank. Tabula rasa. The empty slate taunted her and intimidated her, and whenever she attempted to make even just a single stroke, she found herself hesitating to create her "overpriced and over-hyped art," as the article had put it.

To escape her meandering mind, Serene used her daughter's art as a diversion, so she wouldn't have to focus on her own creation — or more like the absence of it. "What are you painting, poppy?" she asked.

Lily Red scrunched her nose. "I don't know." She shrugged. "I just pick the colors I like and try to make it pretty."

"Lovely," Serene said, and she meant it.

To be fair to Lily Red, her selected colors blended well together and the transitions from one color to the next were smooth, but her work was nowhere near the level of art Serene had been able to produce at that age. Serene was beginning to accept that her daughter's art was more on the music and writing side than it was on the painting and illustration side. She was definitely her father's daughter.

Serene held her stomach and asked God if the life she carried within would lean more on her side of the art industry.

"We should stop." Lily Red put her brush and palette on the table next to her easel.

"Already?" Serene asked. "Are you done with your painting?"

"It's good for now." Lily Red nodded. "Aunt Nova is coming soon, and Claudia and Nate said they would come with her to play with me. We can all paint together." She patted her fingers on the edge of Serene's canvas, smudging it with the paint on her own fingers. "Can they paint on your canvas, Mom? You didn't do anything at all." She eyed Serene's hand on her stomach. "Are you hungry?"

Serene realized they hadn't yet told their daughter about the new baby. She held her tongue from explaining, because Nolan might want to be there to tell Lily Red. "Yes," she said. "A little. Want to go find something in the pantry we can munch on? We can even prepare food for when our guests arrive."

Lily Red's green eyes brightened, the freckles on her cheek deepening. She bobbed her head up and down in response to her mother. "Uh-huh. Rachel and Jenna are coming too, right?"

"Yes, they are!" Serene exclaimed. "Let's get you all cleaned up so you can hug them when they get here." She clasped hands with her daughter and skipped toward the bathroom with her.

"Jenna has never been here before," Lily Red said while Serene washed her clean. "Can I show her my room when she arrives?"

"Sure, but we all have something to talk about when they get here, so you'll have to stay with Claudia and Nate in your room while us grown-ups talk."

"Will Daddy join you too?"

"No, poppy. It will just be us ladies, but we all get to have dinner together after."

"Why are they all coming?"

"Do you remember that play you joined where you were a lost little girl and Uncle Caleb had to find you and rescue you?"

Lily Red nodded. "That was so much fun! Jenna was so pretty when she was an angel in the sky."

"She was, wasn't she?"

"And she was so high up in that hoop and turning and turning and turning, but she never fell at all! Not once!"

"You remember that?" Serene rinsed her out after scrubbing off every bit of paint she could find on her daughter's skin.

Lily Red's gap-toothed grin and bright eyes were an image of unabashed delight. When her eyes glazed, as if she remembered something about the play, Serene had to smile right back. Somehow, the fact that the play had made an impact even on Lily Red was confirmation to her that having a rerun of the play was a good idea. This time, though, Serene intended to revamp all the set pieces, because the last time, she had been too busy with her company to help out. Many commented that the weakest part of the play had been the set pieces. Serene was about to amend that, assuming she would have the opportunity. There was no knowing how the ladies this afternoon would respond to her proposal.

"Pray with me that they will be willing to put up the play, okay, Lily Red? It'll be fun for all of us."

"Since I'm seven now, Mom, can I be the angel and turn and turn on the hoop like Jenna? She can be the lost little girl this time."

Serene laughed. "How about you tell her that when she gets here? Find out if she'll agree."

"Okay." Lily Red lifted her arms and stood on her tiptoes. "I want to be just like Jenna someday. She dances so pretty."

Warmth spread over Serene's heart as Lily Red flitted about her bedroom, careful not to knock anything over. Lily Red might find herself in a completely different industry than her father and mother. Whichever path life would take her, Serene could only lift up her daughter's future to the Lord — uncertainty and all.

After getting Lily Red dressed up and her bedroom cleaned, the mother and daughter duo made their way to the kitchen to prepare snacks for the afternoon. At this point, the sound coming out of Nolan's studio sounded more like music and less like random bits and pieces of halting rhythms and beats caught up in a musician's writing process.

No sooner had they filled several platters with random finger foods when a buzz indicated the presence of a car at their gate. Serene creased her brows. If it had been Nova who had arrived, they wouldn't need to buzz her in, because she had a key to their gate — all members of their family did. Had Jenna or Rachel arrived early? Serene headed for the small screen on the wall to check who was coming.

She gulped. Was that Mrs. P's car? What was Rhoda Petersen doing here? She buzzed the car in and braced herself for the unknown.

"Mom? Who is it?" Lily Red asked as she dangled her feet back and forth on the chair while eating from a small bowl of pretzels on the table.

Serene extended her hand toward her daughter. "Come here, poppy. I think maybe you should stay with your dad for a little bit, okay?"

"But it's Daddy's music time. He doesn't like it when we—"

"I know, I know." Serene nodded. "He'll understand. Come on."

Lily Red hopped off her chair, her bowl of pretzels with her, before clasping her mother's hand. They left the kitchen and walked through a long hallway, passing two other rooms before reaching the back left corner of the house, where Nolan's studio was. As suspected, his door was wide open. With headphones on, Nolan had his eyes shut as he skillfully tapped a staccato beat on the beatbox cajón.

Lily Red scrunched her nose at her mother, hesitant to disrupt her father. Serene pressed her forefinger on her lips and pointed at the sofa in one corner of the studio. "Sit down. I'll come back for you."

Lily Red shrugged and obeyed, climbing onto the sofa, careful not to spill her pretzels.

Satisfied her daughter was in a safe and comfortable spot, Serene made her way to the front door. Upon reaching it, the doorbell rang. Serene braced herself for what was about to happen. She opened the door and gasped when she found Nova and the twins standing on her doorstep. Serene tried to recalibrate her brain to adjust to their presence there. Where was Mrs. P? She stood on her tiptoes and tried to look over their shoulders. There was no one there. Had she imagined Mrs. P's car trying to get into their estate?

"Aunt Serene?" Claudia waved her hand in front of Serene's face. "We're here."

Serene snapped to attention and tried to smile at her niece. "Yeah, it's just—uhh—I thought I saw—"

"Miss Rhoda?" Nova asked. She pointed her thumb over her shoulder and behind her. "Yeah. We saw her car drive out of your gate right as we were pulling up. Did she come to visit you?"

Serene furrowed her brows. "No, actually. She had come unannounced. I guess she changed her mind and decided not to push through with the visit." She blinked her eyes and shrugged. "Anyway, I'm being so rude. Come in, come in!" She embraced her sister-in-law and then her nephew and niece. "You two are growing up so fast! It's like you gain an inch every week."

"We'd be giants by now if that happened for a year," Claudia said as she stepped inside the house. "Where's Lily Red?"

Nate's eyes were glued to his phone, so he barely even acknowledged Serene as he passed through the door.

Nova pulled her coat off as she stepped inside, right behind her twelve-year-old twins. "Nate."

At the sound of his mother's voice, Nate immediately looked up from his phone and smiled at his aunt. "Hi, Aunt Serene." He then put his focus right back to his phone.

Nova clenched her jaw. "Nate, come on."

"I'll just finish this level, Ma, and then you'll have my full focus."

Nova rolled her eyes as she hung her coat on the rack. "Sorry about that. Kids these days."

Serene shut the door behind her. "It's fine."

Nova hugged her. "How are you? Can't imagine you were too thrilled to have Miss Rhoda suddenly come pay you a visit."

"I'm more intrigued than anything. I so wanted to find out why she had decided to stop by."

"Don't let it bother you." Nova waved her hand in the air. "Who knows what's going through her head nowadays?" She hooked her arm through Serene's. "Where's my brother?"

"Studio with Lily Red."

Immediately, Nate and Claudia rushed through the hallway and made their way to Nolan's studio.

Serene bit her lip. They were gone. She couldn't stop them anymore. Hopefully, Nolan wouldn't mind the disturbance. She shrugged. "Do you want to go with them?"

Nova shook her head and squeezed Serene's hand. "I'd rather find out how you are doing. We haven't had a good conversation in weeks, and I want to make sure you're okay. That's why I thought I'd come a little earlier, so I can be here before Rachel and Jenna arrive."

Serene sighed and pointed toward the kitchen. If there was one person she would feel comfortable talking to about what was going on, it was Nova. "Have you read the article?" she asked as they made their way inside the kitchen.

"Yes, unfortunately." Nova placed her bag on top of the table and took a seat. "Hannah and Vienna sent it to me on separate occasions, asking how it was affecting you and Nolan. You, especially."

Serene's heart warmed at the mention of Nova's best friends asking about her, but it was also a reminder of the reach of the article. Hannah and Vienna, after all, were miles away, across the Atlantic, in another country. "I'm lying if I say it doesn't affect me, because it does." Serene set a platter of finger foods on the dining table before sitting next to Nova. "I've been avoiding talking about it with Nolan, and I think it's beginning to upset him that I'm holding back and not letting him in, but—" Serene shook her head "—I don't know what to say to him."

"Wouldn't the truth suffice?" Nova asked.

"Part of me wonders if the article has truth in it. That's what's gnawing at me, and—"

"Seriously?" A grim look was on her husband's face when he stepped under the arch leading to the kitchen. He crossed his arms against his chest and frowned at her. "That article is a bunch of lies. Why would you ever allow yourself to believe a single word in that stupid thing?"

"Nolan—" Serene sighed. She had no idea how to respond.

Nova squeezed her arm for support.

A buzz indicating the arrival of someone at the gate.

Nolan grimaced. He rubbed the stubble on his jaw. "How are you willing to talk about this with my sister, but not me?"

Serene lowered her eyes. "I want to talk about it with you, Nolan. It's just—" she swallowed hard "—it's a lot to process, and it's not easy to express these things to you without feeling like I'm—"

Another buzz interrupted the interrogation. Nolan glared at the intercom system.

"I'm sure Serene can discuss this with you later." Nova stood from her seat and patted Serene on the shoulder. "Right now, you have guests." Nova smiled at him. "Come on. Give me a hug."

Nolan's expression softened, and a smile appeared on his face as he gave in and embraced his older sister. "Hi, Nova. Thanks for being here for us."

"Always." She pulled away from him and patted his arms. "Now, open the gate for the girls."

Nolan huffed before buzzing the ladies in and turning toward Serene. "We're talking about this later. The twins and Lily Red are painting in her bedroom. I'll be back in my studio."

Once again, he walked away and disappeared. This time, he closed the door behind him, his music no longer flowing out of his studio to assure Serene he was still with her. Her lips quivered. "I don't know what's happening to me, Nova," Serene said.

By the time Jenna and Rachel arrived to discuss the possibility of pulling off another run of *Prodigal Once*, Serene was already in a heap of tears.

They all gathered together around the dining table, with Serene and Nova on one side, and Rachel and Jenna on the other. Serene blew her nose on the tissue as she tried to collect herself.

"It's a tough time for everyone." Rachel reached for Serene's hand.

Serene squeezed the hand of her future sister-in-law. "It is." She let out a dry laugh. "Which is why I feel silly about being this dramatic in front of you guys. I have such a blessed life, despite all the trouble happening around me and within me."

Nova shook her head as she ran her hand up and down Serene's back. "We are all blessed, sure, and we are grateful. That doesn't mean we don't have obstacles along the way. We still stumble sometimes or get disheartened. You've been through a lot, Serene. You should be able to vent once in a while."

"Exactly." Jenna bobbed her head up and down. "I can't believe all the things the reporter said about you, especially with your pregnancy. It makes me so mad, what they're putting you through."

Nova's eyes widened. "Serene! You're pregnant?"

Jenna's face drained of color when Serene shot her a glare. "Sorry," she mouthed.

How did she even know? Serene frowned. Rachel was mouthing, "sorry" to her, too.

"What?" Nova asked. "Is it a secret or something? Even from me? But these two know?" She narrowed her eyes at Serene. "You and your secrets."

"It's not a secret, Nova," Serene said. "I've been trying to be careful about whom to announce it to, because my heart's still broken over my last two miscarriages. I don't want to bring people's hopes up, or if I'm to be honest, I don't want to bring my own hopes up."

"Wow." Nova squeezed Serene's hand. "You really are going through a lot, but at least we're all here, right? If anything, one awesome thing about trying to figure out if we can pull off this play is that we have a great reason to meet regularly and pray for one another through this season. We can all use some prayer."

Jenna and Rachel nodded in agreement.

"This is why it would be nice to hold this play," Serene said. "If we can convince the board to give it a go ahead, I really do believe it can bring us all together again, because we're focusing on something other than our own selves. Also, the story is relevant, because we all have been prodigals at some point." Serene pointed at her future sister-in-law. "Except for Rachel. You've been a straight arrow through-and-through."

Nova tilted her head to the side and scrunched her nose. "Serene is right. I can't quite remember any point in your life that you veered away from the faith, Rachel. Gotta give your mother credit for that, despite everything she is putting us all through." Nova rolled her eyes.

Rachel's brilliant smile twitched at that comment, but she didn't say anything in response.

"Didn't they call you Little Miss Perfect at some point?" Jenna asked, nudging her best friend in the shoulder.

Rachel shrugged. "Hey. If the shoe fits."

Serene did everything she could to keep herself from rolling her eyes. Rachel Petersen's confidence was admirable, but this was one of her more annoying traits. It was beyond Serene how this young woman could be okay with being referred to as perfect, but that was likely only because Serene hated that word at the moment.

"So—" Serene pressed her palms on top of the table "—since we're all pretty passionate about putting the play together, would any of you like to pray first before we craft a proposal for the church board?"

"I would love to, if it's okay," Jenna said.

"Sure." Serene nodded. "Go ahead."

All four of them held hands as Jenna prayed. "God, these are uncertain times for us. This year has been a lot of highs and lows. I got married this year, and my best friend is about to get married soon, too. Serene is pregnant, and Nova has got to have the most picture-perfect family at our church. These are things we can be thankful for, but in all of this, there has also been a lot of shaking. Lord, this play we're hoping to put together again once helped reconnect me to my estranged father. Now, we're praying that You could use it to rebuild the bridges our weaknesses have destroyed. Only You can come through for us."

As Jenna prayed, Serene realized that of all four of them, Jenna was the youngest Christian. Despite how much Serene supported her father's decision to put Max as the next pastor of Connect Church, it was so hard to picture Jenna as a pastor's wife, basically the mother of a church. Then again, Serene's standard for the mother of their church was her mother, Mama Aida, and that was a standard no one could ever match in Serene's eyes.

Serene's heart went out to Jenna, so she made a mental note to remember to make good on her word to invite Jenna over once Nolan left. Maybe if she could focus on pouring out love and encouragement to someone else, she would be able to distract herself from the doubt and insecurity taking root inside her heart.

eight

FANTASTIC PAINTINGS & FUTURE PLANS

After waving the ladies and the twins goodbye, Serene shut the front door and climbed the grand staircase, ready to head for the master bedroom. A gentle tug of longing to check on her daughter caused her to meander toward another hallway, where she found Nolan standing under the door frame of their daughter's bedroom, his head leaning against the doorpost. She had gone there to kiss Lily Red good night, not to argue with her husband. She tensed as she debated within herself whether she should approach or turn back.

With her heart a lot lighter after the time of prayer and seeking God with the ladies, Serene decided it would do her marriage good to make it up to her husband for the things she had told him. From his side, she snaked her arms around his waist and leaned her chin on his left bicep, hardened by his folded arms. Lily Red lay in her twig-and-vine wooden bed, all tucked in, hugging her favorite stuffed elephant, Lumpy. The peaceful look on her face made Serene smile. It was such a lovely complement to the fantastical forest theme of her bedroom — the walls having been hand-painted by Serene herself with trees and various woodland creatures.

"She's beautiful, isn't she?" Serene whispered.

Nolan nodded. "Just like her mother."

"And her dad." Serene kissed his shoulder. "I'm sorry, Nolan."

"For what?" he asked.

Serene flinched. It was so like him to pry like this. "For being so stubborn, I guess. For the things I said. I hope you know I appreciate it when you stand up for me. It's selfish of me to think the article only affects me, when this is your career we're talking about. I should have told you from the beginning."

"You should've. After all these years of marriage, I should be the one you run to about things like this, Serene." He turned around to face her, slightly pushing her backwards so he could close the door to their daughter's bedroom. "And this isn't about my career. That's what hurts the most, Serene. Do you really think all I care about is damage control when things like this happen? Serene, when I read that article, I almost broke Max's phone with how angry I was, and I couldn't wrap my head around why you were pushing me away, why you wouldn't receive any help from me." He intertwined his fingers with hers. "Come with me." He cocked his head to the side. "I have a surprise for you."

Serene raised a brow. "Oh?"

Nolan led her back down the staircase, through the foyer, past his studio, and to the backyard garden. To their left was the pool area, and the jacuzzi. To their right, where a flower garden and a playground were, someone had parked a classic red 1950 Chevy truck.

"Nolan?"

"Do you remember?" he asked as he pulled her past the pool area and toward the truck. "This was the exact same truck we used when we shot our first professional video for *Rocking Serene* in college. You were so uncomfortable that day, and when you left me back then, I would always think back to that day and get mad at myself for not realizing soon enough how unsuited you were for my industry." He let go of her hand and ran his palm against the exterior of the truck. "*Red & Ice* was my dream. It wasn't yours, but you followed my dream anyway, because you loved me that much."

Serene got choked up by her uncertainty about taking a stroll down memory lane. "I get the point, okay? We fell apart back then, because I couldn't find the guts to tell you what I was going through, and now I'm doing the same thing. I said I'm sorry, didn't I?"

Nolan narrowed his eyes at her and puckered his lips to give her this expression that he only gave her when he thought she was saying something silly. "Come on. That is totally not the point." He climbed up to the back of the truck and coaxed her to come up there with him. She didn't bother going to the back. She just grabbed his hand and let him pull her up, while she pressed her foot against the side of the truck to propel her upwards.

Once she was on the back with him, she was greeted by fairy lights hanging on the sides, surrounding a picnic spread reminiscent of their first date, after Nolan had returned to the Lord and decided to pursue her.

"Remember?" he asked.

Serene nodded. Where was he going with this, though? Why was he doing this? He was trying to be romantic, sure. She got that, but what exactly was he getting at?

Nolan propped up some pillows. Serene sat next to him. Despite all the questions racing through her mind, she still snuggled against him, leaning her head on his shoulder and holding his hand.

"I guess I'm missing the point here," she admitted, "and I do appreciate all this, I do, but Nolan, it's true what I said to Nova earlier. What if the article was true? What if the only reason I ever succeeded was not because of my own merit, but because of my connection to you? Is that not a valid concern?"

Nolan's grip tightened on hers. He pressed his lips against her temple before responding to her concerns with concerns of his own. "Several things bother me about the things you said, Serene. One, I don't understand why you would ever doubt your own talent, because we both know that with or without me, God has gifted you with so much of it. Two, it's so strange to me you would think there's something wrong about succeeding because of your connection to me. We're married, Serene. My success is your success, and vice versa. Why are none of these fools making a fuss over the role you played in my success? You sacrificed a lot for me to get to where I am right now, and I'm grateful, love. I thank God everyday that you are my wife."

"We have a lot to be grateful for, don't we?"

"We do." He pointed toward the playground Serene had designed specifically for her daughter. "Take a look around you. We are home. We are together. Your fight is my fight, and your pain is my pain, because we are one now. You and me. Isn't that what happened when we said our vows? You don't have to keep fighting your battles alone, love."

Serene swallowed hard. To that, she couldn't come up with an answer. His words revealed something deep inside her she hadn't even known was there until that moment. It was this insidious sliver of pride within her, one that felt the need to compete with her husband and match what he had reached in his career.

"I'm sorry, Nolan," she managed to squeak out. "You've been amazing through all of this, and you've loved me through and through, even when you may not understand me. For all it's worth, I haven't fully understood myself either, but I think I've been pushing myself to match your success as a way to prove myself worthy of the love you've been pouring on me."

"Serene, you don't have to—"

"Let me finish." Serene brushed her thumb against the back of his hand and leaned her head on his shoulder. "I'm just realizing now that I don't need to prove anything to you, to myself, to the media — least of all, to God. I'm already chosen. You're my beloved, and I am yours, and I love that, Nolan. I love you. You're amazing. I'm so proud of everything you accomplished."

"And I'm just as proud of you, Serene," Nolan said. "First of all, you're an amazing mother to our daughter. I see so much of you in her, and I find myself falling in love with you all over again whenever I realize what a wonderful daughter we have. More than that, Serene, you've been through so much this past year. That art exhibit fiasco, losing control of *Thrive*, this stupid article that has no basis in reality, and now, a pregnancy on top of all this drama at church. You've been so strong through it all. Not only that, you've still managed to support me and go on tour with me, with not a word of complaint. You've been my rock, and I've been a fool not to realize how much all these things have been chipping at your confidence. That's unacceptable, because you are more wonderful than any of my best songs could ever express. You're right. You have nothing to prove. Not to me. Not to anyone else."

Nolan's acknowledgment of everything she had been through assured her that it had not gone unnoticed, that she was strong in her own way. She was his counterpart even if it didn't quite look the way she had imagined. His words freed her heart and gave her hope for the future. She giggled even as she snuggled closer to him. "We'll be okay. Right, Nolan?"

"Of course," he said, not a single hint of doubt in his voice. "Serene, we've had a rough couple of years. That last miscarriage was devastating for both of us." Nolan rubbed his palm against her thigh and settled his hold on her knee. "But there's hope of new life growing within you. We've mourned long enough. This is a time we can rejoice. This is good news amid all that's happening. To me, your pregnancy is a reminder that we are still going strong, despite everything we've been through. We may not be the *Red & Ice* performing together on stage anymore, but we're Nolan and Serene, and I don't care what any article says. We may not be perfect, but I've always believed — from the day I asked your father if I could marry you when we were six years old — that we are perfect for each other. And we are, Serene. I don't know why you scoffed at that interview, but I wasn't just speaking in hyperbole when I told them what I did. For me, the family we have, it's as close to perfect as it gets."

His lips found hers and Serene allowed herself to once again melt into his arms. This time though, unlike the times they had spent rehearsing their performances on this truck, her heart was no longer racing when she was around Nolan.

It was steady.

All along, Serene realized that was exactly what she needed her heart to be. Secure in knowing that no matter how many hit pieces the world wrote about her, it would not change the fact that she was deeply loved.

A week later, Serene waved her husband goodbye as the tour bus rolled out of their driveway. Lily Red held Lumpy against her chest, sniffles coming out of her.

Serene ruffled with her hair. Despite all the times their family needed to separate ways for any reason, Lily Red still cried whenever it happened. She held the little girl's shoulder and nudged her toward the door. "Come on, poppy. Let's get inside. You start school on Monday, so let's try to make the best out of our free time until then, okay? Also, Jenna is coming over to hang out with us this afternoon. We get to find out from her whether we can do the play again."

The foyer welcomed them with this calming sense of familiarity. The lavender scent coming from the diffuser Serene had turned on earlier triggered memories of their living room, where her mother used to diffuse the same scent. Serene smiled as she brushed her hand against her daughter's hair. Something had been settled within her and despite all the disappointment she had gone through, Serene had a hope within her anchoring her soul. Along with this reawakened hope, a distinct longing to create seized Serene.

As if to affirm what she found herself wanting to do, Lily Red let go of her hand and threw her arms up. The ears, arms, and legs of Lumpy, stomach clutched by her right hand, flopped in the air. "We should paint today, Mom!"

Serene smiled. "Is that what you want to do?"

"Uh-huh!"

"Let's go do that then."

Ten minutes later, they had two easels — a kid-sized one for Lily Red, and an adult-sized one for Serene — set up in Serene's art studio. Holding her palette in her hand, Serene took a breath and closed her eyes to conjure up a mental image of what she wanted to create that day. Nothing came up, and her mind remained a blank canvas.

Lily Red giggled. "Why do you have your eyes closed, Mom? You can't paint that way."

Serene smiled, but kept her eyes shut. "I can't, can I? Mom is just trying to picture in her head what she wants to paint today."

"Oh okay. I'll do that too!"

Serene snuck a peek at her daughter by squinting one eye open. Lily Red had her eyes shut tight, her little face scrunched up as if she was making a real effort to come up with an image in her head. Serene's gratefulness for the existence of her little girl turned into a desperate prayer over the life of the child she was carrying within her.

"Life," she whispered. "Breathe life unto us, oh God. Preserve my children's lives. Whatever is being birthed right now through this play, preserve it, as well. Today, I ask for Your creativity. You are Creator. The One Who breathed life into us. I trust You to carry to completion what You have begun in us. Let the prodigals return, oh God. Let us all return to You." The shift in the atmosphere surrounding her and the abiding presence of God within her were palpable to Serene. When she opened her eyes, she trusted God to lead her as she walked the artist's path with faith. Without allowing hesitation to hold her back, she dipped her paintbrush in a dab of purple paint and made her first brush stroke.

When Lily Red noticed her mother had already started, she did the same.

Time ceased to matter as both mother and daughter surrendered to this notion of timelessness, both creating their own works of art. It was a grumble in Serene's stomach and a buzz in their security system that alerted Serene to the passing of time. Beside her, Lily Red had a finished painting of a tree flourishing by a river. Its roots, deep and colorful, took up the bottom half of the portrait canvas, almost as if to emphasize the depth of the roots rather than the tree itself. Serene raised a brow. Maybe her daughter was more of a painter than Serene had given her credit for. But where was her daughter? Lily Red had curled herself up on the fainting couch on one side of the room, napping right below one of Serene's most expensive paintings, *Red Hat*, from her first and most successful art show: *One Red Hue*. It was a black-and-white image of a huge crowd and about two thirds from the bottom, smack center, was an obscure figure wearing a red cowboy hat — the only shade of red in the painting.

Another buzz made Serene jolt from where she stood. She checked the screen and found Jenna's yellow car waiting to enter their gate. Serene buzzed her in.

Before heading to the front door to welcome Jenna, Serene glanced at her newest painting. It was of a seed aglow, sprouting from the ground. It was a promise of a new beginning, because they were no longer among the reckless, among the prodigals. They were new creations, and they were about to enter into a new season. The seed had been planted. It had already died, and now it was about to be something else entirely — a tree planted by rivers of water, bearing fruit in and out of season. Serene's painting was the beginning. Lily Red's painting was the promise.

Later, once they sat around the table for lunch, after they had said grace, Serene looked Jenna straight in the eye and said, "I don't think we should do the play," Serene said. "At least not the one we already did. We should do a sequel. We're no longer prodigals. It's time for us to turn over a new leaf."

As she said the words, a surge of faith rushed over Serene. She laid her hand on her stomach, and without a shadow of doubt within her, she believed: this baby would be born.

PART TWO

The One Who Danced Away

JENNA OWENS

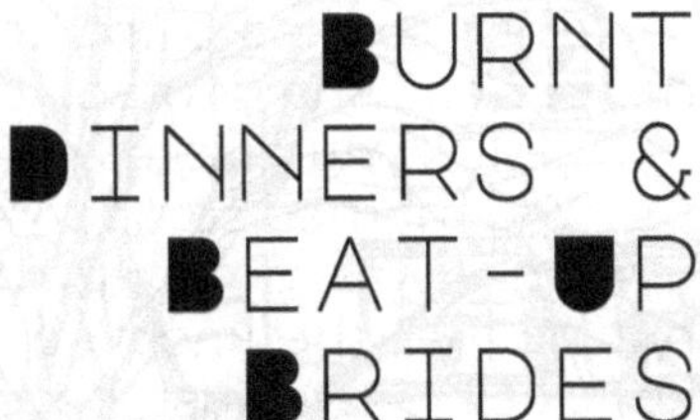

The charred skin fell off of the chicken, mocking Jenna Owens for her failure, as she laid the glass tray on top of the tiled island counter. She threw the oven mitts beside the tray and propped herself up on a barstool. She laid her elbows on the counter and rested her chin on her palms, cupping her cheeks. After a frustrated huff, she narrowed her eyes at the burnt remains of a chicken that had died in vain because of her incapacity to make her husband a good dinner.

A few months into their marriage, and Jenna had already convinced herself she was possibly the worst wife in the world. How was Max putting up with her? The poor guy had roped himself into a lifelong commitment with her, and there was no way he could get himself out of it.

The creak of a door indicated Max walking out of his office studio, where he would often shoot and edit videos for his podcast, *Mad Max Missions*. He had been there for hours, and Jenna had wanted to surprise him with rosemary chicken, but that wasn't how life turned out. Then again, life rarely turned out the way Jenna wanted.

Max sauntered into the kitchen, heading for the fridge, when he spotted his wife still staring straight at the block of charcoal that had once upon a time been a clucking chicken.

Jenna didn't flinch from her position. "Hello, husband."

"Hey, wife." Max snickered. "What did you do, Jen? Burn dinner with your laser vision?"

"That sounds a lot cooler than what actually happened." She pouted. "Let's stick with that story."

"Only if you first tell me what the actual story is."

"You married someone who can't cook a decent dinner. I was going to make rosemary chicken, but now—" she knocked on the chicken with her knuckles "—we just have to make do with this meteorite fragment."

Max laughed. "I like the sound of meteorite fragment." He walked past her to get something from the fridge. "It might give us superpowers."

"What superpower do you want?" Jenna asked as her husband moved around the kitchen behind her.

"Hard question," Max said. "You have to give me time to think about it. How about you?"

"Invisibility, because I'm super embarrassed right now." Jenna pressed her finger against the glass tray. "Ow." It was still hot. Served her right for failing in her mission.

"You? Embarrassed? Didn't think that was possible."

The sound of something liquid being poured into something made her thirsty. "Can you give me a drink, too?"

"Sure." Max laid a glass of orange juice next to her before pouring himself another glass. He then leaned his elbows on the counter, so he was standing beside her, their shoulders touching. "What are you embarrassed about?" He pointed at the burnt dish. "That?"

Jenna kept her chin propped up with her one hand before she pulled the other glass closer with her free hand. She nodded at Max before taking a few gulps of the orange juice. "I can't make a decent dinner." She patted his clean-shaven face with her hand. "You'll starve, because you married me. Poor you."

"Where's all this drama coming from?" His eyes twinkled with amusement as he drank from his glass of juice. "I'm fine with what you've been making so far."

"We can't live our entire lives together eating pancakes and spaghetti."

"Or boxed mac and cheese."

Jenna wrinkled her nose. "See what I mean? I want to do better." She pouted. "You deserve better." She sighed and returned to her original position, staring the dead chicken down. "I get so easily distracted whenever I try to make food, and I also forget random ingredients. Like salt. So many dishes need that to taste good, apparently."

Max chuckled as he stood to his full height, dwarfing her as he finished his drink. He then embraced her from behind and leaned his chin on top of her head. "What is going on with you, Jen? Why are you letting this get to you so much?"

"Did you know Serene cooks all their food herself? They can afford to hire a chef, but she does it all, because Nolan prefers her homemade cooking."

"She cooks only for herself and her daughter right now, so it's not as impressive as you think it sounds. Serene's buttered fried chicken is amazing, though. Have you tasted it?"

"You're not helping." Jenna rolled her eyes. "Do you know I once overheard Mrs. P tell Nova she wouldn't touch anything I cook with a ten-foot pole?"

"When?" Max asked, the heightened pitch of his voice revealing his surprise.

"It was during our engagement party, before they left the church."

"Okay." He let go of her waist, so he could bend his tall frame to lay his elbows on the counter and rest his cheek on his palm. Whether it was to make eye contact with her or to mimic the way she looked, Jenna couldn't tell, but she appreciated how patient he was with her. "Jen, you've always been the one who was immune to Mrs. P's opinions. When we were kids, you never cared what she thought about anything. Since when do you care what Mrs. P. says about you? Not to mention your food?"

"Since I became a pastor's wife." Jenna lowered her gaze, because she wouldn't be able to stand it should she happen to detect even a slight flicker of disappointment in his eyes. Her chin quivered. "I'm not cut out for this, Max."

"Jenna…" He tucked her hair behind her ears, his thumb stroking her cheek. "I had no idea this transition was getting to you so much."

"It shouldn't, right? My focus should be on God. I need to learn to trust in Him through all of this, but between you taking up the leadership of the church and this church split—" Jenna choked. "I feel like I'm under a microscope, like the whole church is assessing my every move, finding out if I can handle the expectations. Even when I was at Serene's place, I would catch her staring at me sometimes, examining me and figuring out if I can fill the shoes her mother left behind. Mama Aida, Max. I'm being compared to Mama Aida! Meanwhile, here I am. Can't even bake a simple chicken dish properly."

"Jen, this is a crazy time for both of us. It's a lot to deal with. Some would say God doesn't give us more than we can handle, but the Bible doesn't really say that. A lot of us find ourselves in situations that prove to be more than we can handle, but God allows these into our lives, so we can learn to depend on Him. He is the One Who handles it all. For all it's worth, I'm terrified too. If not for Pastor Sam reassuring me that he won't retire until the church is in a more stable situation, I would've already given up."

"He said that to you?"

"At Mrs. P's house." Max nodded. "He won't just leave the church to a twenty-seven-year-old without proper and complete support from the elders." He rubbed his palm up and down her spine. "You're not alone in feeling like everyone is assessing us, Jen. They are, but maybe God is just teaching us that all of this isn't up to us. It's all up to Him. We may not be ready to face the demands of pastoring a church, but for some reason, here we are. He is the One Who chose us, so He'll be the One to qualify us and make us ready. That being said, I suggest you stop giving the very much dead chicken your death glare and go out for dinner with me. Sound good?"

Her heart a lot lighter after her husband's pep talk, Jenna relented. "Let's go."

While the night out was a fun distraction, her husband's kind words were only enough to temporarily assure her. The burnt chicken was still inside her head — a symbol of her inadequacy. What if she never got this right? How could she hope to be a mother someday, raise a family, lead a church when she couldn't even follow a stupid recipe? What if no matter how hard she tried, she would never be enough, she would never qualify?

Serene's words circled her head. *"We're no longer among the reckless, among the prodigals. We're new creations in Christ. This is a time for us to overcome."* Jenna had loved the idea when Serene had suggested they focus on the story of the prodigal son contending with the jealousy and criticism of the other brother. It would be relatable to many, but Jenna still wasn't sure which one she was. She still felt like the prodigal in so many ways, and she wanted nothing more than to run away from the other brother.

Problem was that the entire church was beginning to look like the other brother in her eyes.

An epic instrumental arrangement of a classic worship song accompanied the fluid motion of Jenna's body as it transitioned from one form to the next — a moving expression of her need for an Almighty God to be Strength in her weakness. Like she had always done when something became too overwhelming or too painful in her life, she abandoned herself, her qualms, her concerns in a dance. Not one to stay still for too long, the morning after her chicken mishap, Jenna woke up early to welcome dawn with an act of worship.

She had never been one to dwell on her shortcomings. Max had chosen her, and she was now his wife. This was the life she had signed up for, and she wasn't about to go around feeling sorry for herself, just because there were challenges along the way. Movement was her way of fighting back. It didn't matter what she looked like, whether it was graceful or pleasant to an onlooker's eye. Jenna melted into the flow of the music and allowed the Holy Spirit to lead her every movement. In that moment, God's presence was right with her, His glory filling her soul. This was how she would survive — no, thrive — being the wife of a pastor. It wasn't in her own capabilities, but in the ability of her God to defend her, to uphold her, to be her glory and the Lifter of her head.

By the time the music stopped, Jenna was breathless, her muscles throbbing from the intensity of her every move, but she had a smile on her face, and a lightness in her chest that told her she had won the victory. God would be her confidence, she was sure of it. Jenna bent over, laying her hands on her knees, to help her lungs draw breath. Around her, the sun cast a warm orange glow over her surroundings as it rose to announce the morning.

Jenna picked her phone up and paused the music. Six o'clock. It would be at least an hour before Max would wake up. She had time. Jenna puffed her chest, collecting her bravery, as she marched back into their house to take a quick shower before tackling her fiercest opponent at the moment: breakfast. She planned to make muffin pan frittatas, and she was determined to make it the best breakfast she had ever made in her life. That was a low enough bar for her to reach, because it wasn't like she made excellent breakfasts to begin with, so she wasn't shooting for the moon here.

An hour later, Jenna grinned at the cute little egg-based muffins laid on a platter. Triumph! Max ambled along the kitchen, rubbing his eyes awake.

"Good morning, husband."

"Hey, wife."

"Look what we're having for breakfast."

Max yawned and stretched his long arms before looking at her successfully executed dish. "That looks amazing. I'm starving, too." He rubbed his stomach. "Do we have coffee already?"

Jenna winced. How could she forget to turn on the coffeemaker? Coffee was usually the first thing Max looked for in the morning. This was the first time she hadn't been able to make him coffee. "I totally forgot about that. Sorry. Let me brew some now."

"Nah." Max shook his head, pecked her on the cheek, and patted her shoulder. "Let me make it this time. Thank you for breakfast, Jen. You're amazing. Now, it's my turn. I got everything else."

Jenna couldn't help but smile as she watched Max move around the kitchen. That moment stamped the notion in her head that this man was with her. They were a team. He would be strong in the areas she was weak, and vice versa. As she recognized his desire to serve her, in turn, she found herself wanting to serve him to the best of her ability, as well.

She hopped off her seat and began helping to prepare the breakfast table. She could get used to this, her and Max working together. They were going to be okay.

Later, they said grace after pulling up bar stools on either side of the island counter to have breakfast there.

Max took a sip from his coffee while Jenna just held her cup of rose tea and inhaled the sweet scent.

"The youth group is at ten. Are you still heading to your dad's after?" Max asked.

Jenna nodded. "He says he has a surprise." She rolled her eyes.

Max made a face. "Don't get me wrong, Jen. I'm so grateful for his generosity, but if it's another huge gift, I don't think we should accept anymore."

"I know. Hopefully, it's not that, but if it is, then I would have to talk to him about it. He's also been asking about how I've been doing, considering everything happening in church, so it might be good to just focus on that while I'm there."

"Great." He grabbed hold of her hand and squeezed it to affirm her. "I'll follow you there after my meeting with the board, then."

"Sounds like a plan." Jenna took a sip from her cup of tea. "Tomorrow, I have an interview at Frontier Press."

Max creased his brows. "With Caleb Grant?"

"Yeah. He approached me last Sunday to tell me they're short-staffed right now. I didn't pick up on what the reason was, but they need a temp, so he asked me if I'd like to consider working there as basically a girl Friday. I'm not sure if I want to take it, because it's not exactly the line of work I want to get into, but I figured I can show up for the interview anyway." Jenna shrugged. "It would be a good way for me to get to know Caleb and Nova a bit more."

"That sounds great." Max nodded. "They're amazing, and if you're pushing through with this play, it would be good for you to work closely with Nova, because she wrote the first one, and it would make sense if she wrote the second one."

"That's what I thought!" Jenna exclaimed. She then tensed when she realized Max hadn't touched his food yet.

Her doubts about him not wanting to eat her food were quickly dispelled, however, because Max took a frittata from the plate and sliced it straight through the middle. Melted cheese oozed out of the sides, the mixture of parsley, mint, tomato, and ham adding color apart from the egg's yellow. He bit into his toast before popping a bite of the frittata into his mouth. He wobbled his head from side-to-side as he chewed slowly. His eyes lit up before he swallowed. "This is amazing, Jen."

Her ears perked up. Was he just being nice? She placed one on her plate and took a bite. The burst of complementing flavors in her mouth made her eyes pop open. This was excellent. She could even taste the hint of nutmeg she had added to it. She swallowed, smiled, and squealed. "I can't believe I made this!" she exclaimed before jumping to her feet and pulled out a few wild dance moves to celebrate. She then sat on her husband's lap, wrapped her arms around his neck, and pressed her lips against his. "There's hope for us yet."

"Never lost hope." Max grinned. His arms tightened around her waist as his lips grazed her jaw. "Also, I can get used to this every morning."

Jenna laughed. "Yeah? You can, huh?" Suddenly, panic seized her. What were these rashes showing up around Max's lips? His face was bloating up and taking on a sharp shade of red. "Max, what's happening to you? You have rashes."

He tried to speak, but his words came out in a string of muffled words, and his breathing started to wheeze.

Just like that, her hope and her triumph proved to be short-lived. Had she poisoned her husband with a muffin-shaped frittata?!

ten

NEAR-DEATH NIGHTMARE & ANOTHER ALLERGY

Max was allergic to nutmeg and had suffered an anaphylactic reaction to it. They weren't even two months into their marriage, and Jenna already almost killed her husband with breakfast. As they walked out of the hospital, the swelling on Max's face had already subsided. He was no longer wheezing. While that brought Jenna relief, guilt was still trying to weasel its way into her soul, and in response to that, all Jenna could do was laugh at the entire scenario. It seemed she couldn't get anything right, and at this point, the entire thing was simply laughable. She could only go up from here, right?

"Sorry for almost ending your life, husband." Jenna hooked her arm on Max's and leaned her head on his arm as they made their way to their car. "Though you have to admit. It's kind of weird that you didn't know you were allergic to nutmeg until now."

"Right? Have I never eaten a dish that included it at some point?"

"It's a pretty common spice." Jenna shrugged.

"I should call Mom and ask. The doctor did say it's possible to develop an allergy later in life."

"Meh." Jenna nodded. "My theory is I've developed an allergic reaction to certain types of people now that I'm in my twenties, so it's not all that surprising."

Max chuckled as he gave her a side hug and smacked her temple. "Thanks for keeping it together and rushing me to the hospital."

Jenna pointed upwards. "It must have been God. I don't know how I got through that. I was so scared."

Max slowed down their walk toward the parking lot. "You pull through when it matters, Jen. I'm blessed to have you."

She looked up at him and smiled. She was so blessed to have him, as well, and most would probably say she only thought that because they were still in their honeymoon stage, but no, it wasn't just that. God had blessed her by giving her Max, and the idea of ever losing him was now quickly becoming her greatest fear.

When they reached Jenna's car, flashes of her panicked drive to the hospital covered her mind. She had never driven as fast as she had that morning. It had been hard not to panic while Max's face was swelling up in the passenger's seat, but they had made it in time. That she had been able to keep her cool was purely by the grace of God, because there was no other way she would have been able to pull it off without Him keeping her focused and calm. Jenna headed for the driver's seat, while Max rode shotgun.

While they put their seatbelts on, Max asked, "What did the youth group say when you called them?"

A vague memory of him asking her to message the group to let them know they would be running late flitted across Jenna's mind. He had been recovering after being treated with epinephrine and antihistamines, and she had nodded at him that she would, but the doctor had arrived just as she was about to, and she had forgotten to call altogether.

Jenna winced as she stuck the key in the ignition. "I forgot to call them." The engine rumbled alive. "I'm so sorry. Should I drive at lightning speed again?"

Max huffed before narrowing his eyes, shaking his head, and smirking at her. He fished his phone out of his pocket and gave one of his assistants a call.

Jenna sighed with relief as she focused on driving the car out of the hospital parking lot. Really, her saving grace was that this man was still so in love with her and couldn't be mad at her for too long.

"They're fine. Maureen said she figured something might have come up if I'm late to a meeting, because I've never been late before."

"Thank God for your great track record," Jenna said. "So, we're going home first, right?"

"No. Let's go straight to church. Maureen is distracting everyone until we get there, but they're still waiting for us."

Jenna drummed her fingers against the steering wheel. "I'd like to point out, husband, that I'm not the one who's still in my PJ's."

Max perused his black fitted T-shirt, plaid pajamas, and bedroom slippers. "Oh. Right. Hmm." He glanced at Jenna and grimaced. "Let's go straight to church. They'll understand."

Jenna smirked. "I married the right man."

He chuckled. "Glad you think so."

Jenna continued driving. A comfortable silence followed as both of them got lost in their own thoughts.

Max cleared his throat. "Is it a good idea for us to push through with doing an entirely new play?"

"What do you mean? Don't you think it's a good idea?"

"I do, but I'm not sure if it's the right timing. I was heavily involved in the production of the first play, and I know how much it took to put it together. With everything that's been going on, do you believe it will help and not just be another thing people will stress about?"

"Just this morning, you told me you thought it was a good idea for me to work closely with Nova, because it will give me an opportunity to support her as she writes a new play. Why the sudden change of tune?"

"It's not sudden." Max shook his head. "I want to be supportive towards Serene, you, and the other women, because you're so passionate about it, but I do have second thoughts about the timing. With the strain of the transition at church, not to mention Jeremy's and Rachel's wedding, wouldn't pulling this play off be another source of stress?"

Jenna's grip on the steering wheel tightened. "I hadn't actually considered Rachel's wedding. She hasn't talked about it at all, so I'm not sure she would even need much help from me. I mean, this is Rachel Petersen. She probably already has a binder detailing everything that needs to be done for both her wedding and the play. It's not like she's the kind of person who will need us to hold her hand through this entire process."

"You'll most likely be her matron-of-honor, Jen. I'm a hundred percent going to be Jeremy's best man. There's no question about it."

That much was true. There was no way for her to deny that, but then an image of Serene's painting of that seed planted, growing roots, representing a new beginning, captured her mind. Spending time with Serene had made her so sure this play would help the church heal. Practically speaking, however, Max had a valid point.

"So, do you think we should call it off?" Jenna's heart dropped asking the question. She didn't want to do that. "Because we're all pretty excited about it, and if you had just seen Serene— Max, we do believe this can help the church."

"Jen, if you go for it, then I'm with you all the way, but I want to make sure you know what you're getting yourself into. This is a lot of work. With the youth group, this new job you're trying for with Caleb, the wedding, your volunteer work with *Lady Lacey League*, and everything happening at church, do you want to add choreographing and rehearsing for the play to your plate? Is this a priority?"

Jenna bristled. "Well, when you put it like that..." Why hadn't he voiced out his thoughts earlier? He had seemed to be a hundred percent into it all this time. "I would have to bring it up with the ladies. It's not like it's my call."

"Right." Max stretched his arm to the side so he could ruffle her hair. "Either way, know that I think you'll do brilliant work if it pushes through. You are an amazing dancer, and if the play goes on, who knows? I might fall in love with you all over again."

"Please." Jenna grinned. "You're still so in love with me, as it is."

"Can't argue with that logic."

The church came into view. Jenna drove her car into one of their regular spots in the parking lot, which was still quite empty. Once she had stopped the car, she turned to look at Max. Despite all the objections her heart made to him questioning the play, she chose to see him voicing out his concerns in a positive way. "Thanks for trying to look out for me and making sure I don't over-commit myself," she said.

"Of course." His thumb brushed against her cheekbone. "Always." He unbuckled his seatbelt, so he could lean over and give her a soft, gentle kiss. "Whatever you decide, I'm sure it will turn out amazing. Besides, if you do push through with the play, I honestly wouldn't mind seeing you wearing that angel outfit again while you're dangling on a hoop twenty feet from the ground." He grinned. "That scene, the way you looked that night, would forever be etched in my mind."

Jenna grinned back, but at that point, he had gotten into her head. Was this something they should be doing? Could she pull it off? She could barely even keep their household together. Her last dish had sent her husband to the hospital!

What exactly was Jenna getting herself into? Would she be able to just dance her way through all of this?

eleven

FAITHFUL FATHERS & FOSTERED FEELINGS

The couple parted ways with deep sighs constituting an unspoken prayer for grace. Max was off to their home to get dressed and ready for a meeting with Pastor Sam and the church board, while Jenna was off to see her father. Neither knew what to expect from both gatherings.

When Dad had asked her to visit him, hinting on some sort of surprise for her, Jenna had been curious, but skeptical. Because of the divorce and how estranged their relationship had been during Jenna's formative years, her father had tried to make it up to her by giving her extravagant gifts. After driving her to college, he had given her a brand new car. While sick with cancer, he had the entire play — *Prodigal Once* — produced out of his pocket. As a wedding gift, he had paid for a significant share of their wedding expenses, their entire honeymoon, and the downpayment to their first house's mortgage.

While Jenna was thankful, all of it was getting a bit too much. As a teenager and a young adult, it had always felt to Jenna like her father was trying to buy his way into her life. Now that their relationship was in the best place it had ever been, she wanted to assure him he didn't need to do that anymore, but how would she even tell him that without the risk of offending him by implying his generosity was some ploy to buy her affections?

Jenna shut the door to her car and stared at her father's Victorian house — one that was way too big for him, especially considering he lived there alone. Even as she walked along the path leading to his front porch, memories — both good and bad — flooded her mind. That she could spend time with her father and be at ease around him was already a miracle in and of itself, especially considering how at one point, their strained relationship had caused her to hesitate to pay him a visit after having learned of his cancer. As she climbed onto the front porch, she smiled. "Thank you, Lord," she whispered, "for having brought us this far."

She then opened the front door and called out for her father. "Dad?" She passed through the entryway and snuck a peek at the living room. Her jaw dropped. "Mom?"

Eden Miranda? Inside Paolo Marquez's apartment? Would miracles never cease?

Her mother looked up from a magazine she was reading and smiled. "Oh good! You're finally here." She patted the empty space on the couch beside her. "Paolo!" she yelled out. "She's here!"

That's when a waft of something tasty drifted past Jenna's nostrils. Her father was in the kitchen? What was he doing? He shouldn't be over-exerting himself.

"I'll go check on Dad." Jenna pointed toward the kitchen.

"He'll be out in a bit. He's baking cookies," Mom said. "Come sit here with me, and tell me all about your honeymoon with Max."

Jenna wrinkled her nose. Telling her mother about her honeymoon didn't sound like an appealing activity to Jenna. She mostly wanted to go to her dad and reprimand him for baking when he should be resting instead. It had only been a year ago since his full recovery from cancer, after all, but knowing how fickle her mother's moods were, Jenna relented and plopped herself next to her mother. "I'll do better than just tell you, Mom. I'll show you pictures." She brought out her phone and swiped through her gallery of photos with Max during their honeymoon. "The hotel resort was gorgeous."

Mom paused at a photo of them with Rachel and Jeremy. "Who are these people?"

"You don't remember them? They were our best man and maid of honor. They were in the area for other reasons, so we all decided to meet up. Rachel is my best friend, and Jeremy is Max's. I introduced you to them several times."

Mom waved her hand in the air. "Oh, you know me. I'm terrible with names and faces."

"Right." Jenna nodded. She didn't know what to say next, because the foremost question circling her mind was why her mother was there to begin with. No one hated her father more than her mother, and despite all her attempts to reconcile the two, even on her own wedding day, her mother had barely said a word to her father, so this! This was a surprise that Jenna increasingly struggled to process.

Mom smiled when she saw a selfie of Max and Jenna together, where Jenna was giving Max an affectionate gaze as he was smiling at the camera. They were in their swimwear, and the background was a pretty sunset at the beach. "Max is so handsome." Mom patted Jenna's thigh. "You've done well for yourself in choosing him."

"Glad you think so, Mom." Jenna smiled. "He is amazing."

The corners of her Mom's eyes and lips lowered in time for Jenna's father to show up with a tray containing a plate of cookies and three glasses of what looked like pink lemonade. He winked at Jenna. "Were you surprised?"

"I was." Jenna glanced at her mother. "I didn't expect to see Mom here." She leaned her head on her mother's shoulder. "But I'm glad she is. It's been a while since all three of us have been in the same room together."

"Don't be silly, Jenna," Mom said. "We were all together at your wedding."

"Yeah, but there were a bunch of people there, too. I meant us being together. Just us. What brought this about?"

Her mother huffed before giving her father a sharp glare. "To be clear, just in case you're getting ideas in that flighty little head of yours—" Mom patted Jenna's cheek "—your father and I aren't getting back together."

Jenna threw her head back. She creased her brows when she realized: "The notion didn't even cross my mind."

Mom had hated her father so much, it was already too much for Jenna to process them being in the same room without yelling at each other. How could she go as far as to think they would ever get back together? Part of her grieved at that revelation. The idea that these two had once been so in love, they had decided to get married, only to be where they were now, shook her in a different way. There was no possibility whatsoever of that happening to her and Max, right?

Dad laughed, a sound that broke the tension formed by her mother. "Eden, why don't you tell Jenna why you're here?

Mom rolled her eyes, reminding Jenna of all the times her mother acted like more of a teenager than she ever had. She could sometimes scarcely believe this was the woman who had raised her.

The expression on her mother's face softened, her brown eyes lowering. "Your pastor said something in your wedding that struck me," she said. "And I don't know why it did, because my parents were Catholic, and they've told me that many times before, but he said your lives — Max's and yours — were beautiful stories of God's grace, forgiveness, and redemption. That hit me—" Mom used her thumb to jab at her chest "—right in here. What was my story like? Would it be something people would refer to as beautiful? It was circling my mind so much that when your father asked me to dance, I said yes, just so I could talk to someone about what was running through my heart and mind at that time." Mom shifted in her seat and fidgeted with her fingers on her lap. She cast a look at Jenna's father, as if she was unsure what to do.

Dad nodded at her to encourage her to continue, but she bit her lip and shook her head instead, like whatever it was she wanted to say was far too difficult to voice out.

Not knowing what to do or how to react, Jenna reached toward the coffee table in front of them to grab a glass of pink lemonade to offer to her mother. Mom readily took it and drank several gulps as Jenna prepared a coaster for her to place it on after quenching her thirst.

The surrounding atmosphere grew thick with something that made Jenna feel like they were achingly close to a breakthrough, but whatever it was her mother wanted to say, it had to happen in her time, not Jenna's. So, Jenna waited in silence, even as inside, she lifted the situation to God. *I believe it was You, God, Who touched her heart at my wedding. Whatever you're doing inside her right now, let it be for Your glory, let it be a means for us to lay down all the bitterness of the past, so we can heal as we walk into the future You have for us.*

Mom placed her glass of lemonade — halfway finished — on the coaster. She then blew out a long breath before refilling her lungs with a sharp inhale. She nodded and squared her shoulders, as if she was pumping herself up to do something. Whatever that something was, Jenna was about to find out.

"When we were dancing, your dad asked me for forgiveness. I asked him what he thought my story was, and—" Her mother teared up. Jenna grabbed the box of tissues on the coffee table and handed it to her mother, who quickly wiped away her tears, before saying in a broken voice, "Your father said the kindest things."

Jenna looked at her dad, whose face was lighting up with a smile — not one of pride, but one of compassion.

"I told her she was amazing for raising a daughter like you," Dad explained. "After everything

I put her through, after all the times I cheated, she managed to pick herself up after the divorce and become a good mother to you. I thanked her for not only raising you, but eventually, allowing you to be a part of my life, even if I know that may not have been the easiest thing for her to do."

The tug of conflicting emotions inside Jenna's heart at all the things her father said made her body tremble. Was any of what he said true, though? On one hand, she was grateful that her parents were in a place where they could communicate again. On the other hand, all her father's statements highlighted how absent he had been throughout Jenna's life, because he had no idea what having Eden Miranda as a mother had been like. Jenna couldn't say it out loud, of course, but to say that her mother had raised her was false. Eden had provided for her, but Jenna had raised herself, and probably even her own mother.

Mom took hold of her hand, and Jenna needed to summon all of her will not to pull her hand away, but what Eden said next gave her the release she needed. "I know everything your father said wasn't true. When I teared up, he thought it was because I was moved by his appreciation, but that wasn't why. I got emotional, because when I looked at you and how beautiful you were on that day, the one thing on my mind was how much I dreaded the idea of you and Max ever turning out like your father and I did."

Jenna's lips quivered. She barely noticed she was crying until the tears pooled in her chin and fell on the back of her trembling hand. Her mother had unknowingly addressed the fear this unexpected reunion had formed in Jenna.

Clasping Jenna's hand between both of hers, Mom said words Jenna never imagined she would ever hear from her mother: "I'm so sorry, Jenna. As much as I wanted to believe your father's story about me was true, I returned home knowing it wasn't, so I called your father and asked if all three of us can meet up, so that we can start to truly heal. I want the children you will have someday with Max to have grandparents who get along, a family that's whole — something your father and I deprived you of." Mom swallowed hard. "It took me a while to get to a point where I can admit this, but it's true, sweetie. I let my anger against your father deprive you of the opportunity to have a relationship with him. I made you bear a share of my fears, insecurities, and bitterness when I should've helped ease yours. Thank you for putting up with me all these years, Jenna."

Each of her mother's words felt like a stab to her chest, only because it re-opened scars Jenna had forgotten were even there. Jenna hadn't even realized until this very moment how much she needed to hear these things from her mother, but now that she had, she could sense the healing God was doing toward her freshly opened scars.

Choked up, Jenna laughed through her tears before responding, "Mom, you did the best you could. You were broken, too, and we were both lost together, but I'm glad we both found our way here. Thank you for coming. Thank you for reminding me why I followed God in the first place."

Her mother let go of her hand, bristling. "I'm not sure how I feel about God yet, Jenna. My experience with your father's church wasn't very pleasant, and it's something I don't know how to open my heart to just yet."

"It's okay, Mom." This time, Jenna took hold of her mother's hand, her fingers brushing against Eden's knuckles. "God is patient with us. I'm just grateful He brought us to this moment."

Later, as the three of them prepared dinner together in an attempt to make good memories to replace the bad ones, Dad pulled Jenna in his arms to embrace her. "Surprised?" he asked.

"The best surprise you've ever come up with. Thank you, Dad."

"We are no longer prodigals," Dad said, kissing her forehead.

The truth hit Jenna right above the bridge of her nose. She threw her head back at the impact, a big smile hugging her entire being. "Awesome."

The doorbell rang.

Sure that the person waiting outside was her husband, Jenna exclaimed, "I'll get it!" The moment she opened it, without having even seen who was actually standing outside, she blurted out, "We should do the play!"

At the front porch, Max stood, staring at his feet. He lifted his brown eyes and gave Jenna a lopsided smirk while a tear rushed down his cheek. "I can't do this, Jenna. I can't be the pastor of Connect Church."

twelve

PESKY PASTS & SUDDEN SCRUTINY

Short, steady strides moved them along the cul-de-sac near her father's house. The white laces of Jenna's red Converse shoes bounced with her every step forward. The savory, charred smell of barbecue wafted in the air, teasing Jenna's taste buds. Her stomach ached. She began craving the *arroz valenciana* and the buttered fried chicken they had been preparing for dinner.

However, her husband was going through something, so here she was, taking a stroll around the block with him, waiting for him to tell her what had made him doubt his calling to become a pastor. Hopefully, she would be able to focus and listen to whatever he had to say, assuming he would ever actually say it.

"I'm glad you weren't there." Max sighed. "It got ugly, Jen. Pastor Sam had to take a stand and fight for his decision to name me as the next lead pastor of Connect." He bowed his head. The pain in his eyes was breaking Jenna's heart. She had never seen Max like this before, not since that night by the campfire, when he had let her in by telling her about his past. His broad shoulders were tense, his arms taut as it swung back and forth as he walked. His hands were balled into fists.

Her soft touch pried his fist open so she could hold his hand. She leaned her cheek on his arm, her cheekbone brushing against his shoulder. "I should have been there."

His hold on her tightened as he shook his head. "I'm glad you weren't; otherwise, you might have been placed on the hot seat as well. Neither one of us have stellar pasts."

Jenna winced. "Is that what happened? They put your past under scrutiny?"

"All of it." Max clenched his jaw, the gentle curves of his face taking on an edgier, more angular form. "Marcus and Naomi — God bless them — tried to be peacemakers. Their hearts were in the right place, but I'm not sure I could say the same for everyone else, myself included. It was a disaster."

A sinking feeling came over Jenna as a picture formed in her mind of what might have happened. Marcus and Naomi Grant were pillars of Connect Church. They were well-respected and loved by everyone. Their children — all of whom already had families of their own — were valuable members of the congregation. If even the Grants struggled to keep the peace... She shook her head to ward off the unwanted images attacking her brain. She didn't need memories of an event she hadn't even attended. "They brought Mr. and Mrs. P to the meeting, didn't they?"

Max nodded. "Not only them. A lot of the people who also decided to separate from the church were with them."

Jenna gulped. "I can imagine how that wouldn't turn out well."

"It was okay, at first. Everyone was trying to be respectful and cordial, but you know what Mrs. P can be like. The moment she was given her turn to speak, it all bubbled out of her. She brought up how she had been teaching me in Sunday School since I was a kid, and how she had always liked me, but—" Max scoffed, this dark expression coming over his face.

Jenna gripped his hand, her thumb brushing against his knuckles. She didn't need to pry any further. That 'but' said everything she needed to know about what had happened next. She turned her head to the side and leaned her chin against his arm before brushing the tip of her nose against his bicep. "I'm sorry, Max."

"She got to me, Jen. Whenever I think about everything she said, how she pitted my past against the experience and qualifications of Pastor Sam and her husband to emphasize how unqualified I am, how young I am—" He gritted his teeth. "What if they're right? It feels like we're in way over our heads right now, and it's not even like I asked for this. I want to trust that Pastor Sam was listening to the Lord, and the Lord gave him this direction. Also, it confirms God's call for my life, so it makes sense, but what if we got it wrong? You and I have barely started out in life. How can we lead a church?"

Jenna leaned her head on his arm and swung their arms forward and back. "I have so many Christianese answers I can give you, but you've already heard every single cliché answer I can think of. We can do it by God's grace. God doesn't call the qualified; He qualifies the called. God's Redemption at Christ's Expense. Pray Until Something Happens."

Max chuckled. "So, are we just spitting out random acronyms now?"

"We can twist all of them and make them applicable to this situation." Jenna shrugged.

Max squinted an eye at her.

"What? You know I'm right!"

The smirk on his face was enough to make her feel better. "Fine. That's true enough."

Jenna lifted his hand in front of her, her arm supporting his as she traced a finger against the tattoos on his arm. "You're right. We don't have stellar pasts." She smiled as she traced her finger against the word, *abide.* "As much as a lot of people have come against you because of these tattoos on your arm, it is still a testament to how something beautiful and creative can come out of our weakest moments."

"That defense won't work with Mrs. P at all."

"Mrs. P is no longer a part of our church, though, sad as it is to say that. We can't operate under what Mrs. P approves or doesn't approve. Imagine if we have to do that—" Jenna rolled her eyes "—it'll drive me insane."

"Heh. Me too."

His downward gaze squeezed Jenna's heart. It was so unlike him to doubt himself this way. Jenna closed her eyes for a few seconds. *Lord, give me the right words to encourage him.* "You've never cared about what Mrs. P thinks, Max."

"Right. I shouldn't let this get to me, but it did." He winced. "I think it's because she compared me to Pastor Sam. She listed down all the things that made him an effective pastor and how her husband measured up to all of that and how I didn't. It was hard to hear, Jen, because she basically said out loud all the fears I had in me about not measuring up to Pastor Sam's legacy."

Jenna understood all too much what he was going through, because she felt the same way about Mama Aida. Especially after Pastor Sam's wife had passed away, she had reached legend status at their church because of how universally loved and respected she had been. How could Jenna ever live up to that? However, this moment wasn't about her. It was about Max and what he was going through. If she was to ever become anything like Mama Aida, she could start by supporting her husband.

"Max, for all it's worth, I see a lot of Pastor Sam in you," she said. "You may have different styles and ways of going about things. I also don't know what kind of teenager Pastor Sam was, or if he made the same wrong choices you might have made in the past, but I see a lot of his character in you."

Max creased his brows, a smirk appearing on his face. "What makes you say that?"

"You care about people, Max — genuinely care. You have such a big heart, and you do everything in your power to help people you love succeed. The patience you had for Jeremy — even through all the times he stole your money or lied to you or took advantage of your kindness — that's not something everyone has for people, especially broken ones. The young people at church love you and your creative ideas have allowed them to see Jesus as He is. That's what makes you a great youth pastor, and what will make you a great lead pastor at Connect Church someday. You don't need people to be dependent on you and recognize you for your credentials, because you point them to God." Jenna smiled and winked at him. "You pointed me to Him, remember?"

Max narrowed his eyes. "I thought that was Rachel."

"Okay, fine. She helped, too." Jenna waved her hands in the air. "Let me put it this way: Rachel kept pointing out that I was in darkness and was telling me all the things I could do to get to the light. You, however... Max, you didn't even make me feel like I was in darkness, because you brought the light to me, and when I was away from it, I recognized how much better it was than darkness."

"Wow, Jenna." Max smirked. "That's almost poetic. You sure you want Nova to write the play? Maybe you should do it yourself."

"Haha. Most scatter-shot play ever."

"Scatter-shot, but interesting, especially if you shoe in a scene with you dancing on a lyra loop twenty feet above air."

"Favorite scene?"

"Made me fall in love with you, didn't it?"

Jenna wrinkled her nose. "My favorite too, then. Seriously, though. We'll make it through this, Max. God didn't allow this to happen, only to make us fall on our faces."

"Where is all this optimism coming from? You were also having your own doubts about our ability to do this just yesterday."

"I've been giving it some thought, and I've come to the conclusion that it was mostly my ability to cook that I was doubting. I mean, I do love you, husband. How sad would it be if you starved or got killed by nutmeg under my watch, but I realize I can't be too hard on myself, can I? God's got me. I'll keep giving it my best, and He will sort it all out in His perfect time."

"Right." Max embraced Jenna. "It's amazing to hear you say all that, Jen. It's a good reminder."

"Max, right now, my mom and dad are in the same room together, and neither one of them hates the other. They're even cooking our dinner together, a dinner I'm actually excited to eat. Don't get me wrong. I would rather be nowhere else than right here with you, but my mom is so close to giving her life to Christ, so how can I not be astounded by how God works in our lives? As Mrs. P was hurling the past at you like a weapon to discredit you, God was reminding me of a past that we have already moved away from. Look how far we've come, Max. When you were a kid struggling to get through each day, did you ever imagine you would get to where we are now?" She skipped ahead. With their hands still clasped together, she started walking backwards so she could take a better look at his face. "He has made all things beautiful for us, Max. What we have right now — you and me — it is so beautiful."

"I agree." Max grinned, "but what exactly has this got to do with me leading a church?"

Jenna scrunched her face at him. "Everything, husband," she said incredulously. "Dad said this to me earlier right before you arrived: we're not prodigals anymore. All the reckless living without God as our compass, that's gone now. We are in a better place than we've ever been before — at least I am. Aren't you?"

"You're here." His grip on her hands tightened. "How can I not be?"

She winked at him and drew closer, her arms wrapping around his waist as she leaned her weight on the strength of his arms supporting her. "We both have a lot of room to grow, but I personally love where we are right now."

"I do, too," Max said.

"So, let's just enjoy this moment, this season of our lives and of our marriage. Sure. This is a new thing we're getting ourselves into, and it will be hard. We both already knew that, even before we signed up to get ourselves into this entire mess, but we've already gone from the worst points of our life to multiple moments of redemption, and we're still standing. We'll get through this as well."

"My wife is inspired today," he said. "Does what your father said have anything to do with you believing we should push through with the play?"

Jenna nodded. "Partially, yes, but now, after what you've told me, I am even more convinced we need it now more than ever. The other brother needs to remember that the prodigal son is also the Father's, and vice versa." She took both his hands in hers and tried to twirl him around the sidewalk, but instead, he just stopped walking and stared at her as she leaned backwards, her spine slanting diagonally, both her hands holding onto his. His strength and his grip kept her from falling to the ground. "I don't know every detail of what happened at that meeting, Max. Whatever words were said, I'm sure they weren't pleasant — words meant to wound rather than restore. I don't need to know the highlights and the lowlights. All I need to know is whether or not you believe we are obeying God by taking this on."

Max didn't respond immediately. He just stared blankly at her with this reserved smile on his face as she swiveled from side-to-side, her toes positioned between his feet as she relied on his support to keep her from toppling over. "I do believe this is what God wants us to do. Out of obedience and trust toward Him, and toward Pastor Sam, we can't really back down from this, can we?"

"We certainly can't, Pastor Max."

He cringed. "Pastor Max. Still doesn't sound right to my ears."

Jenna laughed as she pulled herself up to a straight standing position. "You'll get used to it. Right now, what we need to do is get back to my dad's house so we can eat." She once again came alongside her husband, linking her arms with his and strolling around the cul-de-sac. "My mother's *arroz valenciana* is calling my name."

"What is *arroz valenciana*?"

"You've never had that?" Jenna huffed. "You are in for a treat."

Ahead of them, her father's house came to view.

"So, are your parents getting back together?"

Jenna sighed. "No. Not yet, at least. Maybe someday. Right now, I can only hope my mom would come to know Jesus."

Max rubbed his palms together. "Let's wait and see what God will do tonight."

His statement somehow morphed into Max sharing God's Word to her mother after their dinner conversations naturally led there. By the end of the night, Eden Miranda finally decided to give her life to the Lord. And it was a reminder to Jenna of why her husband would someday make an amazing lead pastor.

Everyone else would eventually start seeing him the way Jenna did, and once that happened, hopefully, Jenna had also grown enough to be the kind of woman able to support and challenge him to be God's intended version of Max Owens.

thirteen

LITHE DANCERS & LOOMING DANGERS

In the wee hours of the morning, Jenna shifted in their bed, cautious about her every movement, careful not to wake her husband up, as she tried to slip out of Max's arm laid over her waist. The stroll along the cul-de-sac shared with Max and the dinner conversations shared with her parents flitted across her mind and placed a smile on her face. However, deep inside, something was astir. She couldn't quite place what or why it was. All she knew was this strange sense of foreboding was unsettling her, so as she often did when unsettled, she prepared herself to surrender whatever was going on within her to a God Who often met her amid motion, in the abandon of a dance meant only for her King.

Jenna nimbly moved along the bedroom to dress herself as quietly as possible. Minutes later, in dark leotards, an over-sized sweater reaching up to her thighs, and black boat socks, Jenna stepped into the moonlight, right in the middle of their backyard. The dark embraced her. It took a little getting used to for her eyes to adjust to the dimness, but she didn't need to see for her to move. An orchestra played a song on her phone — set on a stand on the grass — as Jenna executed a slow and deliberate pirouette. She savored the cool night air on her skin and the smell of fresh dew — a promise of a new beginning, of new mercies every morning.

The music intensified bit by bit, and as Jenna moved along with it, the rising urgency in her soul matched the music. It planted a conviction within her about the future ahead. The battle would intensify further before it would subside into peace. What it all meant, Jenna didn't know, but she allowed the music to carry her steps and tug her toward a breathless surrender to the God of the Universe. Her God was the Only One Who would be able to deliver them and give them the victor. Along with the sense of urgency and panic building inside her was a promise of the power to overcome.

The intensity of the music halted almost all of a sudden before it played a few more notes and then there was nothing but silence and the sound of Jenna's breaths. Her chest heaved up and down as she stayed bent over on the ground, crumpled up to her smallest form, bowing before a great God. When she opened her eyes, the sun's rays were already kissing her skin. Still kneeling on the ground, she faced the sun and welcomed God's light.

"Your kingdom come," she prayed. "Your will be done. On earth as it is in heaven."

That last statement, she didn't say alone. Behind her, Max stood barefoot and still in his sleeping clothes, arms folded over his chest, a pensive look on his face as he set his eyes on her. "That was beautiful," he said, as he sat next to her, cross-legged.

She settled on the grass, her legs tucked beneath her thighs, as she leaned against him. "How long were you watching?"

He shrugged. "I woke up and discovered my wife missing, so I figured she's dancing out here, and I was right. Looked like there were some intense prayers going on."

"Can't explain it," Jenna said. "Ever get this intuition that things are about to get much worse before they can start getting better?"

"No, but it concerns me to know that's what your instincts are telling you right now."

Jenna nodded. "Can't shake it. Something bad is about to happen. I've never felt this way before, but somehow, there's also peace. Everything will be okay."

"He's still God, no matter what. He will protect us," Max said, his warm tone veiling the slight tremor in his voice. "He's fighting for us."

"We don't need to be afraid," Jenna said, but it was all beginning to sound empty. Trite. Cliché. It didn't help ease the sense that she needed to brace herself for whatever lay ahead.

What was going through Max's mind, she could only guess, because he changed the topic in a pensive and careful tone. "Mom is coming over this morning. She said she'll bring breakfast."

Jenna stifled a giggle, amused because he made what he was saying sound so ominous despite how mundane it actually was. "Rachel will come over, too. Now that we're both back, Mom wanted to discuss something about *Lady Lacey League*."

"Do you think that might be what's bothering you?"

"Why would that bother me?" Jenna flinched, as she flipped her head to the side to look at Max's profile. "Is there something going on with your mother?"

"Not at all." Max stretched his arms forward and balled his hands into fists. "She's excited about the league, so I'm thinking she may have quite a number of projects planned. With your interview this morning and the play..."

"I can handle it." Jenna nodded. She had to learn how to handle it all, right? This wasn't the worst it could get, and diving head on to this would only help develop her muscle for what life would be like in the future. "I'm sure Mama Aida went through a lot more than this, so I need to be able to do the same, right?"

Max frowned. "Is that what's getting to you? Trying to live up to her legacy?"

"A little. Yes." Jenna fidgeted with her fingers.

"Okay." Max's brows furrowed. "You know you don't have to, right?"

"I know, but I want to. It feels like I need to."

"Why?" Max grimaced. "Mama Aida was something else. I don't think you're doing yourself any favors by making her the standard you have to live up to."

Jenna bristled. She recalled what she had told Max yesterday when he had been struggling with being pitted against Pastor Sam. Did he not see anything that could compare Jenna to Mama Aida? "Don't you think I can live up to her legacy?"

"It's not a matter of whether you can or can't, Jen. It's a matter of whether you should."

"That's what people expect from me, Max."

"Since when do you care about what people expect from you? You're Crazy Jenna. Even when we were kids, you danced to the beat of your own drum, and that's what I've always loved and admired about you."

Jenna winced. Was she that careless in his eyes? The sun rising made the dew in the grass shimmer. Crazy Jenna. Why did that term make her heart ache so much? She had been known at Connect Church as Crazy Jenna her entire life. It had ceased to bother her long ago, but this time, it hurt to hear Max call her that again. "Aida Sinclair is Mama to everyone in the church. I don't even know why she's called that by everyone, but she certainly lived up to it. She was a mother to so many of us. On the other hand, I'm still Crazy Jenna, right?" She was unable to keep the slight edge in her tone.

Max's shoulders tensed. He glanced at her. "Jenna, all I'm saying is Mama Aida is different. No one has ever been able to live up to her standard, and no one needs to. She's completely different from you, from any of the women in church. Why would you put it upon yourself to live under the pressure of being like her?"

Jenna hopped to her feet in an attempt to diffuse her tension by moving around. The first thing she did was a cartwheel.

"You're upset." Max stayed where he was, but his eyes followed her every move. "Why?"

"I'm not."

"You are."

Was she? She couldn't tell through the growing hurt in her chest as she began to realize how far away from the standard of a good pastor's wife she was, so far away that Max couldn't even draw even a single comparison between her and Mama Aida to encourage her. "Let's just drop this, okay?" She picked up her phone and marched toward the house.

"Jenna, I don't understand why you're mad." Max scrambled to his feet to catch up with her.

She was already inside their house when he was able to get a grip on her elbow. He spun her around and looked straight at her face. He threw his head back upon seeing her expression. "Wow. You're really angry about this."

The doorbell rang.

Jenna sighed. "That must be your mother. I'll go take a quick shower first. Please tell her I'll be with her to help with breakfast as soon as I'm done." She wiggled away from his grip and ran up the stairs until she got to their bedroom. Was she being irrational by acting this way? Why had the things Max said triggered her so much? A lot of them were true. She shed her clothes and stepped inside the shower. The moment the water hit her, she let out a sob, and the tears followed.

Hopefully, a good cry in the shower would make everything better. Unfortunately, it didn't, and she faced the rest of the day, feeling like the girl she used to be: Crazy Jenna.

fourteen

EXPECTED **E**XPECTATIONS & **O**VERWHELMED **O**NES

nnette Owens was nothing like Jenna's mother. Instead, in more ways than one, she was what Jenna kept praying her mother could become someday. Annette represented hope that someone who might have had seasons of failure as a mother could still turn into someone who could mother and nurture in a way that honored God. Around her mother-in-law, never had Jenna felt unloved, uncared for, or out-of-place. That morning was no different, despite the tension brewing between Jenna and Max.

"There you are!" Annette exclaimed when Jenna appeared half an hour later, fully dressed, hair dry, and ready to face the day. "How is my beautiful daughter?" She tossed the oven mitts on the counter, so she could go over to Jenna to wrap her in a warm hug.

Jenna melted into her mother-in-law's embrace while casting a glance at Max, who gave her a look she couldn't quite decipher before he put on the mitts and brought out a pan from the oven. Jenna pulled away from Annette whose smile drew hers out. "How are you, Mom?"

"I am blessed beyond measure. Everything is great, apart from how I've missed you and Max." Annette held Jenna's hands. "I hope you both had a wonderful time on your honeymoon."

"We did." Jenna nodded. "The time away helped." The savory aroma coming out of the pan highlighted the grumble in her stomach. "What's cooking? I wanted to help, but I was dancing this morning, so I had to rush to the shower when you arrived."

"Oh, don't worry about it." Annette stroked her back. "Max helped me make the quiche. He's getting pretty handy in the kitchen. Is that your doing?"

"Probably." Jenna snickered. "He always has to help with the damage control whenever I mess dinner up, which is why I want to cook with you. I want to learn from the best."

Annette squeezed Jenna's hand. "We'll make time for it. I can't wait to spend that time with you. For today, it was my pleasure to serve both you and Max. I have a lot of time to make up for with Max, anyway."

"Thanks, Mom. This is a lovely breakfast," Jenna said, noticing the quick tossed salad and toasted slices of a buttery baguette on the counter. "Let me get the drinks. Coffee? Tea? Orange juice?"

"Coffee," Annette replied. "Black with half a teaspoon of sugar, please."

Jenna headed for the coffeemaker and found it already full of hot coffee.

"I started it," Max said. "Also made you a cup of tea."

"Thanks." Jenna tried to smile.

Max tugged on her ponytail and carried the basket of bread and bowl of salad to the dining table.

"Do forgive me if I came in too early," Annette said as she rummaged through their cabinets for plates. "Rachel mentioned she has to go to the city to help Nova out with something, so I figured it would do us well if we start early."

"Oh yeah? Hmm." Jenna pursed her lips as she retrieved two coffee mugs from the mounted rack wall hanger. "I have to go meet Nova's husband for a job interview. Rachel and I can probably go together after the meeting."

Annette's brows met as she leaned back on the edge of the kitchen counter, a stack of four plates in hand. "Job interview?"

"Just a temp position."

"Hmm." Annette's raised brow gave way to a curious glance toward her son as Max returned to the kitchen.

"It's a temporary thing, Mom," Max said as he reached for the plates in her hand. "She wants a job related to social work, but doors aren't exactly opening right now."

Mother and son exchanged this look that made Jenna uncomfortable. What were they hiding from her?

Annette tilted her head to the side before lifting her brows. "God bless you in your interview then, Jenna."

"What are you guys not telling me?" Jenna asked.

"It's nothing," Max said. "Just a conversation Mom and I had before we got married."

"I just didn't think you would want to work immediately after your honeymoon, honey," Annette said. "It seems I'm mistaken."

Jenna shifted her weight from one foot to the other before bringing the pot of coffee and two empty mugs to the dining table. What exactly had they been expecting? Was Max expecting her to be a full-time housewife? They had never actually discussed this in detail. During the marriage counseling sessions they had attended with Pastor Sam, Max had mentioned it being ideal if Jenna stayed at home once they had kids, and she had said she would be open to that when the time came. That time hadn't come, so was there some sort of unspoken expectation happening here that he had failed to mention to her?

The couple exchanged glances. Part of Jenna wished Max would at least mouth an apology toward her, but he mostly just seemed confused. He was being so dense, and he didn't even know it. This awkwardness building around a job interview for a temporary position — one that Max had told her was okay — wasn't helping either.

Jenna swallowed back her disappointment over her husband's insensitivity and forced a smile instead as all three of them stood around the fully prepared dining table.

"Should we wait for Rachel?" Max asked.

The stare he was giving the food only further chipped at Jenna's insecurities, because he had never looked at her cooking that way before. She swayed her head from side-to-side to get rid of the negative thoughts piling inside her mind. What was going on with her? Why was she being so needy and petty?

The doorbell rang.

Jenna sighed out of relief. "Must be Rachel. I'll go get it." Had Rachel sensed that breakfast was ready and that Jenna needed someone to break the ice between mother, son, and wife? She hurried toward the door and swung it open. At the front porch stood Rachel with this brilliant smile on her face. Wearing a crisp, white shirt over straight pants and heels — her hair held up by a fancy bun — she was the model of sharp and sophisticated. Jenna's gaze drifted down to her brown pants hanging a couple of inches above her ankles and held up by black suspenders over a yellow turtleneck shirt.

"Jenna!" Rachel exclaimed before hugging her. "This has been an exhausting two weeks. I don't know how I'm still holding up."

"Holding up? That outfit is amazing on you. It's like you're planning a conquest of the corporate world."

"Please. I haven't conquered much of anything lately." Rachel shook her head. "Caleb and Nova hired me to help organize her new book's launch party. Between this, the play, my wedding, and all the church drama, I'm beyond overwhelmed!"

Overwhelmed? There was no sign of that in her countenance whatsoever. Jenna gritted her teeth. Why had Max broken up with Rachel again? And how did he end up with a wife who couldn't even make him breakfast? She closed the door and put on a smile. Her mind was telling her she was being ridiculous, but for some reason, no matter what her brain was saying, the sickening sensation in the pit of her stomach only grew as the morning proceeded.

Little comments here, a bit of laughter there — it chipped away at her confidence, but Jenna wasn't one to sway under such pressure. She would prove them all wrong. She could do this, and no one was going to tell her otherwise. Not even Max. He may not believe Jenna could be the next Mama Aida, but she would show him. Jenna could do this. She just had to believe what the Word said about her, right? Right.

Why then did she still feel like she should run away, lose herself in a dance, and forget she ever agreed to be the wife of Pastor Max Owens?

fifteen

DISCIPLING DEER & DISTRESSED DINOSAURS

"You're not still mad at me, are you?" Max nudged her arm as they finished putting away the dishes.

Behind them, Annette and Rachel's chatter as they headed for the living room only deepened Jenna's growing irritation. While mildly aware of the irrationality of her soul's responses to what was going on around her, she couldn't seem to fight the frustration building within.

"For the hundredth time, I'm not mad, Max." Even to her ears, her tone made it sound like his name was a bad word. "I told you to drop it."

"Sure, Jenna. You don't sound mad at all." His jaw tightened as he washed his hands. "This is ridiculous. I'll see you tonight." He dried his hands and walked past her. "Have a great day."

"Where are you going?" Jenna asked, turning around, her hands still full of suds from not having finished rinsing.

"I'm spending the day with Jeremy. We'll probably come back here this afternoon to work on stuff at the studio, but I'm honestly not sure."

"Why didn't you tell me you were meeting up with Jeremy?"

"I didn't know I had to, Jenna." His tone was now beginning to mirror hers.

Jenna gritted her teeth. Should she back down? She tried to dull the edge in her voice. "You don't need to. I was just expecting you to be in your studio all day."

"You were going to be in the city for that interview of yours."

He made the interview sound like some sort of extramarital affair. She gasped at the way her anger morphed into heat rising from her chest to her cheeks.

Max was oblivious to her ire as he shrugged and told her why he was hanging out with his best friend. "You're not going to be around, so I figured I'd make my own plans. There's nothing I need to do at the church right now, and I'm pretty much done with most of the content I need for my Podcast. It's good to go for at least two weeks, so—"

"Sure, whatever. Can you just tell me what is with the shade?"

"Shade?"

"Why do you talk about my interview like it's some sort of sin?"

"What?"

"I told you about that, and you even said you thought it would be a great way for me to connect with Nova about the play."

"I meant that."

"Then why the push-back now? Were you expecting me to just be a stay-at-home wife? That was never something you mentioned before the wedding."

"No! That's not it at all, Jenna. And I'm not pushing back. I'm just—" His jaw tightened. "Never mind. Let's discuss this another time."

Jenna wanted to push further, but he was right. They had guests, and their whispers were getting sharper and sharper, very close to becoming a full-on argument.

She relented. "Fine."

"Fine." Max climbed up the stairs to get ready for the day, leaving Jenna with suds on her hands and anger in her soul.

This was weird. She and Max had been friends for years, and they had never— Jenna scoffed. How had she forgotten? Max had always pushed her boundaries and challenged her decisions. He had been the one who had constantly guilted her into going home to visit her father when he had been fighting cancer. She hadn't wanted to then, but he had pushed her. He had been right, and even is he had been upset with him at first, she could only be thankful that he had drawn her out of her own hurt.

But this? Now? He was being unreasonable, and she wasn't about to let him make her feel inadequate about yet another thing. Then again, she didn't quite fully understand what was upsetting her so much — was it the idea that Max might not think she was good enough? Or the fact that Jenna was afraid of the exact same thing? After all, she wasn't a church girl like Rachel, who had all the social graces required to flourish at their church. Jenna barely even spoke church lingo yet. She loved God, and she loved Max. That's why she wanted to be his help mate. The rest? It felt like all of it was above her pay grade.

Jenna held on to the edge of the kitchen sink before turning around. She straightened herself to her full height and took a few steps forward, ready to start this meeting with Rachel and Annette. She faltered and held on to the wooden post supporting the kitchen counter.

"Jenna?" Rachel entered the kitchen. "Hey. Everything okay?"

"Yeah, of course." She tried her best to sound convincing. "I'm fine."

Rachel narrowed her eyes. "You don't seem fine."

Jenna huffed. There was no point in hiding from Rachel. After everything they had been through, Rachel was one of the people who knew Jenna well enough to detect when she was lying. "Okay, sure. Whatever. I'm not fine, but I have to find a way to keep a smile on my face, because my mother-in-law is waiting, and that's what Mama Aida would have done."

"Mama Aida? What does she have to do with any of this?"

Jenna flinched. Should she have brought this up with Rachel? After all, Rachel's mother was notoriously critical of Mama Aida, and the irony of it was Rachel was about to marry Mama Aida's son.

"Nothing." Jenna shook her head. "Let's go."

Just as Jenna was about to brush past her best friend to get through the kitchen door, Rachel grabbed hold of her hand. "You're not making her into some sort of standard for yourself, are you?"

Jenna's lip twitched. This woman knew her too well. "Look. I know I shouldn't do that, okay? We're so different, and she's like this sage owl familiar with all the ways of the forest, while I'm this stupid bunny hopping around, lost and trying not to be devoured by a fox. Spare me the lecture, Rach."

Rachel giggled. "What's with the forest analogy?"

Jenna smirked. "I don't know. It was the first thing that came to mind. I don't even know if foxes eat bunnies."

Rachel linked arms with her. "If we're sticking with the forest analogy, I think Mama Aida is more like a doe panting for the waters. Maybe you're a doe too — you're as graceful as a deer when you dance anyway. But you're not quite the same as Mama Aida, because you're still just a fawn. You still need to grow in the Spirit some more. We all do."

They crossed the entry way to head for the small living room, where Annette was waiting.

"Sorry, Mom," Jenna said. "We were talking about forests and woodland creatures."

Annette smiled. "Interesting conversation starter."

"Yes." She nodded. "It was nice, even though Rachel compared me to a fawn, and there was this old cartoon movie about deer that traumatized me as a kid. It was so sad!"

"How are you traumatized by that, but *Jurassic Kingdom* was perfectly okay?" Rachel asked.

Jenna shrugged. "*Jurassic Kingdom* wasn't sad."

"People got eaten by dinosaurs!"

They plopped themselves on the longer side of the L-shaped sofa, with Annette already comfortable on the shorter side.

"Only the people we don't like, though."

Annette cleared her throat to get their attention.

Jenna stifled a giggle as she and Rachel tried to focus. Rachel was right. They both had some growing up to do.

"So, since both of you ladies have somewhere to go this morning, this meeting shouldn't take too long," Annette said, "but I do want to hear from you both and find out how you are doing. Before that, shall we say a prayer? Jenna?"

Jenna hesitated. She didn't want to pray, mainly because she didn't know what to pray about. She had been feeling out of sorts from the moment she had woken up, and her morning had progressively gone worse. Also, her mind was full of deer and dinosaurs. Not wanting to cause a fuss, however, Jenna relented. She nodded. "Sure." All three ladies bowed their heads as Jenna reached deep into her heart for words to say. "God, I don't know what's going on right now. I feel like so many of us have been going through such upheaval, and it's so strange that we are, because we're all in a season of life where we should be rejoicing. I just married a wonderful man, and Rachel is about to get married as well. These are men of God, and yet all the celebrations we should be having is somewhat overshadowed by this cloud of resistance. I don't know why it's so hard right now, why we're struggling so much, but help us rejoice, God. No matter what happens today, anoint us with the oil of joy."

At those words, Rachel flinched beside her.

Jenna squinted her eyes open to find out what was happening, and she discovered Rachel wiping away tears from her face with a tissue. Jenna wasn't sure what to do. Should she end the prayer before comforting Rachel? What was the right protocol here? She shifted in her seat and reached for her best friend's hand, squeezing tight. God was right there, and this wasn't about formalities. This was about relationship. Her heart went out to Rachel, knowing that it couldn't be easy to be in love with Jeremy, while her parents were now actively splitting their church apart. She had no idea how to comfort Rachel or make things better for her friend. She didn't have a Bible verse to give or a wise piece of advice to say. All she could offer was her presence and hope that would be enough.

"We're right here for you, Rachel," she said. "We're family."

Somehow, her focus on Rachel's dilemma made it easier for her not to focus on her own. It took several minutes for Rachel to recover from her tears and explain to them what was going on with her.

"It's just hard," Rachel said. "Everyone is on edge, and I'm so heart-broken by everything, but on the other hand, I'm also so excited about this wedding. It shouldn't be weird, right? I shouldn't feel guilty that I am anticipating my own wedding."

Jenna couldn't help it. She giggled.

Rachel looked at her and pouted. "I must sound so shallow."

"Not at all." Jenna let go of her hand. "Those are real and valid concerns, Rachel, and I'm glad you're able to process them out loud."

"Jenna's right," Annette said. "What's going on at our church has been hard for everyone, because we're family. All of us. Your parents included."

"What do you think about all this, Annette?" Rachel asked. "It can't be easy to see your son going through this, especially considering he's newly married." Rachel brushed her fingers against Jenna's shoulder.

Annette sighed. "Most would think that I would be on my son's side, and I am — don't get me wrong — but I also do understand your parents' point of view, Rachel. I don't agree with their decision to split the church, of course, but Max is young and inexperienced, and I don't know what went into Pastor Sam's decision to ordain Max as the leader of the church, but I can understand why so many of us feel hesitant about making him our spiritual leader. And I say that as a person whom my own son led to Christ. Aida, especially, had such a huge impact on me as a young Christian. I'm sometimes jealous of you young people, because you all get to call her Mama Aida. It would have been strange for me to call her that, because she isn't that much older than I am. She was a good older sister to me, though, and I do miss her."

All of what Annette said rippled into Jenna's heart. Max had been right. How could she ever live up to Mama Aida's legacy?

"All that to say—" Annette smiled "—while I believe Max can be a great pastor someday, I also question the timing. I worry about you and my son, Jenna. This is a lot to put on your shoulders, especially when you're only a few months into your marriage. Still, I trust that if this is the Lord's will, He will get you both through."

Jenna bristled. Was it God's will?

Rachel sighed. "I think Max will be an amazing pastor, Annette. I do, but it's also a relief to me to hear you say that, because I have the same concerns, and when I listen to my parents and their side of the story, I understand why they're hurting. It hurts me that there's division, when it would be so much easier for all of us to just unite and find a solution to this problem together."

Jenna clenched her jaw. "So, none of you think we can do this? You would rather have Mr. and Mrs. P pastor the church?"

"That's not what we're saying," Rachel said.

"What are you saying?" Jenna asked.

"Only that maybe there's a way to go about it where all parties win."

"It's your parents who aren't cooperating, Rachel. They're the ones who decided to just abandon the church and bring as many people with them as they could." Jenna then shot a look at Annette. "I'm surprised you didn't go with them, Mom."

Annette flinched. "Jenna." The name was said in a sweet but controlled tone. "There's no need for the temper. What has gotten into you? No matter the concerns we mentioned, we're on your side. Yours and Max's. We're just longing for a better solution than division. That's all."

All worked up inside, Jenna reeled in the anger that had been triggered within her. What was happening to her? It's like she didn't have any self-control left. "I'm sorry," she said. "I shouldn't have burst out like that."

"For all it's worth—" Rachel stroked her back, right along the spine "—I'm glad you did. Otherwise, you would've just held all of that in your heart and it's not a burden that's healthy to carry."

"This whole mess has been affecting us in different ways, and we're reacting because we care." Annette reached forward to both of them, so she could take both their hands in hers. "I love both of you with all my heart. You have been such a blessing to me and the girls of *Lady Lacey League*. Your testimonies have encouraged so many of the girls who come to our meetings to live Godly lives."

Jenna's heart sank. Why was Annette making this sound like a goodbye? Was she shutting the non-profit down?

"I started *Lady Lacey League* to honor the memory of my daughter, and it has done that. It has reached more lives than I could have possibly imagined, but—" Annette sighed "—I've been praying, and I do feel God's leading elsewhere. I can no longer do the work required to keep the non-profit going, as I am about to enter into a new season of my life." She smiled. "Unless either one of you would be willing to keep it going, then I would have to shut down the organization by the end of the year."

Jenna hadn't expected the storm of emotions that burst through her when Annette said those words. The outreach they were doing toward inner-city women, encouraging them towards abstinence and pursuing God, had been one of the ministries at church that Jenna had held close to her heart. Before she could think it through, Jenna spoke out loud what was on her mind. "I'll take it on, Mom," she said. She regretted the words the moment they came out of her mouth. What was she doing? She already had more than enough on her plate!

Before she could say anything else, however, the delight in Annette's face stopped her from taking it back.

"I'm so glad you said that, Jenna," Annette said, "because when I was asking God if there was anyone who could take the mantle of leading this ministry, yours was the face that immediately flashed through my mind."

Jenna gulped. There was no going back on this now. What had she just done?

sixteen

∇ILLAGE HELP & ∇IRTUOUS HEROES

How had she gone into a meeting feeling overwhelmed by everything in her life and walked out of it with even more reasons to be overwhelmed? How could she run a non-profit organization while putting on a play, taking on a temp job, trying to become a decent pastor's wife, and learning how to cook all at the same time?

Jenna's grip on the steering wheel tightened. What would Max say about all this? Would it convince him that he had ended up marrying a complete nutcase? Once upon a time, she had been fuming over everyone calling her Crazy Jenna, only for her to eventually prove them all right.

"I can't believe you just did that!" Rachel squealed in the passenger's seat.

"Neither can I." Jenna's jaw tightened.

"It makes perfect sense, though. You have a degree in social work. You have training on how to deal with at-risk children and young people. This is a great match. It's so obvious! You came in clutch, Jenna, especially since I was still reeling with shock over Annette saying she wanted to shut the org down. She had poured so much of her heart and soul into it. Do you have any idea why she would retire from the work she's doing there?"

Jenna shrugged. "Your guess is as good as mine. Mom's reasons are her own, but I'm sure if God is calling her elsewhere, then it must be for a good cause."

"Has Max not mentioned anything about this?"

"I wouldn't be surprised if he doesn't know yet. He would have said something if he did."

"That's a lot to take on, though," Rachel said. "Especially with everything going on. I admire you for being willing to step up to the plate."

"I'm in way over my head, Rachel," Jenna admitted. "Part of me wishes I could take it back, but Annette was so happy, and I don't have the heart to tell her I might have made a mistake."

"I hear you." Rachel nodded. "But you're aware you're not alone, right? We're right here with you, willing to support you all the way."

Jenna didn't know how much stock she could put into those words, because everyone was clearly dealing with something. "So, you're leaning into this event coordinator thing pretty hard, huh?"

"Kind of, yeah." Rachel shrugged. "Nova was so impressed by how I put together your wedding, she requested that I do this for her, which of course, I had to say yes to, because come on! Other than it's a paid job, I love Nova's books."

Jenna shifted in her seat. She hadn't even read any of the books Nova had written. "Are they good?"

"Unbelievably good. They're bestsellers for a reason, Jenna. I'm surprised they haven't been turned into movies yet. Nova's work is perfect for the big screen. Of course, I may be biased, because I know the author, but still. They're awesome."

"I should get a copy then."

"What are you doing at Caine Tower today, by the way? You mentioned it earlier, but I might have missed it."

"Interview for a temp job with Caleb."

"Oh wow. Really? You sure you're going for a temp job, considering you've already committed yourself to *Lady Lacey League*?"

"It's not like Mom is dropping the organization on my lap today. I just need to learn to steward my time well between commitments. It will be good training ground for me. Besides, Caleb must need the help if he's desperate enough to ask me to volunteer."

"Oh, come on. You'll do fine." Rachel wrinkled her nose. "Though I must admit, it's hard for me to imagine you in an office environment."

"Why's that?"

"You're more the free-spirited, artsy, creative dancer type, Jenna. More like Nolan and Serene. It's hard to imagine you stuck in a cubicle eight hours a day, five days a week."

"I guess that makes sense, but hey, assuming I get the temp job, then at least I can say it's something I experienced."

Caine Tower came into view. The skyscraper looked like it had been taken straight out of a comic book. The idea of working there made Jenna's skin bristle, as she entered the outdoor parking lot and parked her car.

Ten minutes later, she was inside Caleb Grant's office, and the first thing she ended up saying was, "Hi, Caleb. I'm sorry if I'm wasting your time, but I'm not sure this is where God is leading me at the moment."

Jenna let out a huge breath of relief, because for the first time that day, it felt to her like she had just done something right.

Caleb Grant grinned at Jenna. "Out of pure curiosity, can you at least tell me the reason? I would love to hear it."

Jenna shrugged. "It's only because something came up this morning. It's not quite a job, or maybe it is. I'm not even sure yet. I guess what I'm trying to say is that I can't prioritize this job right now, because God is leading me to other things."

"Do the circumstances at our church have anything to do with your decision?" Caleb asked.

Jenna nodded. "Kind of. Yes."

"Well, that I can understand." Caleb nodded. "Thank you for coming here to inform me in person. I'm sure God will provide someone capable of filling the spot we need." He stood up and shook hands with Jenna. "If I may, do you have any plans for today?"

Jenna shook her head.

"You should go three floors down, then. Pay Nova a visit. I'm sure she would love to see you."

"I'll do that. Thank you for thinking of me for this, Caleb."

"No problem. I trust Max's recommendations. Your husband cares about you."

"What do you mean? Max recommended me for this job?"

Caleb nodded. "Didn't he tell you?"

Jenna's head spun at the revelation. "No, he didn't." She frowned.

"He probably has a lot on his mind." Caleb shrugged it off like it was nothing.

Meanwhile, Jenna struggled to process the information. She stood stock still in the middle of the elevator as it descended three floors down. Her mind was lost in a sea of questions. Why was she on her way to meet Nova when she had already said no to a job here? Why had Max been acting so strange lately? What was going on with him? She brought out her phone to text her husband.

> **Jenna:** Hey. I'm done with the interview. I told Caleb I won't take on the job. You recommended me for it? I don't understand.

The reply came quickly. The elevator door dinged, and Jenna stepped out, her face glued to her phone as she exchanged messages with Max.

> **Max:** Why didn't you take the job? It seemed like you wanted it.

Jenna: Long story. I'm a little confused right now, Max. I don't know what you want

Max: I want you to be happy, Jenna. I want you to feel supported, and I don't understand why you would think otherwise.

She read the message over and over again. Her mind began to reel as she replayed the events of that morning. What exactly happened? Max had tried to remind her that she shouldn't have to live in Mama Aida's shadow. She could be herself, and God would use her still. She had taken offense to that. He had been concerned about her over-committing herself to multiple things at once. Again, she had taken offense to that. Had she just misinterpreted the glances between mother and son, their actions filtered through the lens of her own struggles? Had Max been the one acting strange? Or had it been her all along? It was like she had sensed something bad was about to happen when she had woken up, so she self-sabotaged and actually made bad things happen. This could have been a beautiful day!

Jenna responded to Max.

Jenna: I'm sorry for being so snippy and oversensitive, Max. Was just needing a bit of assurance, I guess. I love you, and I'll see you at dinner.

Max: I may not always have the right words to say, but I'm in your corner, Jen. Don't ever doubt that. Love you too and see you later!

With squared shoulders and a smile on her facWith squared shoulders and a smile on her face, Jenna marched past the bustling office, which represented a world that had never been her own. When she reached Nova's office, she found Nova pacing the floor, listing down things for Rachel to do.

"Okay, so what was all that again?" Nova asked as she counted out each of the things she was saying through her fingers. "We need to secure a venue, finalize a guest list, send out invites, figure out an appropriate aesthetic as far as decorations go, find a caterer, and basically make sure all the books are there on time." Nova sighed. "Well, that last part, we can do nothing about. That's more Frontier Press's problem."

Jenna knocked on the open door.

Both women cast a glance at her. The looks on their faces made her feel like such a nuisance.

"Caleb said I should come see you?"

Nova let out a huge sigh. "We need all the help we can get. Do you mind assisting Rachel in whatever she needs to get done? We need to pull this off in less than two weeks."

Jenna hadn't actually expected to be given work, but she had nothing planned, so why not? Within the next hour, they briefed her on what was going on. The release date for Nova's newest novel had been delayed for weeks before suddenly, they pushed it to this current date. With Nova heading the marketing department of the publishing company, she was in charge of making sure her own launch party would proceed without a hitch, but this was proving to be a challenge, considering she already had a lot of other ongoing projects. If Rachel could take the bulk of the pressure off her, then it would greatly help. Since all of it was on short notice, Rachel basically needed someone to assist her as they ran errands all around the city.

Because they had driven there together in Jenna's car and Rachel still had her car at Jenna's, she needed someone to drive her around the city to find venues, so she could send images and thoughts to Nova.

"You could also just drive me back to your place, Jenna," Rachel said.

"Then you'll drive back to the city and go to all the venues?" Jenna shook her head. "No need. I'll take you. It would be my pleasure. Besides, it would be great to spend the day together. We haven't done that in quite some time."

Nova clapped her hands together. "That sounds perfect. You have no idea how much this helps, ladies."

"It's our pleasure, Nova," Rachel said. "I personally can't wait for your next book to come out, so I'm thrilled and honored to be a part of this."

"You know what they say." Jenna smiled and shrugged. "It sometimes takes a village. We're your village."

Jenna cringed at what she had said. She wished she could have said something more about Nova's work, but she couldn't remember the last time she had enough of an attention span to read a fiction book. She had been wanting to read Nova's books, if only to relate to the people at church raving about them, but she had been putting it off. Yet another thing she was failing at. Meanwhile, Nova had a full-time job, two teenagers to raise, and a successful writing career. Why she wouldn't just retire from her corporate job and focus on writing and raising her family at home was beyond Jenna, but to many of them, Nova had always been a picture of someone who had it all.

"Isn't she amazing?" Rachel gushed as she got on the passenger's seat as Jenna pulled on her seatbelt to prepare for an afternoon of driving around the city. "It's like she can do everything. How she juggles it all — work, home, church — is mind-boggling to me."

Jenna was about to retort that Nova wasn't exactly involved in many church activities, but remembered that Mama Aida had passed the women's ministry to Nova, who had been faithful in making the ladies' gatherings happen every week. "Some people seem to have it all, don't they?"

With Rachel agreeing to the sentiment, that was the last they spoke of Nova for the rest of the day, as they got swept away by a trip from one venue to another, trying to tick off as many items on Rachel's checklist as possible, while catching up with each other.

After the first venue, they broached Jenna's job interview with Caleb and the commitment she had given to Annette earlier.

"I told Caleb I don't think this is what God is asking me to do. The odd thing is that he told me it was Max who recommended me for the job."

"I thought you said he didn't seem to want you to take it on?"

Jenna shrugged. "I might have misinterpreted? My emotions have been all over the place lately. It's been a roller coaster trying to figure out how to manage what I've been feeling and what I should be doing. There's a real possibility I'm overthinking everything, when I shouldn't."

"That, I can understand." Rachel huffed. "This is such a strange season for us all. I don't think any of us know what to do or how to react. We're all winging our way through it."

Jenna smiled as she slowed the car down, so they could park by a quaint café-restaurant. It was nice to know she wasn't alone in feeling the way she did.

After the second venue, the topic of Rachel's wedding and what was going on between her and her family was next.

"We have a weird dynamic going on right now, that's for sure," Rachel said. "Mom is upset that I'm still attending Sunday services at Connect Church instead of going with them. She says we're family, and we should stick together, but Connect Church is also family — especially now that Jeremy and I are engaged. Why don't they just come back to the church we have treated as our family all my life?"

"Can't imagine your mother is pleased with that line of reasoning."

"It's not like I'm able to say that to them. The truth is, I do want to just go with them sometimes. The vibe towards me at our church has been strange. It's like most people aren't sure how to interact with me. They don't know why I'm there instead of with my parents. Jeremy helps soften the blow, but it definitely hangs a cloud over our engagement. It's exhausting."

Jenna sighed. "I wish I could hug you right now. If it helps any, Max and I do find the vibe in church iffy. We sometimes wonder if people see us as the ones who split up the church. Hearing Annette say earlier that even she had reservations about Max becoming lead pastor hit me hard. It's difficult to realize that he's about to take leadership of people who can't see themselves under his authority."

"All this makes me wonder if we're thinking about what other people are thinking too much, but it's hard not to. This is our community. As I said, our family. In my head, I know I should focus on what God is saying, but in practice, it's not that easy to pull off."

Jenna nodded as she slowed down in front of a boutique bookstore, their third venue.

By the time they drove back to the parking lot of Caine Tower, there was this overwhelming sense of peace in Jenna's heart. The time spent with Rachel and being able to talk through what they were both going through provided her a space for release. It seemed Rachel was on the same page.

"Thanks for this time, Jenna," Rachel said. "I miss all these talks we have. Even when we were back in college, talking to you makes everything so much lighter."

"Same, Rach. I'm always encouraged whenever we chat. We'll get through this." Jenna tapped on her steering wheel. "Do you want me to go inside with you?"

"No. I'm sure Nova and I can manage from here on out."

"How will you get home?"

"Jeremy will pick me up. We're going on our—" Rachel put on air quotes "—first official date."

Jenna laughed. "At least you're having one of those. Max and I didn't even go on a single date before getting married. We got engaged, then we had three months of rushed wedding plans, and then bam! We're married."

"Oh, trust me. I know." Rachel chuckled. "I planned your wedding, remember? I thought you both were crazy for doing it that way, but now, look at us. Jeremy and I are almost in the same exact predicament."

Jenna shrugged. "What can I say? Max and I make good role models for both of you."

"Ha!" Rachel's face blanked. "That's a way to look at it — not sure about its accuracy, but you helped me out so much today, I can't complain much, can I?"

"Yeah, yeah. It was my genuine pleasure, Rach."

Rachel was about to open the door to her car when her phone began buzzing. "It's Jeremy." She answered the call. "Hey. I'm here at the parking lot already... Yeah. I'm with Jenna." She paused. "Oh okay. Sure. I'll tell her. Right. Bye." She hung up. "Max is apparently with Jeremy. They're waiting to pick us up once I finish updating Nova about the venues we found." Rachel grinned and flicked her brows up and down. "Seems like tonight has turned into a double date."

A shot of excitement rushed through Jenna. "That sounds great." She bit her lip. "If that's okay with you, that is."

"Are you kidding? It'll be so much fun."

Jenna mirrored her best friend's grin. Whatever negative sense of foreboding she had that morning must have been just the enemy trying to ruin what was turning out to be an amazing day.

They both got out of the car, and immediately, Jenna wondered if she had jinxed herself, because something sharp and pointy pressed against the small of her back and a deep voice spoke behind her, "Give me everything you have, or I'll kill you."

seventeen

HOLD-UP RISKS & HEROIC RESCUES

A hard palm pressed the back of her head before thick fingers dug against her skull and yanked her back by the hair.

"Please," was all Jenna managed to say.

"Give me the keys to the car." His grip tightened, making her brain whirl from the pain of her scalp. "Do as I say, and I might let you live. Don't try anything stupid, girl. I'll make your regret it. The keys. Now."

Trembling, she tried to fish the keys out of her pocket. The stranger hissed at her impatiently. She cried out when his knife broke skin.

The sound made him throw more than a few unsavory words at her, his breath hot against her ear.

"Hey. What's going on here?"

"Go away! She'll pay for it, if you come near, I swear."

"Get away from her. Now."

The voice of whoever was intervening rang familiar, but the wild thumps of her heart were ringing in her ear, making it difficult to place who her rescuer was. It didn't matter. Right now, the mugger was distracted. She should take the opportunity to fight back. She clung to her car key and slipped its pointed end between her forefinger and middle finger, her hand forming into a fist. After a sharp intake of breath to draw her courage in, she spun around to stab the mugger with her key. His knife sliced through the side of her waist at the same time her key hit the side of his neck, throwing him off. He cussed loudly and backhanded her with so much force, it threw her several feet away, her head hitting the edge of her car with a resounding thump. She landed on the pavement, the concrete scraping her skin as she gripped her bleeding waist. The stranger was about to lunge for Jenna to stab her when someone intervened and leaped forward to take the criminal down. Jenna blinked her eyes, her brain struggling to comprehend the scene unfolding before her. Her vision blurred, filling her mind with deers and dinosaurs, before she drifted out of consciousness and found herself in a fantastical forest of her own mind, basking in sunlight, a deer panting for living waters.

Jenna gasped for breath. The forest and the waters got sucked into the vortex of reality, presenting to her a confusing and discombobulated scene. She was still at the parking lot, sitting on the concrete, her back against her car. Rachel's cries as she called out for help on her phone drowned out Jenna's concern over the sharp pain on her waist and back. Jenna lifted her palm and found blood on it. The wooziness in her head continued to blur her vision. She leaned back against the hood of her car.

Not far from her, Rachel was crouched on the ground with a phone in hand. She was pressing her palm hard against someone's stomach. Blood was squirting out of somewhere. A man lay still on the ground right in front of Rachel, while another in a ski mask limped away, cussing, as he tried to get away from them.

The bleeding man Rachel was trying to help had saved her from getting stabbed, but who was he? She winced in pain as she tried to crawl forward to find out.

"Jenna, you have to come help! He's bleeding so much!" Tears rushed down Rachel's face as she put the phone on speaker. "What do I do? There's so much blood. Oh God. Please, please. Spare him." She lifted his arm over her shoulder. Blood kept squirting out of a gash in his arm, and Rachel let go of his stomach to put direct pressure on the cut on his arm with both her hands. "Please hurry!" she cried out.

"The ambulance is coming," the voice on the phone said. "Just keep elevating his arm and putting pressure."

"Jenna, help! Please!" Rachel cried out. "We'll lose him if we don't do something!"

Whoever that man was, it was someone they knew. Rachel wouldn't be acting this way if it wasn't. Panic shot through Jenna. Was it Jeremy? She swallowed hard and shook her head at the possibility. Was it Max?

Forgetting the pain on her waist, she scrambled forward, crawling to get to the man who had come to their rescue. Her heart sank when she recognized the face of the man who had saved them. There was no relief to be found in discovering that it was neither Max nor Jeremy lying on the ground, bleeding to his death. Jenna's heart sank.

On the hard pavement, fighting for his life was Caleb Grant.

PART THREE

The One Who Wrote Away

NOVA GRANT

eighteen

SUDDEN PAIN & SHAKEN PEACE

- ONE HOUR AGO -

With countless deadlines and one project piled after another, Nova didn't think she could pull this launch party off, but as she swiped through the pictures Rachel had sent, her hope grew. She might be able to pull this off! She walked out of the elevator and smiled at the familiar bustle of the twenty-third floor of Caine Tower, which housed *Galactic*, the speculative fiction imprint of Frontier Press, where her husband was not only an agent but also the editor-in-chief.

Nova weaved through the office cubicles, stopping by a few to say hi and catch up a little, before arriving at Caleb's corner office. When she got there, the first thing she saw was the empty space behind his desk. Where was Caleb? She creased her brows as she walked in and found him seated on a leather chair, leaning back, with a thick, loosely bound pile of paper in his hands. With reading glasses and a laser focus on a new manuscript, Caleb Grant was the very picture of the man Nova had fallen in love with and married thirteen years ago. If what he was reading was riveting enough to garner that intense, eagle-eyed expression on his face, there was no way he was aware she was standing right there. Despite all her deadlines and all the pending tasks she had going on, Nova paused to take in the sight of her husband falling in love with a new book.

When Caleb's mouth dropped open as a reaction to whatever it was he was reading, Nova couldn't help but speak up. "Is it that good?"

Caleb's shoulders jolted straight, and he sat up on the leather chair, eyes darting from side-to-side, as if he just now realized he was still inside his office. "Nova! How long have you been standing there?"

"Not long." Nova shook her head. "Is that the new author you were raving about last night?"

"No, actually." Caleb creased his brows. "It's an unsolicited manuscript. My assistant read it and loved it, so she printed it out and gave me a copy. When my interview with Jenna fell through this morning, I picked it up and started reading. Nova, I haven't felt this way about a new book since I read your first manuscript of *Edge of Darkness*."

Nova wrinkled her nose at the memory of her first book. In so many ways, it had been the story that brought the two of them together, but it was also a reminder of how amateur her writing had been back then. She sauntered forward to take a seat on the couch perpendicular to the chair Caleb was in. "That novel was the one that started it all."

"You should read this once I'm finished reading it, Nova. It will blow your mind. This writer reads like a young Alex Orwell."

Nova laughed at her pen name. While she had gone with her maiden name, Nova Stone, as the author behind all her books, between her and Caleb, they still sometimes referred to her with the nom de plume she had originally used with her first manuscript. "It's been a while since I last heard you use that name."

"Yeah, well, it's been a while since we talked about your writing." Caleb shrugged.

"Really? I feel like that's all we talk about when we're not talking about church or the twins."

Caleb set the manuscript on his lap before leaning over to squint an eye at Nova. "You haven't written in a while."

"What do you mean? I have a book launch coming up."

"For a book you wrote… what? Three or four years ago?"

Nova bristled. She was hoping Caleb hadn't noticed, but Caleb had a way of zoning in on things he cared about and his wife was certainly high on top of that list. "What happened earlier? Jenna's been driving Rachel all over the city to find a venue for my launch party. Why didn't she push through with the interview with you?"

A smirk appeared on Caleb's face. "Changing the subject, are we?"

"It's okay to take a break from writing, Caleb."

"Sure." Caleb nodded. He sounded like the furthest thing from convinced. "Jenna said she didn't feel like an office job was what God was calling her to do. She made a commitment with Annette to take over *Lady Lacey League*, and she wants to support Max more now that Pastor Sam is transitioning leadership of the church to him. Add to that the play you all are working on together, and—" he lifted a shoulder "—I can understand why she doesn't think she can take on an office job right now."

"Interesting." Nova lowered her eyes. "About the play, though—" She twisted her toes against the hardwood floor of his office, her knees rubbing against each other as she tried to speak out. "I don't think I can go through with it."

"What do you mean? I thought you wanted to take it on, so you can get writing again. Why are you backing out now?"

"It's all too much. Not just here, but also at home." Nova sighed. "Nate has been retreating, more so than usual. Claudia is— well, she seems fine. No issue there. But with the twins getting into their teen years, and all the work I have piled at the marketing department, not to mention a possible book tour, I don't think I can add another thing to my plate. Maybe we're better off staying away from all this church drama anyway."

Caleb stared at her long and hard. "Is that what you came here to say?"

"No. I just wanted to drop by to thank you for sending Jenna. She and Rachel have come to my rescue today. Rachel, especially, is taking a lot off my plate by helping organize the launch party. It was your idea to tap into them as resources, and it helped. So—" Nova nodded "—thanks."

"Is that all?"

Nova winced. Why did he sound so stern? "Do you mind picking up the twins from school? We need to finalize the details for the book releases we have scheduled, and Rachel is about to get back here to discuss the venues with me. I won't be able to pick them up."

Caleb tilted his head to the side. Melancholy glazed over his blue eyes as his stare on her deepened. He nodded slowly. "Okay, Nova, I'll pick them up, but first, please reconsider dropping the play, because I have this strong sense that it might help unite rather than divide. Also, do me a favor, will you?" He handed her the manuscript in his hands. "I can't wait to find out what happens next, but I think you should read it."

Nova stared at the pile of paper he was handing her. Was he joking? Did he not hear what she had just said about how busy she was and how much she needed to get things off her plate, not add to it? "Caleb, I don't have time. Weren't you listening to anything I said?" There was a sharpness in her tone that revealed her frustration.

"Trust me on this, okay? I believe with all my heart it might inspire you to get writing again."

The statement grated at her nerves. Was this what he was upset about? The fact that she hadn't been writing? "Caleb, I don't understand why you're making an issue out of my writing — or lack of it, I guess. I've produced an entire book series since I met you — a book series that, let's not forget, is basically the flagship series of the imprint that you are heading. The last book in the series is about to launch, so I don't understand why you're suddenly so concerned about my writing. Why can't you just let me start writing again when I want to?"

"What do you mean? You don't want to write anymore?"

Nova flinched. "That's not what I meant! It's just that things have been hectic and there's no time to write."

"Nova, when you wrote your first novel, you were juggling family drama, night classes, a few part-time jobs, and an obsessed stalker."

"Know what? No." Nova rose to her feet. "We're not doing this. I came here to thank you, but for some reason, you're picking a fight with me over writing."

"I'm not picking a fight with you, Nova. All I'm saying—"

"You are, Caleb. You're picking a fight with me over something that shouldn't even be any of your business. It's up to me when to write again. That shouldn't be up to you."

Caleb's shoulders sagged. To her relief, he backed off. "Okay, Nova."

Nova frowned. This wasn't how she had expected this visit to his office would go. "I'll see you at home later. Don't forget to pick up the kids." Without bothering to hear what more he had to say, she walked away to return to her office. Work consumed her the moment she sat behind her desk. So engrossed in it all, she barely noticed when Caleb dropped a pile of paper on her desk.

The move grated her nerves further. Why was he pushing this? "I told you, Caleb. I don't have time."

"Read it once you find time, then," he said. "Thank me later. I'm going to pick up the twins."

Nova huffed, not even daring to look his way. "Just leave me alone, Caleb. Go."

"I love you, Nova," he said, before walking away.

With her husband gone, she returned to her work, unaware of the clock ticking along. Upon realizing Rachel hadn't yet shown up, she checked the time. What was taking her so long? Why wasn't she here yet? It shouldn't take her twenty minutes to get here from the parking lot. Her phone started buzzing. Rachel's name was on the screen.

Nova answered, "Rachel! Where are you? I've been—" The sound of an ambulance behind Rachel alerted her senses. What had happened?

"Nova, you have to hurry. We're at the parking lot. I'll drive you to the hospital. Caleb and Jenna are already on their way there. They're both in an ambulance."

Unaware of the extent of their injuries, the irritation she had felt for Caleb earlier mixed with the anxiety over what could've happened that her husband was suddenly in an ambulance. Upon reaching the parking lot, she found Rachel soaked in blood, with a manic glaze over her blue eyes. Only then did Nova recognize an alarming but very real possibility: she could lose the love of her life that night.

nineteen

SHIFTED **P**RIORITIES & **S**OOTHING **P**EACE

Nothing in life could prepare anyone for a loved one's brush with death. Everything ceased to matter — all her concerns about her family, her career, her church, none of it mattered compared to that one life-threatening moment. Nova paced the floor of the waiting area outside the operating room, where the doctors were trying to save Caleb's life. Policemen were still taking Rachel's statement. Jeremy stood beside her, stroking her back.

Nova wished she could send everyone away — especially Rachel. This woman, whose body, hair, and clothes were soaked in her husband's blood. On one hand, Rachel was the one who had done everything she could to save his life. On the other, she was one of the two people Caleb had risked his life to save.

Why was she still there?

"Nova." Someone touched her arm.

Nova flinched and turned to her side to find Jenna and Max standing there. The blood on her clothes and the ugly bruise on her face told Nova she had been hurt as well, but why was she standing there and Caleb wasn't? She pushed Jenna's hand away.

How had God allowed this to happen? She backed away from all of them until the back of her knees hit the edge of a chair, and she fell into it, shaking. Max and Jenna immediately rushed beside her, with Jenna sitting next to her, careful not to touch her, and Max on his knee on the floor beside her.

"Nova—" Max's voice broke.

God wouldn't let her lose Caleb, would He? What was she going to say to the children? The children!

"The twins." Nova gasped the two words out. "Caleb left the office to pick up the twins from school. I have to go pick them up. No one told them. No one even called. I need to go see my children." Her hands trembled as she brought out the phone from her pocket. She could barely even see the screen through the tears blurring her vision.

Max held her wrist. "Nova, I'll pick them up," he said. "Jenna will call your mom and Caleb's parents. Everything will be okay."

How could anything be okay in a scenario like this? Her lips quivered. Rachel approached to hand her a tissue. Nova stared at it, but all she could see was the blood soaking Rachel's dress. Her husband's blood. She took the tissue, hoping it would make Rachel leave her alone. More tears rushed down her cheek. Why was she so shaken up? Caleb wasn't dead. He wouldn't die. God wouldn't let that happen. Nova had to believe God wouldn't let such a thing happen.

Panic rushed over her, and she gripped Max's arm as Jenna stood up to make phone calls.

"I think I'll take Rachel home," Jeremy said. "She's more than a little shaken up, so it might do her well to go home and take a shower. We'll be back with food. We can also drop by your house, if you want. Get some stuff for you. Is there anything you need?"

Nova couldn't think. Was there anything? Were the cops gone? Weren't they going to wait to take Caleb's statement?

"Maybe it would be better if Nova's mom gets the things she needs. She would know their house better," Max told Jeremy. He then looked at Nova straight in the eye before gripping Nova's hand. "We'll be fighting in prayer for Caleb, okay?"

"I can't lose him, Max," Nova blurted out. "I can't lose my husband."

"Shhh…" Max shook his head. "No one is losing anyone tonight."

Max gathered her in his arms and brushed his palm up and down her back. Nova melted into his embrace. All the fear, apprehension, and stress burst out of her. The sight of her husband as they had wheeled him into the operating room kept running through her head. She clung to Max like he was a lifeline, like doing so meant holding on to Caleb.

In her ear, Max whispered a prayer. "God, Caleb is in Your hands right now. His life is in Your hands. Don't take him away from us. Give Nova the peace, assurance, and comfort she needs. This isn't the way Caleb will go. This isn't the way. Reach into Nova's heart and mind right now, and speak peace into all this chaos."

Nova didn't know if it was his soothing voice or the fact that holding on to him enabled her to draw from his strength, but the simple prayer Max had uttered did bring with it a wave of peace that started from the top of her head and cascaded down to the tips of her toes. "Amen," she said. "Amen." Her sobs subsided. She pulled away from him and tried to collect herself.

"I'll go get the twins," Max said.

Nova nodded at him. "Thank you, Max."

"No problem." Max rubbed her shoulder. "Jenna will be right here with you."

Rachel squeezed Nova's shoulder. "We'll be back."

Nova looked up at her. She was still here? Hadn't she and Jeremy said they were going minutes ago? She nodded at them.

Jenna sat next to Nova and took her hand. "They're coming, Nova."

She was being nice, but all Nova could feel towards Rachel and Jenna was irritation. If it weren't for them, Caleb wouldn't be in this predicament. A vague awareness of her own irrationality tugged at Nova's heart, but her anger was begging to be directed at someone, and the man who had stabbed her husband wasn't there.

The operating room's doors opened, and a doctor stepped out.

Nova gasped for breath as she stood up. "What happened? How is my husband? Will he be okay?"

The doctor's stoic face didn't tell her much. "Your husband lost a lot of blood because of the punctured artery. He also suffered from a concussion when the back of his head hit the pavement. He is stable right now, Mrs. Grant, but we will keep him under observation. We're hoping for the best. If he wakes up within the next twelve hours, that will be a good sign."

"If he doesn't?"

"We will cross that bridge once we get there, Mrs. Grant. Right now, he's in the recovery room. We'll keep him there until he is stable for transfer to his suite. Right now, I suggest you get some rest and perhaps a meal, if you intend to stay here to watch over him tonight."

Nova nodded. The last thing she wanted was to eat. All she wanted to do was to go see her husband, but for now, knowing he was alive should be enough.

"He's okay, Nova," Jenna said as she squeezed Nova's hand. "He's alive."

Nova let out an exhale of relief, even if she still wanted to be able to see Caleb. She sat back in the chair and Jenna sat next to her.

"I'm so sorry for everything," Jenna said, still holding her hand. "I had an inkling this morning that something might go wrong, but I couldn't have imagined something like this would happen."

Nova forced out a smile only because the knowledge that her husband was alive allowed her to think a little straighter. "He's okay now. That's what matters." She gave Jenna a quick look-over. "How are you doing?"

"A little bruised and beat-up, but grateful to still be alive, thanks to Caleb."

This deep-seated selfishness took over Nova, because she was angry, but it wasn't with Rachel or with Jenna she was angriest. It was with Caleb. Why had he done what he had done? Why did he have to go and be the hero? Nova shut her eyes as guilt consumed her over such a thought, but she knew it in her heart to be true.

Her mother arrived, and Caleb's parents followed not long after. Max then arrived with the twins, followed by Jeremy and Rachel, who were both carrying bags of Chinese takeout for everyone to share. The mood was almost festive as Nova told them Caleb had survived and was in the recovery room. They were just waiting for him to stabilize before transferring him, but he should wake up any time now.

That was what Nova had told everyone. The problem was that when the nurses wheeled Caleb out of the recovery room to transfer him to a suite, he was still unconscious. When dawn broke the next morning and Nova opened her eyes, her first instinct was to check on him. He was still unconscious.

As the day went on, it had become increasingly clear — and the doctor confirmed this to her later — Caleb was in a coma.

twenty

ΛNCHORED HOPE & ΛCCEPTING HOME

Time neither crawled nor ran. For Nova, it ceased to exist. Minutes turned to hours and hours to days; it meant nothing to Nova. Stuck in a hospital suite with her unconscious husband, the passing of time, as well as all her other concerns, took a back seat to this one obsession she now had: the desire for Caleb to come back to her.

A warm orange glow filled the suite as the rays of the morning sun woke Nova up. She squinted her eyes against the light and tried to reorient her thoughts to where she was. The white-washed ceiling reminded her, triggering a rush of anticipation inside her. She sat up on the couch that had been her bed for whatever number of days she had been in that hospital suite. She groaned at the ache in her back and her joints. It was as if the hospital couch was taunting her age, reminding her she was past forty and shouldn't treat her body like this anymore.

Nova did a few stretches as she slipped into her slippers before making her way to Caleb's bedside, whispering a desperate plea as she approached: "Please wake up, Caleb."

Nova took a seat on the cushioned metal stool by his bed. She stared. There he still was — breathing, but unconscious; alive, but lifeless. Whatever shred of optimism Nova had was fading away as she intertwined her fingers with his and pressed the back of his hand against her lips. "Caleb, I need you to wake up. I need you to come back to us, okay?" Her voice came out hoarse. She had already spoken variations of the same words to him multiple times. Not once had he responded. No matter what she had tried to do — cry, scream, beg for him to wake up, try to pound the doors of heaven to return him to consciousness — none of it helped to jolt him out of his unconscious state. He remained within her reach, but still so distant from her.

Nova clasped his hand between hers, gripping him tight, as a rare winsomeness came over her. "You leave me no choice, Caleb. I have to resort to this now." She stood up, the stool creaking against the white, tiled floor. She then shut her eyes and inhaled deeply before letting go of his hand and bending over to plant a soft kiss on his unmoving lips. The moment their lips touched, a wave of embarrassment tickled her senses. What was she doing? This was so stupid. She was a woman in her forties, with a genuine wish that true love's kiss would wake her unconscious husband up. She propped herself back up on the stool and sighed. As foolish as she felt at the moment, it was worth a try, at least once. Anything to wake Caleb up.

"I'm desperate here, Caleb," she said as she brushed her fingers against his arm. "I miss you so much. Come back to us, honey. We need you. The twins and I need you, so fight to get back to us, okay?" She stared at his still form, willing him to move. When that didn't work, she closed her eyes and tried to imagine him talking to her. What would he say if he was awake?

The knowing look he would give her accompanied that reserved smile of his when he made her feel like he was seeing right through her. It would sometimes rub her the wrong way, how known he made her feel. That had certainly been the case during their last encounter. She couldn't understand what he had been trying to get at, but it had affected her the way it had, because she had been so aware of how well her husband knew her mind, her personality, her heart. Right now, as uncomfortable as it sometimes made her feel, she would give anything to have him look at her that way again.

Her phone started vibrating against the wooden bedside table. Nova winced. Who was it this time? She rolled her eyes. Most likely Nolan. She picked it up and checked the name on the screen. She was right. It was her brother. He had been calling every day, and as much as Nova knew he meant well, she didn't want to answer the same questions all over again. Still, of the many people trying to "support" her, Nolan was among the ones she could still bear to listen to, so she answered his call.

"Nolan?"

"Nova, I am saying this with a lot of love in my heart." Nolan drew in a deep, long breath. "Go home today, okay?"

"Huh? What are you talking about?"

"Ma says she will be there today to watch over Caleb, so you can go home, spend time with the twins, take a shower, and get a night of decent sleep in an actual bed. Your limbs are no longer compatible with couches." Nolan snickered. "Those weren't Ma's exact words, but you get the sentiment."

This was why she felt better about talking to Nolan. He could at least make her smile. Nova slid out of the stool and plopped herself back on the couch. "Ma is talking to you about how old I am?"

"Not exactly. Just that she's concerned over how you haven't been home in days. Nova, you can't just stay there until he wakes up."

"How do you know he hasn't woken up?"

"Has he?"

Nova released a breath. "No. He hasn't." She clenched her jaw before spilling out the truth. "I'm scared, Nolan."

"You're Super Nova, remember? You may get scared sometimes, but you overcome. This time isn't any different, and remember, Nova—" Nolan chuckled "—your husband is a literal hero. Caleb saved both Rachel's and Jenna's lives. He'll get through this."

Nova winced. "Is it bad that I'm angry at him for doing that? I know he probably acted on instinct, but what was he thinking? Didn't he think of me? The twins?"

"Nova..." Nolan sighed. "This is the exhausted version of you speaking. Go home. You can come back tomorrow to relieve Ma from the watch, but right now, you need to take care of yourself. Do you want your hero of a husband to wake up and find you all stinky?"

"I do wash myself while I'm here, Nolan." Nova rolled her eyes as she stood up and looked out the suite's window. "I just don't want him to wake up and find that I'm not here."

"That's fair, but there's no way of knowing when he will wake up. You've been there for three days now. You need rest too."

"Three days, huh? It feels so much longer than that. Why are you the one calling to give me this information, anyway? Why can't Ma tell me all of this herself?"

"Beats me. For some reason, she thinks there's a better chance you will listen to me instead of her. She says she's tried to convince you time and time again, but you refuse to budge."

Nova snickered. "Seriously? It's insane that she would think you have more sway than she does."

"That's what I said, but hey—" Nolan paused "—at least her misconception got you to laugh."

"I wouldn't call that laughter."

"I'll take what I can get. For real, though. Nova, you have a community willing to help you. Remember that. You don't have to go through this alone. You are both so loved, so allow those who love you to help, okay?"

Nova took a deep breath. His words rang true, but the very thought of leaving Caleb's side was giving her anxiety. "I'll think about it."

"Whatever you decide, Ma will be there this afternoon, ready to relieve you of your watch. You two will just have to talk it out."

"Fine. Thanks for the heads up, Nolan."

"Take care of yourself, Nova. Bye."

Nova hung up. She stared at her phone as she returned to Caleb's bedside. This time, she sat on the edge of the hospital bed, her focus still on all the unread messages and missed calls on her phone. She returned the phone on top of the bedside table and tried not to think too much about any of it.

Her last words to her husband drifted across her mind. *"Just leave me alone, Caleb. Go."* Why had she been so short with him? If she had just picked up the twins instead, would this have happened? Somehow, every minute Caleb stayed unconscious shifted Nova's anger from Rachel and Jenna to Caleb to herself. Was she to blame for all of this?

Before that thought could eat her up, a knock on the door made her jolt to attention. Expecting the doctor, she was met with disappointment when Pastor Sam, Jeremy, and Rachel walked in instead. Every day since Caleb had been hospitalized, a steady barrage of people had shown up to bring her food and keep her company. At some point, it was getting exhausting for her, because she felt like she was entertaining them more than they were bringing her any comfort whatsoever.

Still, she put on a smile for her guests, because at least they helped get her mind off her culpability in Caleb's current predicament. "Hi, guys. Thank you for coming," she said as she hugged Pastor Sam, then Jeremy, then Rachel.

"We brought you breakfast," Rachel said, placing a brown bag and a coffee cup on the other bedside table across from where Nova was sitting. "Coffee and a bagel with cream cheese. I hope you like cappuccino."

"It will do. Thank you, Rachel. That's thoughtful."

"He hasn't budged at all?" Jeremy asked as he leaned on the metal railing at the end of the hospital bed.

Nova shook her head. What a stupid question. Did it look like Caleb was any different from the last time Jeremy had seen him?

"What are the doctors saying?" Pastor Sam asked.

"There's not much they can do at this point." Nova shrugged. "Caleb is stable. No signs of internal bleeding. His wound is healing. But for some reason, he's just not coming to. All we can do is wait."

"How are you dealing with all this, Nova?" Pastor Sam rubbed her shoulders. "Clara told me you refuse to let anyone take a turn watching over Caleb. Not even his parents or his brothers and sisters."

Was Ma talking to everyone to get her to take a break? Nova repeated to her pastor what she had said to Nolan earlier. "I want to be here when he wakes up, Pastor."

"Why is that?"

Nova winced. What did he mean, why? Why wouldn't she want to be there when he woke up? She was his wife! "Not to be rude, Pastor, but can we talk about something else, please? It doesn't help to keep talking about Caleb's situation, and everyone who comes visit kind of focuses on that, and I have to explain the same thing over and over again."

Her three guests exchanged glances.

Pastor Sam nodded. "Of course. I can understand how that can be exhausting."

An awkward silence followed as everyone present tried to figure out what they could talk about. Nova was in no mood for small talk, nor did she want any talk about God being in control, so she welcomed the quiet.

It was Rachel who eventually broke the silence, her shoulders perking up as she tried to put on a smile. "Your boss had a talk with me, by the way. Ethan Caine?"

"Yeah?" That triggered Nova's curiosity, at least. "What did he say?"

"Just confirmation about your launch party being postponed until further notice. Also, he mentioned that if you need anything from the office, you can let me know. He gave me a temporary pass to the office, so I can assist you as much as you need."

Nova threw her head back. "Thanks, Rachel. That's helpful to know." She smiled at the thought of their boss. Ethan Caine had been one of the major influences in both Caleb's and Nova's lives. "God really has blessed us to have Ethan as a boss. He's the one paying for the suite."

"Wow. Praise God!" Pastor Sam exclaimed. "Has he come to visit yet?"

Nova shook her head. "He sent flowers with an apology, saying he won't be able to visit. Something about finding it hard to be in hospitals, but we should take all the time we need for Caleb to recover."

"He's quite intimidating." Rachel frowned. "It's good to know he has some kindness in him."

"He's a good man. Even tried to date Serene once."

Pastor Sam and Jeremy exchanged glances.

"Did you know about that, Dad?" Jeremy asked.

Pastor Sam shook his head. "As far as I know, your sister has only ever dated Nolan."

Nova winced. "Well, technically, Serene declined Ethan almost immediately. He did mentor her when she started her incubator."

"Oh yeah." Jeremy nodded. "I remember him. He was in her first art show, too."

"Wow." Rachel cast an affectionate glance at him. "It's still so amazing to me how you manage to remember details about people like that."

Jeremy shrugged. "As you said, he comes off as intimidating. He's hard to forget."

The interaction between the couple reminded Nova they were actually getting married; it had been so easy to forget with everything going on. "How are the wedding plans going so far?"

The delight that appeared on Rachel's face made Nova regret asking. Could she really handle all the gushing about to happen? She would have to, because it was she who had brought this upon herself by asking the question.

"We have an idea for a wedding venue and a theme, so we're excited about that," Rachel said. "It's just really hard to talk about it with anyone, that's all."

"Yeah." Nova winced. "I can see how it would be difficult to get people excited about a wedding when everything around us is falling apart. It honestly surprises me you two are getting married in the middle of all this chaos. Can't you wait until after all the things happening at our church blows over?"

Rachel's mouth opened as she exchanged looks with her fiancé.

Nova immediately recognized how brash she had been. "I'm sorry. That's stepping out of line. I shouldn't have said that."

"No, it's good, Nova," Pastor Sam said. "You're voicing out something a lot of people are thinking but don't have the guts to say out loud. Especially not to Jeremy's and Rachel's faces. You saying it gives them a chance to respond."

Rachel hunched over and sank on the edge of the couch, hiding behind Jeremy, clearly withdrawing herself from the conversation.

It was Jeremy who spoke up. "We've definitely considered postponing the wedding, Nova, but even before we flew back here, we already had this strong conviction that we should push through with the wedding no matter what we come home to. It's something we believe can help unite rather than divide. Kind of like how you ladies feel about putting on the play."

That gave Nova pause. What was she doing here? Was she pushing this couple to suspend their life plans because of troubles other people were going through? What difference would there be between her and Mrs. P, then? Her husband's face while talking about the play drifted through her mind. "Interesting you would say that," Nova said. "That's what Caleb said about the play. Those words exactly. Something about it helping unite rather than divide. Has he spoken to you at all, before—" she glanced at Caleb's motionless form "—this?"

"Not at all." Jeremy shook his head. "Caleb and I have barely spoken a word to each other since I returned."

"We're postponing all work on the play, right?" Pastor Sam asked. "Given the circumstances we are in, that may be the wise recourse."

"No." Nova set her foot down. "I'll write the script. We'll push through with it even if we end up having all the meetings here at the hospital. That's what Caleb would want, so when he wakes up, I'd like to be able to tell him I've been writing. Also—" she turned to Rachel "—can you do me a favor?"

Rachel swallowed hard and pointed to herself. "Me? Sure, Nova. Anything."

"There's a manuscript in the bottom right drawer of my desk. It's a thick, spiral-bound pile of paper. I actually don't know what the title is or who the author is, but I would appreciate it if you bring it here, please?"

"Of course." Rachel seemed to perk up at the idea of being able to help.

"Thank you." Nova winced. "And I'm sorry about snapping at you about your wedding. I did ask, so I shouldn't have shot you down like that. It's just difficult for me to process the idea of being happy over something while Caleb is in the state he is in."

"I understand, Nova, and Pastor Sam was right. A lot of people are thinking it but not finding the guts to ask it, so it's almost a relief that you did."

"Thank you for understanding."

"If you need anything else, just let us know," Pastor Sam said.

"I will. Thank you, Pastor," Nova said.

They all said a prayer together before the three of them said their goodbyes, leaving Nova alone in the room once again.

The first thing Nova did was say a quick prayer for the food before eating the breakfast that Rachel had brought for her. Once satiated by a good meal, Nova still had a hunger in her soul, amplified by the silence surrounding her.

In the solitude, in the quiet, there was no one Nova could run to other than a God she wanted to believe could see her right at this moment of desperation. So many prayers had already been uttered on Caleb's behalf — by her and by other people — but God remained silent; their prayers remained unanswered. Why? Her searching heart brought her to her knees in front of the couch that she had slept in for the past three days. With her phone in front of her, and her knees on the bottom edge of the couch, she asked God to come through for her. When she ran out of words, she opened the Bible app on her phone and happened upon the first book of Thessalonians. A specific passage jumped at her.

Rejoice always, pray continually, give thanks in all circumstances; for this is God's will for you in Christ Jesus. 1 Thessalonians 5:16-18

It triggered her indignation. Rejoice always? Give thanks? How? How could she possibly do something like that in a circumstance like this? It didn't make sense to Nova, and yet, that's what the Word was asking her to do. Hands clasped together, Nova leaned her forehead against the back of her thumbs as she searched for something to thank God for.

"Thank You, God," she said when she couldn't think of anything specific to be grateful for. "You are good. My lack of understanding doesn't change Who You are. I'm confused and hurt right now, but God, You are still good. I declare Your goodness over the situation we are in, because it could have been much worse. Thank You for giving us a community who loves us and wants to support us. Forgive me for not recognizing that I am not alone in this, that there are people willing to bear this burden with me. No matter what I'm going through, it doesn't change the fact that You, God, are good and will always remain good. Most of all, Lord, thank You for sparing my husband's life. He may be unconscious right now, but he breathes yet, and I'm thankful for that. If in this coma, he is somehow with You, tell him we still need him with us. Bring him back to us. There's so much yet that we need to accomplish before You can take any of us. Please hear my cry, hear my plea. No matter what is happening in my life, I love You, God, and I can only say that, because I trust that You love me. You love Caleb, and everything will happen as You allow it to be, so Lord, please… bring my husband back to me. In the Name of my precious Savior, Jesus, amen."

Her amen brought about a sense of surrender in Nova, a deep trust that God had everything under control and that Caleb's life was in God's hands. She read more from the Word, trying to stay conscious of God's presence. A nurse dropped by to check on Caleb, and then the doctor. They said the same thing to Nova. All they could do was wait, but the jadedness had left Nova. In its place was a hope serving as the anchor to her soul.

Once again losing track of time, Nova's breath hitched when the door opened and Rachel peeked in.

"Rachel!" Nova smiled. "You're back."

"I have the manuscript you asked for," Rachel said. "I hope I brought the right one." She entered the room and handed Nova what she had asked for earlier.

Nova stood up to take the pile from Rachel. "Yes. This is it." She nodded. She thumbed through the pages before looking at Rachel. "Thank you. I hope it wasn't too much of an inconvenience."

"Not at all. I mentioned what you said about the play to Jenna, and Jeremy also mentioned it to Serene, and I think all three of us are ready to work on the play if you're up for it. Just let us know when."

"Oh." Nova raised her brows as she nodded. "Right. The play. What day is today?"

"It's a Saturday." Rachel checked her phone to make sure. "Yep. Saturday."

"I see." Nova wrinkled her nose. "Monday, maybe? I'll keep you guys updated on whether I'm still here by then. Hopefully, Caleb would have already woken up, but if not, we'll have it here. Otherwise, would my place be okay?"

"Either way is fine with us. We'll adjust to you."

"Thank you."

"I actually have to go. Jeremy and I have several appointments for our wedding, so—"

"Right. Sure." Nova nodded. "Go. Go."

Rachel turned to leave.

"Rachel." Nova took hold of her elbow before she could reach the door. "I'm sorry again about what I said about your wedding. I think it's sweet that you and Jeremy are so sure and so determined to push through with it. It took years for Caleb and I to tie the knot. We'd been dating for so long, and we were sure we wanted to be together, but we were always waiting for the right timing. As a couple, we were both so cautious. Whether or not we could admit it at the time, we both wanted things to be perfect first." A soft smile tugged at the corners of Nova's lips. "It's why it's difficult for me to understand why you guys can just rush into marriage. First, Max and Jenna; now, you and Jeremy. I do believe God is leading You, so—"

Rachel clasped Nova's hand. "I've always admired you and Caleb, Nova. It means a lot to me to hear you say all of that. Jeremy and I understand where you're coming from. Personally, I've always wished I could have a longer engagement. There's a great part of me that still resonates with what you and Caleb wanted — something perfect, but I've learned over the past months that perfection is God's job, not ours. It's interesting to me that God brought me to this path, and if I wasn't a hundred percent sure this was His will for us, I would balk too. Yet, here we are. Thank you for trying to understand us, Nova. It means a lot."

"I wish only the best for you and Jeremy." Nova sighed.

"We know."

"Now, go. Your boyfriend is waiting."

Rachel blushed at the term. She twisted her heels to head for the door, and Nova smiled at how in love Rachel seemed to be. A sudden tug of urgency made Nova sit up straight, the manuscript still clasped in her hands.

"Oh, Rachel," Nova said. "One last thing before I let you go."

"Yes?" Rachel asked, turning slightly.

"Thank you for having enough presence of mind to do what had to be done to save my husband. The doctor says it could have turned out much worse had it not been for you."

"Anyone in my situation would have done the same, Nova. Besides, it's Caleb who came to our rescue." Rachel glanced at Caleb. "He'll come back to us."

Nova's hope grew. "He will."

Rachel left the room, leaving Nova on her own.

There was nothing left to do other than to read the manuscript Caleb had asked her to read. It was the least she could do for him, considering the state he was in, so she opened the first page. The title of the book was *Orphaned Souls of Wonder*. The author's name was one Nova had never heard of. Naveed Clancy. A ring of familiarity came with the name, but Nova couldn't quite place it.

She opened the first page and read the first line, and then the next line. Within a few minutes, the book had completely hooked Nova, and as she read through the next paragraph and then the next, something sparked within her — the desire to create. No wonder Caleb had wanted her to read this. It wasn't the most well-written book she had ever read, but it had with it a freshness that re-ignited her sense of wonder — something Nova hadn't even been aware she had lost.

She had just finished reading the first chapter and was eagerly awaiting to dive into the next one when the door creaked open and in came her mother, her twelve-year-olds, as well as Max and Jenna. Nova reluctantly put the manuscript down and got up on her feet to welcome them.

"*Iha*!" Ma used her fingers to tuck Nova's unruly hair behind her ears so she could clear Nova's face. "How are you doing?"

"I'm fine, Ma," Nova said.

Nate and Claudia immediately went to their father's bedside to check on him.

"He hasn't moved a muscle yet?" Nate asked.

Claudia placed a bag of food on top of the bedside table. "We brought lunch. I'm starving."

"We also have fruits." Nate lifted his hand to show a plastic bag full of an assortment of fresh food.

"They wanted to visit their dad," Ma explained. "Since it's a weekend, I couldn't find a reason why they shouldn't."

"We finished all our school work," Nate said before fishing out his phone from his pocket.

"Nate, you're not spending your time here playing games on your phone," Nova said.

"That's not what I'm doing, Ma." Nate lifted his phone up. "I just want to take a picture of Dad."

"Why?" Nova frowned.

Nate shrugged. "So he knows what he looks like when he comes to."

"Unnecessary." Claudia rolled her eyes.

Nova waved to Max and Jenna. "Thanks for coming. Rachel and Jeremy were here earlier this morning. They visited with Pastor Sam."

"Yeah." Jenna nodded. "Rachel mentioned it. We thought we could give Clara a ride here and then give you and the twins a ride back home once you are ready."

Nova's shoulders sagged. "No. I want to be here. Ma, come on. You can't handle sleeping on the couch here."

"It's not just me who'll look after Caleb, Nova." Ma shook her head. "There will be a bunch of us who will do it."

Nova creased her brows. "What do you mean?"

Max smiled at her. "We'll be taking shifts. Your mom will be taking a shift after you leave, and then Caleb's parents will come to relieve her. Jenna and I will also return to keep watch at midnight. Then Rachel and Jeremy volunteered to come early morning to be here until you return. If you want to be able to attend church tomorrow, then we can arrange—"

"No." Nova shook her head. "This isn't necessary, Max. It's not like this is all exhausting to me. It will stress me out more to not be here with Caleb, and—"

Ma squeezed her hand before whispering to her, "Take all the help you can get, Nova. You're not just a wife. You're also a mother."

Guilt hit Nova as she looked at her children. They both seemed okay, like they were taking this in stride, better than she ever could. Was she missing something here? Nova glanced at her mother, then at Max and Jenna, and finally at her husband.

Aware that there was no fighting this, Nova relented. It would be a good time to get herself together and at least have a conversation with her twins about what was happening. It was time for her to accept the help and go home.

twenty-one

DEPRESSING HOMES & DESPERATE HEARTS

Gratitude often came over Nova whenever she entered the little cul-de-sac within their gated community. The Spanish-style villa that she and Caleb had bought together right after they had gotten married was a home she was proud of, but as Max took a turn around the cul-de-sac to stop at their house, Nova shifted uncomfortably in the back of Max's SUV.

Knowing she wouldn't find Caleb there filled Nova with more dread than she could imagine. Every bit of her wanted to go back to the hospital to be with her husband, but it was just one night. She could bear a night without Caleb, couldn't she?

Nova bristled. What was happening to her? When had she gotten so dependent on him she couldn't imagine spending a night without him? She fidgeted with her fingers, her hands laid over her lap. Claudia took hold of her hand and leaned her head against Nova's shoulder.

"It will be okay, Ma," Claudia said, her dark curls brushing against Nova's arm.

"I know, Claud," Nova said as she laid her arm over her daughter's shoulder and pulled her in, giving her a soft kiss on the cheek. "We'll get through this. Your dad will be all right. I believe that with all my heart."

Nate looked up from his phone as Max pulled over in their driveway. "Here we are."

As the twins alighted the vehicle to get to their home, Nova reached forward to rub Max's and Jenna's shoulders. "Do you guys want to come in? We can have dinner delivered."

Max and Jenna exchanged glances before Jenna twisted her torso to face Nova. "We're fine, Nova. We want to get back home, so we can ready ourselves to take over Caleb's watch later."

"You'll call me immediately if he wakes up, right? No matter what time of the night it is, it's fine. I'll answer the call." Nova dropped her hands and rubbed her jeans with her palms.

Jenna nodded. "Of course. We'll call you, Nova. We also informed everyone who will take a shift tonight to do the same."

"Thank you," Nova said. "I do appreciate everything you guys are doing. Please forgive me if I'm not able to express it better."

Jenna's expression softened. "You've gone through a lot. This is the least we can do after what Caleb did for me. If you need anything, don't hesitate to call, okay?"

"Sure. You both take care." Nova scooted over so she could get out of the SUV through the side where Nate had kept the door open for her. Nate walked her up the deck leading to their front door, which her son opened wide to let her in. The moment Nova stepped inside their house, a wave of sadness hit her. Caleb wasn't there. He was still in a coma. He wouldn't descend the stairs to greet her. Their bedroom would be empty. Nova gripped her son's hand tight as Claudia emerged from the living room to their entry way.

"Ma," Claudia said, taking a hold of her mother's free hand. "Come see what we've been working on."

Something about Claudia's cheery tone sounded forced to Nova. Why were her children the ones trying to cheer her up and not the other way around? Nova gritted her teeth. She had to snap out of this. She wasn't the only one in pain. Her husband's life might be hanging in the balance at the moment, but these were her children. Why did she feel so disconnected from them, like she didn't know how this was affecting them, and she barely seemed to care?

Claudia pulled her toward the living room, where a huge blue banner with white letterings was hanging over the room, silver streamers curling beside it. The banner read, *Welcome Home, Dad!*

At the sight of it, Nova swallowed hard.

"He's coming home, Ma," Nate said.

"We're sure of it." Claudia's voice cracked. "Right, Ma?"

Unbidden tears trickled down Nova's face as she dropped the purse containing the manuscript on the floor and hugged her children. This wasn't about her anymore. She had been going through all of this on her own, at the cost of the people around her who also loved Caleb.

"You're right," Nova said. "Your father will be okay. I believe with all my heart that he will be."

Claudia sobbed into her shoulder while Nate pulled away and sat on the edge of their beige leather sofa. He took a pillow and hugged it against his chest.

Named after Nova's older brother, so much of her son reminded him of the brother she had lost. Even at such a young age, Nate had an intensity about him that Claudia didn't have. He had a way of processing things with so much depth that it sometimes scared Nova.

"Nate?" Nova stroked Claudia's back as she gave her son a questioning look.

"Ma, why did he do it?"

Nova's brows creased. She wiped her own tears away and used her thumb to wipe away Claudia's. She gripped her daughter's hand and led Claudia toward the sofa, so they could sit with Nate.

In the middle of her two children, Nova braced herself for a conversation she wasn't sure she was ready to have.

"What do you mean, Nate?" Nova asked.

"I'm awful for saying this, but why?" Nate frowned. "Why did Dad risk his life to rescue Jenna and Rachel? Wasn't he thinking about us?"

"Nate." Claudia frowned. "Wouldn't you have done the same if you were in that same situation? Would you have just let that criminal stab Jenna?"

Nate shrugged. "I don't know. We read about heroes in books, but that's not real life. We're not supposed to actually be heroes, are we?"

Part of Nova wanted to reprimand Nate for having thoughts like this, but then a swift recollection of how she had felt while waiting outside the operating room for news on Caleb returned to her. How could she fault her son for feeling this way when she herself had struggled with the same thoughts? "First of all, I can't blame you for asking the questions you're asking. For a while, I felt the exact same way. I was so mad at your father for doing what he did, but in a lot of ways, that's also what I love about your dad. He's selfless. I want to think he did consider us when he jumped in to rescue Rachel and Jenna. I would never want to believe your dad didn't take us into consideration, but we often need to count the cost when doing the right thing. Your father did the right thing. He put his life on the line to do the right thing, and isn't that what the Bible tells us to do? Isn't that what God says is the greatest love we can offer? To lay down our lives for our friends?"

"Dad is a hero," Claudia said.

Nate shifted beside Nova, his body stiff as he leaned back and let out a sigh. "I don't care if he's a hero. I just want Dad to wake up. Why is doing the right thing always so hard?"

Nova laid her hand on Nate's knee. She couldn't begin to process what was going on in his head. "Where are these questions coming from, Nate?"

"It's true, Ma, isn't it? It's hard to do the right thing; doing what's wrong is so much easier."

Nova bristled. It was rare to hear Nate talk this way. Most of the time, he kept to himself or stayed on his phone. That he was the one talking like this right now and not Claudia surprised her. "Why do you say that?"

"Ma, we're supposed to believe that we're sinners, right? And that Jesus came to save us? And when we follow Him, we are saved from our sins, and we become a new creation. That's what Pastor Sam preaches at church all the time. That's what we were taught in Sunday School."

"Right."

"Then why don't I feel any different? I still get mad at Claudia sometimes."

"All. The. Time." Claudia huffed.

"I can't help it." Nate shrugged. "She can be so annoying!" He frowned. "And why is it that Mrs. P can get away with being mean to everyone, and she's doing all right? Meanwhile, Dad is always trying to do what's right, and he's the one in a coma now? It isn't fair, Ma. That's not how it should be."

Nova's brain scrambled to catch up with what her son was saying. What did Mrs. P have to do with all this? That's when it hit her. With Nate slouched back in the sofa, already almost taller than Nova, and Claudia slouched forward, her elbows over her knees as she twirled absent-mindedly with her curly hair, Nova realized her children were growing up. She had been so caught up in the routine of everyday life that she had barely realized it. In a few months' time, Nate and Claudia would enter into their teens, and even now, they already had their eyes wide open. They weren't just children anymore, oblivious to what was going on around them. They were attentive and observant and smart, and now they were able to ask hard questions about their walk with Christ.

Nova herself hadn't even paid much attention to what was going on at church, but apparently, Nate was up-to-date on everything, actively observing. How had it taken her husband's coma for Nova to take a pause from the rush of her own life to take enough time to listen to what was going on in her children's lives?

Nova closed her eyes. *God, what do I say?*

She opened her eyes and held her son's hand. "You're right, Nate. It's not fair, but God doesn't always work to make things fair, as much as He works to make our hearts right. We may not always understand how He acts or moves or why He allows certain things to happen, but we go through these trials so He can mold us into who He wants us to be. These are opportunities for us to respond in a way that glorifies Him."

When Nova had woken up that morning, she hadn't expected to end the night discussing with her soon-to-be teenagers what was happening at church and why God wasn't punishing Mrs. P for it, but that was how the day unfolded and in the middle of her marriage's greatest tragedy, she discovered something beautiful.

Not wanting to spend the night in their rooms alone, they all decided to set up their own little sleepover in the living room, setting up mattresses and piling blankets and pillows there.

"We missed you, Ma." Claudia said as she drifted off to sleep, snuggling against Nova. "I'm sad this happened to Dad, but it's nice to have a night like this with you."

That hit Nova right in the chest. Where had she been? Hadn't she been here all along? Had she been moving on autopilot all this time, and had that been the reason Caleb had been pushing her to write again?

With her two children asleep on either side of her, Nova retrieved the manuscript from her bag and started reading again. As she read the story of two orphans who had two very different lives — one rich and one poor — she saw the story of the prodigal son and the other brother in the novel she was reading. Now, more than ever, she was convinced that the play had to happen. It needed to happen for the sake of her kids and the generations to follow.

twenty-two

SOULFUL SUNDAYS & SUDDEN SHAKE-UPS

The hum of the air conditioner nearby and the lackluster worship on stage heightened Nova's awareness of the fact she didn't want to go to church that Sunday. Still, there she stood as one of Connect Church's noticeably lessened attendees. The controversies behind the exit of Miss Rhoda from the church were taking its toll on their attendance. Part of Nova was aware of how much this should be bothering her — she didn't want to be indifferent — but her mind was still too preoccupied with her immediate concerns to make space for church issues she didn't have control over.

Nova swayed absentmindedly to the music beside Claudia, whose hands were lifted up, tears rushing down her eyes. Next to his twin, Nate was on his knees, his face buried in his palms. Nova winced. Was the worship lacking or was she simply detached? Moved by her children's surrender to God, Nova forced her mind from Caleb's hospital room to the worship service she should be a part of. As hard as she tried, she couldn't concentrate. Despondent, she sank back in her chair. Why was she even here? She should be with Caleb.

The twins had begged her to attend, that was why. Nova couldn't say no. Also, Caleb's sister,

Hannah, and her husband, Knox, had just returned from their overseas trip and had volunteered to take their turn to watch Caleb, so Nova was without an excuse. She needed to show up at church.

So, here she was, struggling to pay attention as the worship leader said something about God being in control of every situation. Control. Nova scoffed. She hadn't had much of that lately, although for a season there, she had deluded herself into believing she had some semblance of control over her life.

The plot of the manuscript she had been reading lingered in her mind. Why had Caleb wanted her to read it? What had he seen in her that Nova had failed to recognize? Had she been spiraling all this time without even realizing it? While she had gone about her daily comings and goings, believing everything was under control, had she been missing the signs that her life was on the verge of falling apart?

The worship leader asked everyone to rise, and beside Nova, Serene stood up, her hand on her stomach, reminding Nova of a hope for new life. Nova stood next to Serene and breathed out a sigh. Serene brushed her hand against Nova's back, her eyes brimming with tears as she nodded at Nova. "God has got you."

Nova squared her shoulders as her lips trembled. She had tried to keep everything together all this time, but all she had accomplished in it all was to numb her heart. The words the media hurled at Serene in that stupid hit piece taunted Nova. They had called Serene and Nolan far from perfect. At first sight of the title, Nova's immediate thought had been that Nolan and Serene may not have a perfect family, but Nova had felt like she did. Nova had brushed what she had perceived to be an arrogant thought and read the article, fearing for Serene and how she would handle it. But her younger brother and his wife had withstood the attack. Now, witnessing Serene stand there in worship to the Lord, it challenged Nova to face one of the biggest storms in her life with peace in her heart and courage in her soul.

"This has been a tough season for many of us," the worship leader said, "but in it all, it doesn't change Who God is." He then started singing an old song — one Nova had forgotten even existed. It spoke of God's tender mercy calling from behind even when one couldn't recognize His closeness. It spoke of a dependency on a God Who's ever present, but not always felt. The song's chorus expressed God's goodness and his enduring mercy.

Each word struck Nova like lightning to her soul, a reminder of how dependent she needed to be on God. By the time the worship leader got to the chorus, Nova was already choking on her tears, despite her longing to sing along.

Had she forgotten His tender mercy? Had she failed to recognize Him calling her?

Was what happened to Caleb God's way of calling her attention? No. That couldn't be the case, could it? God was a good and loving God. He wasn't the kind Who would harm His children simply to teach them a lesson. But, He had allowed this. He allowed Caleb to get hurt. Why hadn't He protected Caleb? Or even Jenna and Rachel?

The questions came to Nova as she continued singing the song, the music cushioning the questions her soul was hurling at her spirit.

Her pain was unfathomable, and yet, deep inside, Nova recognized its uses. Had she made an idol out of her husband, her career, her family, and how perfect she had perceived all of it to be? Had she not made room for a God Who had been the source of every good thing in her life?

Nova dropped to her knees, the tears still flowing down her cheeks. Yes. He was good. She would declare it until the day her breath would run out and declare it even beyond that throughout eternity. The God her family served was good. Not even Caleb's coma could change that. Not even his death could change that.

Once again, Nova surrendered her husband's predicament to the Lord, but more than that, she surrendered whatever sense of control she was still holding on to.

Nova had lost track of how long she knelt there. She had no idea what music was playing, when Serene knelt beside her and embraced her, tears were also coming out of Serene's eyes. Whether Serene's tears were about compassion for her or something else no longer mattered. All that mattered was that Serene's presence made Nova feel like she wasn't alone. It reminded her that God had sent others to surround her and support her.

She could never fathom the idea of losing Caleb, but she could certainly entrust his life to God, knowing that God would take great care in holding the life of His son.

By the time the worship service ended, Nova and Serene had both calmed down. When Nova opened her eyes, she found Jenna and Rachel by the aisle, the younger women holding her shoulder and Serene's. Rachel quietly handed her a pack of tissues.

Nova took a tissue and blew her nose into it before getting on her feet. Her knees wobbled at first as the sudden rush of blood circulation sent pins and needles down her leg. She stumbled on to the edge of her seat, supported by Jenna, as Rachel helped Serene get to her own seat.

"Thank you," Nova mouthed to Jenna, her stomach turning upon seeing the bruise on Jenna's face. How had she been oblivious to it these past days? Jenna and Rachel returned to their seats right in front of where Nova and Serene sat. The speaker on stage gave the Sunday announcements and asked everyone to prepare their tithes and offering, so Nova rummaged through her purse for the money she needed to put into the offering basket. Instead, she found multiple missed calls and a new message on her phone.

Hopeful that the message indicated good news, Nova opened it and found a message from Hannah.

Hannah: I promised I'd give you an update. He's stable now, but he had a seizure earlier. The doctor is still trying to figure out what's going on. The good news is his stab wounds are healing quite nicely. Have a blessed time with the Lord. Everything is okay right now, so don't think too much about it. See you later.

Nova's immediate instinct was to tell someone she needed to rush over there immediately, but something arrested her and kept her from doing that. It wasn't like she had the power to prevent him from suffering further complications.

So, Nova settled herself back in her seat and listened to the preacher talk about God working all things out for the good of those who love Him. To be at rest in God's presence was the best thing Nova could do for her husband.

To Nova, Knox and Hannah Cartier were living embodiments of God's power to change hearts and transform lives. Knox had once been Nova's stalker and the inspiration for her stories' villains. Despite a broken past, God had redeemed him and brought him and Hannah together through the most unlikely of circumstances. Their story never failed to make Nova thank God for giving her — and Knox — a new life.

This time, however, upon seeing them by the bedside of her unconscious husband, Nova was taken aback by the barrage of powerful emotions — mostly resentment — that struck her at the sight of them. With all the risks this couple had taken in bringing their family wherever God led them, how was it that Caleb was the one who was now unconscious?

"Nova!" Hannah's face lit up when Nova entered the hospital room, the twins trailing right behind her. Both were carrying bags of takeout pasta and chicken.

"Uncle Knox!" Nate slipped his phone in his pocket and hugged his uncle, while Claudia hugged Hannah.

"Your tan is so pretty, Aunt Hannah," Claudia exclaimed. "I wish we could visit you again in Ancoria. It was so fun the last time we visited." She turned toward Nova. "Mom, can we go?"

Nova smiled at her daughter, before raising a brow and casting a glance at Caleb.

Claudia winced. "When Dad wakes up, of course."

"We'll talk about it when he wakes up," Nova said.

"God will wake him up." Claudia nodded at her aunt.

Nova could only be fascinated by how confident Claudia was about her father's chances of recovery. Nate, on the other hand, remained quiet as he started bringing out the food they had ordered, despite having had a lot to say about the situation the night before. Though almost identical with their dark, wavy hair and similar facial features, her children couldn't be more different, and yet, both were beautiful in their own ways.

"Claudia, help your brother with the food," Nova instructed, to which Claudia obeyed. Nova then glanced at Knox and Hannah. "We bought food for everyone." She smiled. "It's so good to see you guys. Welcome home." She squeezed Knox's arm before hugging Hannah. "I didn't expect you two to be here. I was so surprised when Rachel told me to go to church instead, because you took over their watch. When did you arrive?"

"Just yesterday," Hannah said. "It was a last-minute trip, really. We're spending a week here, then we have to go back to Ancoria. Knox has to be here to deal with some issues regarding his grandfather's estate. Since he was coming here, anyway, I figured I might as well take the trip to check on you and Caleb."

"And the children?" Nova asked, referring to their three kids — Cameron, Jaxon, and Eliana.

"They're back home," Knox replied. "We have friends looking out for them. It's good to have community back there, and still find community here, despite everything going on at church."

Nova sighed. "Tell me about it. How old are they again?"

"Cam is nine," Hannah said. "Jax is turning seven in December. Lia just turned three last July."

"Food's ready!" Claudia announced, before showing off the spread of pesto pasta and baked chicken on the one table available in the suite. She pointed at the paper plates and plastic forks. "It's a buffet."

"Go ahead, honey," Hannah said. "You kids eat first. I'm not that hungry yet." She shot a nod at Nova. "Are you hungry?"

Nova shook her head. "I've been forcing myself to eat these past days, but anyway, enough about food." She braced herself for what Hannah had to say. "What happened earlier?"

Hannah frowned as she grab hold of Nova's hand and led her to the cushioned bench before they both sank into the seat. Knox, on the other hand, stood by Hannah, leaning his shoulder against the wall, his arms crossed over his chest.

"Knox and I were debating on whether to call you immediately after Caleb started convulsing, but everything was happening so fast, and they were able to stabilize him immediately, so we messaged you only once he was stable. We're still waiting for the doctor to come back to give us the findings. The doctor did say that it can happen to comatose patients within the first week of coma. Especially when it's a head injury."

Nova nodded. "That makes sense. They suspect the loss of blood from his severed artery, coupled with his head hitting the pavement, might be the cause of the coma. It is a miracle he even survived, considering the extent of his injuries."

"Someone's watching out for him. That's for sure." Hannah gripped her hand. "All of this must be taking its toll on you. How are you?"

Nova sighed. "Better. The worship service this morning helped. There's a lot I don't understand, but I'd like to believe God's hand is in all of this. Caleb and I have had our fair share of tragedy throughout our lives, so I have faith we'll get through this."

"That's a great way to look at it, Nova," Hannah patted her knee. "When Dad called to tell us what happened, I was a wreck after. You can ask Knox how I took it." She pointed at her husband, who nodded to support her statement. "I was so worried. Did they ever find out who the mugger was?"

"No. The surveillance footage from the parking lot did little to help. The mugger knew how to hide himself. It was a simple case of being in the wrong place at the wrong time, and it could have happened to anyone in that parking lot. Too bad it was Jenna and Rachel there. Part of me still kind of wonders if things could have been different, if I had gone instead of Caleb. It was my turn to pick up the kids that day, and I was just so swamped with work, so I asked him to go instead, and you know Caleb." Nova frowned. "Of course, he went. We even kind of had an argument before I sent him out of my office, and I just feel horrible every time I think of how rude I was to him."

A lopsided smile appeared on Hannah's face. "Don't do this to yourself. You can't lose yourself in what-if's. It doesn't help. Besides, if you had gone instead of Caleb, then it might be you in that bed right now. Or it might be Jenna or Rachel. I think Caleb wouldn't have been able to forgive himself if it was any of the three of you."

"I guess."

"Rachel told us it was almost impossible to get you out of this room," Hannah said.

"Rumor has been going around, huh?" Nova cringed. "I mean, is it so bad that I want to be the one who is here when he wakes up?"

"No, of course not, but it's kind of bad that you're not willing to accept help from people who love your family. Also, you have a lot on your plate, as it is. Cut yourself some slack."

"I honestly feel like I'm cutting myself too much slack. If not for Ma practically forcing me out of here, I wouldn't even have realized how little time I've spent with the twins, or how this has been affecting them. My entire focus zoned in on Caleb, and everything else just fell apart."

"And yet, you're still willing to write a brand-new script for this musical production you guys are brewing up." Knox smirked as he narrowed his eyes at Nova. "You're on hero mode."

"Ha!" Nova scoffed. "I wouldn't call myself a hero, though Caleb definitely is."

"That is true." Knox chuckled. "He is the type who always comes to people's rescue." He flexed his jaw. "I would know." He winked at her.

Nova had to smile at how her friendship with Knox had already gone through so much healing and reconciliation that they could joke about their jaded past. Yet again, it was a reminder of God's ability to transform and restore. Knox was an example of what could happen to a prodigal son willing to return to the Father's embrace. The concept of prodigals led Nova to the play she had to write.

"Hannah," Nova said. "Have you heard of the new play we're trying to produce?"

"Rachel did mention it." Hannah's eyes widened. "Can't imagine Miss Rhoda would be happy about it."

How could Nova forget? Few people in church were fans of Miss Rhoda. Hannah was one of them. Nova sighed in response. "Your mentor hasn't been happy about a bunch of things lately."

Knox and Hannah exchanged glances. Hannah lowered her gaze. "I gathered. Do you think the play will help somehow?"

"I hope so. It's why we're doing it." Nova's brows quirked up. "Oh! Speaking of the play, I'm not sure what your plans are, and I know you said you'll only be in the country for a week or so, before you have to fly back, but Serene, Jenna, and Rachel are coming here tomorrow. We're meeting to discuss the play and also catch up with each other and spend time praying together. Would you like to come?"

"Oh yes." Hannah bobbed her head in quick succession to show her enthusiasm. "I am there, Nova. I wouldn't miss it."

"Wonderful. It's good to have you back, Hannah. Hopefully, Caleb will wake up before you leave."

Hannah cast a glance at her brother. "He'll wake up when the time is right."

Right then, the doctor walked in with clipboard in hand. Nova braced herself for another round of hearing all this medical jargon and all the unknowns of a coma. This time, however, she was ready to receive whatever the doctor was about to tell her, because she fully intended to lay it all at the feet of the One holding Caleb in the palm of His hands.

twenty-three

PRAYER CHAINS & PRODIGAL COSTUMES

A hospital room wasn't the most ideal place to plan a musical play. That much, Nova could admit, but she hadn't quite expected to be shooed away from the room, because they had too many visitors and guests. Was it their fault Caleb was beloved by many?

Nova huffed as she made her way to a café nearby — one that Hannah and Knox owned — while Hannah ended up looking after Caleb, so Nova could meet with Serene, Jenna, and Rachel.

Chimes clinked as Nova pushed the wooden door leading to Café Perivóli, the aesthetic of which reminded her of their trip to Ancoria. The Mediterranean garden design had a lot to do with the culture of the island kingdom Knox and Hannah had made a residence out of, which was strange, because Ancoria was in the Atlantic. The strong aroma of coffee made Nova smile. Her favorite part about their coffee shops was how they managed to maintain a sense of home, despite the foreign aesthetic.

A server behind the counter smiled and waved at her. Lucy, her name was. Nova remembered because her family had already gone to that particular branch enough to know the names of several of their staff, their manager included. As if already knowing what she was there for, Lucy pointed toward the table where Serene, Jenna, and Rachel were waving at Nova.

"Someone will be there to take your orders in a bit," Lucy said.

"Thanks, Lucy," Nova said, before making her way to her friends.

"Where's Hannah?" Rachel asked.

Nova sighed. "She plans to catch up with us after our mothers arrive to look after Caleb. Plans and schedules got mixed up when the hospital staff finally noticed how visitors were almost always with Caleb for an entire twenty-four hours."

"How is he?" Serene asked, taking hold of her hand.

Nova sighed. "Not much has changed. Apart from the seizure he had yesterday, he hasn't moved at all."

"Do they know what caused the seizure?" Jenna asked.

The bruise on her face still made Nova wince. She couldn't wait until Jenna got fully healed. "They say it happens to a lot of comatose patients. Right now, it's mostly waiting and uncertainty, neither of which I'm good at handling."

"You're doing great, Nova." Serene squeezed her hand. "I wouldn't know what I would do if I were in your place."

"Come on." Nova smiled. "Serene, you're dealing with your fair share of troubles. Don't downplay it. How's your pregnancy? And where's Lily Red right now?"

"Dad and Jeremy have her for the day. They wanted to give me a break. I've been painting a lot more these past weeks, so I'm grateful to at least have that back in my life. It's been a while since I've been able to paint this much, so that's one great thing going for me."

"That's awesome." Jenna smiled. "The last painting you showed me was amazing." She started thumbing through her photos on her phone. "Look. Isn't it beautiful?" She showed it to Rachel.

"That's gorgeous." Rachel glanced at Serene. "This will make an amazing poster for the play."

"Right?" Serene grinned. "I have several more that we could use, but I'm still waiting on Nova to finish the script before I get carried away with all the planning of the set pieces and the backdrops. I have so many ideas."

"About that—" Nova winced.

Before she could continue speaking, a server came to take their orders. After everyone had their choice of drink and a snack, Nova started speaking again.

"I have ideas about the play and how it should go. It's still the basic idea of how the prodigal son and the other brother relate to each other once the prodigal son returns home. I will, of course, take a lot of creative license and will try to flesh out the characters a bit more. To be honest, I'm falling in love with the idea of exploring their dynamic. I think I'm more than a little inspired by a new novel I'm reading by some unknown author. It was Caleb who recommended I read it. He was so pushy about it too, but anyway, it really has given me a lot of inspiration as far as where I want the play to go. It's the story of two brothers with a father, but they don't relate to their father very well, so they see themselves as orphans, and—" Nova paused, catching herself. "I'm sorry. I'm blabbering, aren't I?"

"No." Rachel shook her head. "I like what I'm hearing. Please go on."

The other two ladies agreed. Before Nova could continue talking, however, she had to take note of how, among the three of them, Rachel appeared the freshest. Both Serene and Jenna looked like they had just gone through battle — most especially Jenna, who had been literally beaten, but Rachel? She looked like she was about to host a diplomatic dinner. Nova sighed. Must be nice to have her life right now. Nova pushed away the threat of resentfulness coming over her. It wouldn't help anybody for her to think this way about Rachel.

Nova focused instead on what she was saying. "I've been talking a lot about the play, like I've actually been working on it, but it's all just ideas at this point." She winced. "I don't have anything solid yet, because honestly—" Nova swallowed hard "—I've been in denial, and I think Caleb has been seeing right through me all this time. I didn't want to admit it to myself, least of all to him, that ever since I took on the job as department head of marketing at Frontier, I haven't been able to write at all. Sure, I have my journals and notes, but creatively? I haven't written in four years. It took me this manuscript by this unknown author and this play to realize how much I've missed it, how much it has been lacking in my life."

"I hear you," Serene said. "It's been years since I was able to paint, and it took a shattering hit piece against me and this pregnancy, which honestly has me scared out of my wits, to get painting again. I don't want to undermine what you're going through at all, Nova, but I'm starting to wonder if everything happening to us is somehow God's way of once again fueling our creativity by placing us in positions where we need to seek Him, where we need to ask Him what's next."

"That makes sense," Jenna said. "I've been dancing a lot lately, but it's like it's all repetitive, routine, and I'm unable to come to a release or complete abandon like I was able to before. But after what happened to Caleb and me, there's this desperation that has fueled my 'flow', so to speak. It's strange, actually, how it has all turned out, but I am thankful for this season, and the ability to dance again without worrying how everyone perceives me."

All eyes went to Rachel after Jenna started speaking. What was she going through other than having Miss Rhoda as her overbearing mother? The obstacles she was facing seemed to pale in comparison to what everyone else was going through. She cleared her throat and lowered her eyes, like she was embarrassed about not having more problems. "I'm not much of an artist," she said. "Jeremy is more the artist in our relationship, and I'm more like the subject of his art, so I can't quite relate to this talk about losing creativity and gaining it back."

Jenna grabbed hold of her hand. "You're an artist too, Rachel. What you did for my wedding, that couldn't be anything but art, and I'm sure the play will be so much more beautiful and organized and pleasant for everyone, because you are a part of it."

"Heh." Rachel smiled and squinted her eyes at her best friend. "I doubt Max will agree with you. The last time we produced a play together, I'm sure I stressed him out."

"First of all, you made that play happen — he would be the first to admit that — second, you are not the same person you were back then. You've grown a lot." Jenna smiled. "I think we all have. At least I hope I have."

Serene laughed. "I've seen the way you were before, Jenna, and you're certainly different."

Jenna feigned a huge sigh of relief. "Good to know. It would be awful if I hadn't changed at all."

Right then, the server came with their food, and a few minutes were lost in just trying to get the right orders go to the right person. Serene said the prayer right after.

With the coffee and food there, it was time for them to get to the point of their meeting. "So," she said, "one good thing about this situation our family is in is that our boss was gracious enough to give me time off work until Caleb recovers. It has allowed me a lot of space and time to just be quiet and recalibrate, so I now know how to proceed with this play. I will start writing it this week." Nova looked at Serene. "I also have been in touch with Nolan. He's willing to write the music for the play, just like last time."

"Oh, believe me." Serene nodded. "He's beyond excited about this. He has even convinced Lily Red that they'll be writing a song together for the play. I think my daughter is expecting a starring role now."

Nova chuckled. "Lily Red's voice is lovely. I'm sure I can write her into the play if you and Nolan are okay with that."

"I don't see why not, as long as we take precautions and make sure the press won't show up to snap pictures of her. That's my primary concern.

Nolan and I are trying to keep her out of their radar for as long as we possibly can."

"I'll see if we can organize some security." Rachel was taking notes about everything being discussed. "We'll make sure to have an official media team. Only they can take photos and videos.

Nova smiled. Things would work out just fine with Rachel around. "So, for now, I'm working on the script, and Nolan is working on the music. Jenna is working on her dance moves, so she can choreograph. Serene will take care of set design and whatever other art pieces we may need. Finally, Rachel will take care of costumes and pretty much everything else. Am I missing anything?"

"I think that covers it." Rachel nodded. "I'm already talking to Jeremy about stuff we may need, but I do think all will fall into place once Nova finishes the script."

"It will be ready." Nova nodded, but she might have spoken too soon, because her phone started vibrating. Hannah was calling. Nova answered. "Hello? Hannah?"

Hannah's breathless voice came through from the other side of the line. "Nova, come back here now."

Whether she was excited or panicked, Nova couldn't tell. "What do you mean? Is everything okay? Are you not coming here anymore?"

"No, you come here," Hannah said, before saying three words Nova had been longing to hear for days: "Caleb is awake."

The sight of Caleb's blue eyes wide open almost made Nova want to get on her knees in worship right then and there. With tears trickling down her face, she rushed to his bedside and immediately pressed her lips against his repeatedly, giving him short, but deep kisses.

"You're back!" she exclaimed before clasping his hand between hers and kissing the back of it. "You scared me so much. I was afraid you weren't going to return to me anymore. How could you do that to me?"

Caleb chuckled. "Nova, as you said, I'm back. I did nothing to you."

"Exactly. You did nothing but breathe for days, and it was terrifying!"

"I'm here now. No need to be afraid." He brushed his fingers against her hair. "Where were you?"

"I had to meet with the ladies to go on with that play you refused to let me back out of."

He grinned. "So, we're pushing through with that, huh?"

"You're perky for someone who just came out of a coma."

Caleb shrugged. "Well, I woke up to a world full of surprises." He pointed his hand at Hannah. "My sister is here all of a sudden, and I was afraid something might have happened to my wife, but then, here she is." He cupped her face with his hand. "Still as beautiful as the day I first met her. I love you so much, Nova."

"I love you too."

They lingered in that moment for a few seconds before Caleb scanned the room. "So, what did I miss? Where are the twins?"

"They're in school. I couldn't let them drop out of school, just because you're refusing to get out of dream world to come back to us. They would have wanted to drop out though, if given the choice."

"Good call on your part, and it sounds like them, though I'm guessing Claudia didn't miss a beat at all."

"She's the most confident among all of us that you will wake up. It was Nate who was struggling with all the existential questions because of what was happening."

"Yeah." Caleb nodded. "Not much has changed then, has it?"

"You can say that." Nova shook her head. "I have, though."

"Have you? It's been what?" Caleb looked at Hannah. "A week? What day is today?"

"It's Monday," Hannah said. "Less than a week, actually."

"And you've already changed?" Caleb asked Nova.

"I've been missing out on so much, Caleb. You were seeing it happen, but I wasn't. It's time for a change. I wasn't seeing it before, but I see it now."

"Yeah." Caleb's smile faded. "I've been feeling it for a while now, too, and I haven't had the heart to tell you, but it's where we're headed." Their eyes met. Where they were headed? What was he talking about? Were they really thinking the same thing?

Nova bristled before she said out loud what she was thinking of doing, "I want to quit working at Frontier Press, stay at home, and focus on the kids and my writing."

Caleb still withheld his smile, his seriousness giving her goosebumps. "I was hoping you would say that, and that's a huge move, but I might top that."

Nova narrowed her eyes at him. "What do you mean?"

Caleb narrowed his eyes right back at her. "Maybe it's better if we talk about this after we get back home?"

"Why not now?" Nova asked.

Caleb looked past her shoulder and waved. "Hello, ladies."

Nova turned to find Serene, Jenna, and Rachel waving back at her husband. She smiled and nodded. "Yeah. We should talk about this later," she said, but her heart skipped a beat, because something was telling her that her husband was way ahead of her and whatever he wanted to do, the thought probably hadn't grazed her mind yet. Still, there was a time for everything. She would know in due time what he had in his heart for their family.

Right now, all they had to do was celebrate, because finally, God had answered her prayers and brought her beloved back to her.

twenty-four

ΔNSWERED
PRAYERS &
ΔWAKENED
PATIENCE

- ONE MONTH LATER -

All four of them agreed they were too old for a fort made out of pillows and blankets, but they took great enjoyment in building their flimsy structure anyway. Exhausted — mostly from laughter — their family of four sprawled themselves in the living room, underneath their fort, inhaling the mild floral scent of their fabric softener. Caleb and Nova were in the middle, with Nate by Nova's side and Claudia by her father's.

"I'm glad you're alive, Dad," Claudia said. "Mom wouldn't be much fun to live with if you had died."

"Hey." Nova wrinkled her nose. "That's mean. I would've been devastated, but I would have been able to recover."

"After at least ten years," Nate said. "Sometime after Claudia and I have already finished college, and you won't have to worry about us anymore."

"I'm your mother. I will never stop worrying about you." Nova chuckled, but she couldn't deny the truth behind her children's words. She held on to Caleb's hand. The idea of ever losing him was not something she was ready to entertain. She leaned her head on his shoulder. "Not going to lie. When I feared I might lose you, I didn't think I could stand it, but while you were in a coma, I could still see God's grace for us all."

"That's because He's with us," Caleb said. "He will give us plenty of grace should we ever face the possibility of losing each other." He pressed the back of her hand against his lips. "Though I don't want to think about that right now."

"Same," Nova said.

"Claudia was the one who brought it up!" Nate announced. "Trust her to come up with the most morbid of conversation starters."

"What does morbid mean?" Claudia asked.

"Seriously?" Nate shook his head at her. "You should read more books."

"Amen to that," Caleb agreed. "Do you have any idea how many books I've already read by the time I was your age?"

"Probably by the thousands. You read too much, Dad." Claudia huffed. "I'm more a visual person, so I want to make movies someday."

Caleb and Nova exchanged glances. Neither of them would be surprised if Claudia found a way to do just that. Nova's heart ached, however, at how different a world her twins were growing up in. Nova's childhood had been a lot more liberal and exposed to the world than she would have wanted, and because of that, she had always wished her children's upbringing would be more conservative, like Caleb's. Today's society certainly provided a lot more challenges and hurdles to parents who wanted to raise their children according to God's Word.

"Even if you do end up becoming a filmmaker, Claudia," Nate said. "You still need to understand what makes a good story. Reading helps a lot with that."

"I read!" Claudia exclaimed. "I read what you wrote, didn't I?"

"Claudia!"

An awkward silence followed before Nova turned her head to the side to give her son a look. "You've been writing?"

"A little." Nate shrugged. "Nothing worth talking about, Mom. Claudia shouldn't have blurted it out."

"What have you been writing?"

"He's good, Mom," Claudia said. "Not as good as you are, but he's twelve years old. His brain isn't fully developed yet, so that's understandable."

"Hey. My brain is a lot more developed than yours."

"You wish!"

"I would love to read some of what you've written, Nate."

"No way, Mom. I wouldn't be able to sleep until you finish reading it. I'll be a nervous wreck the whole time."

"Speaking of reading," Caleb said, "how's your progress with the manuscript I asked you to read?"

"Oh yeah." Nova bit her lip. "Did I not tell you I was done with that already? I've been finished for weeks. I guess it kind of fell through, because of all that's been going on." Over the course of the month since Caleb had woken up, Nova had been transitioning her job at Frontier Press, so she could start working from home as a full-time writer and housewife. After having prayed together, Caleb and Nova felt that this was the best move for their family, especially as the twins were entering into their teenage years. With the focus on the play and the transition, Nova had forgotten to tell her husband about the book. "It's a great story. It has an interesting take on what it means to be an orphan, not just from the outside, but from within. I can tell whoever wrote it is young. Not only in age but also in the writing style, but whoever Naveed Clancy is, he is a good storyteller. With a great editor working with him, that book would be a wonderful read for kids of all ages. Have you found out who the author is?"

"My assistant told me today," Caleb said.

"Yeah? Who is it?"

Caleb chuckled in response.

"You're not going to tell me? Is it someone I know?"

"Mom, come on." Claudia blurted out. "It's so obvious who wrote it!"

"It's not obvious to me. It's—" The wheels on her mind began turning. She shot a look at Nate, whose cheeks were beet red. She ruffled with his dark, wavy hair. "Is it you?!"

"I know nothing about what you speak of," Nate said.

"Oh, please!" Claudia exclaimed. "Just say it already, Nate! Come on. The name of the author is like our initials combined. Naveed Clancy. Nate, Claudia. Nova, Caleb."

"Claudia helped," Nate said.

"I read what he wrote and told him everything he should fix to make it better, but everything else is all him."

"Nate!" Nova's head was spinning. "Why didn't you tell your dad and me? I can't believe I missed this!"

"You weren't supposed to find out. Claudia betrayed me."

"I gave the manuscript to Dad's assistant, because all Nate wanted to do with it was hide it in his shelf to collect dust."

"You should have asked me first!" Nate scowled. "I can't believe you did this."

"Mom liked it, didn't she?"

"Nate, why didn't you want us to find out?" Caleb asked.

"If you had known who the writer was, you would've only said good things about it."

"That's not true. We would've been honest," Nova said.

Nate shot her a look.

She winced. "Okay. Perhaps I would've only showered you with praises, but you heard me earlier. I had no idea you wrote it, but I still said you did great work. It's a wonderful story. I'm proud of you, Nate."

"Did you really not know it was me?"

"Not a clue."

That brought a smile to his handsome face. "Thanks, Mom. That means a lot coming from you."

"What did you think about it, Dad?" Claudia asked.

"Me? I read the whole thing in one sitting before I practically forced your mom to read the manuscript. I had forgotten about it after I woke up from the coma, but I mentioned it to my assistant earlier, and she told me how she had gotten her hands on it."

"Aren't I a genius? You can thank me now, Nate." Claudia sat up and grinned at everyone. "Every time I told him how good it was, he kept telling me I was only saying that because I'm his sister. With all the bookish genes in our family, is anyone surprised? Everyone should be more surprised that I didn't get the reader bug."

"Yeah," Nate said, "you are so the odd one out. Mom, are you sure Claudia's not adopted?"

"Claudia's the splitting image of your father, so no. She definitely isn't."

"I'm practically dad as a girl with dark hair, brown eyes, and Mom's bone structure."

"That visual sounds strange in my head." Nate snickered.

"Wait." Nova reached across Caleb's waist to grab hold of Claudia's hand. "So, you contacted your dad's assistant, so she could get the manuscript to your dad?"

Claudia nodded slowly, her smug smile showing how mighty pleased she was with herself.

"Why didn't you ask us about it earlier?"

"I wasn't sure what either of you thought about it. I didn't know you were reading Nate's novel. Also, if you were, I didn't know whether you liked it or not, so I was kind of afraid to ask."

"I liked it. I did." Nova brushed her fingers against her son's cheek.

Nate blushed. "Thanks, Mom."

A soft smile appeared on Nova's face. "I love that I get to spend this moment with you guys. We've had a tough year, but we got through it, and I praise God that we have all come out of it stronger. I wish I could just freeze this moment right now."

"Or we can make more moments like this," Caleb said.

"I'd love that." Nova smiled at her husband.

Caleb shifted his position as Claudia lay back on the floor next to him. "There's something I want to talk to you guys about. It's something that's been stirring in my heart for a while now, something we have to decide on as a family. It's the reason why I wanted us to spend time together this evening."

"What is it, Dad?" Nate and Claudia asked at the same time.

For some reason, panic shot through Nova. There had been so many changes happening, and she had only just begun to get used to it. Caleb sounded like he was ready to rock the boat again.

"After the summer we spent in Ancoria earlier this year, I couldn't get rid of the idea of living there. At first, I told myself it might only be because your Uncle Josh and Aunt Hannah and their families are there, but after a while, I realized it was something else. Something about the country drew me in, so I'd like all three of you to start praying about the possibility of all of us moving there."

Nova gulped. He not only rocked the boat, he managed to blow it all the way to another country.

"Wow," Claudia said. "That's huge."

Nate whistled. "Epic."

"What do you think, Nova?"

"I don't know what to think," Nova said. "You've mentioned how much you loved it there several times, but I never thought you would seriously consider moving. I mean, what will we do there? What will you do for work?"

"I've floated the idea of running *Galactic* from there, and Ethan has been open to the possibility, because Caine Corp has several of its businesses active in Ancoria, and Frontier press is looking to expand to international waters, so—" Caleb shrugged "—I can more seriously pursue talks about that with the boss once you guys agree." Caleb intertwined his fingers with hers. "When you decided to quit your job and stay at home, it was confirmation for me."

"I do love how traditionally conservative the culture is out there," Nova said. "And we already have family there, so the transition won't be too shocking, but still, it's a big move."

"It's not like we'll go now. You're still in the middle of a book launch, and you're working on a church play. Nate and Claudia still have to finish their school year. I need to make sure the transition from here to there will work for both us and the company."

"I don't have any friends there," Claudia said.

"Heh." Nate scoffed. "You'll make friends the moment you land at the airport, Claudia."

"True, but it won't be the same."

"Since when are you a fan of the same?"

"True again." Claudia sat up. "I'm warming up to the idea, Dad, but I still have to pray about it."

"Same." Nate nodded.

"Nova?"

"We'll pray about it, and let you know," Nova said, but deep in her heart, it already felt like it was a done deal. They were moving their family to the island kingdom of Ancoria.

The clacking of the keyboard and a playlist of only instrumental piano music provided Nova company as she focused her entire attention on the project she was working on in her new home office. With the twins in school and Caleb at work, a rush of inspiration had pulled Nova out of doing laundry and in front of her computer to finalize the script of a play people were still waiting on.

Nova typed in the last words of the script. *Once Upon a Prodigal* was the story of two brothers — both with orphan hearts — longing to discover why they struggled with fatherlessness when they had a father who loved them. Set in a fantasy kingdom,

Nova had allowed herself to run away with the themes of the story set against a backdrop of an adventure shared by two brothers, who were no longer reckless, both deeply loved, but still longing to find their way through life.

The elation that came with finishing any large piece of work was still unmatched. It was a unique kind of satisfaction, and Nova would never get tired of that feeling. She launched her email program and jotted down a quick email to the ladies in charge of the play, announcing that after weeks of waiting, they finally had a script. They could move forward with this project and present an actual proposal to the church board. She attached the script to the email and clicked on the send button, hopeful that God allowed her to finish the play just in time.

As far as the play's ability to unite their church, Nova was no longer sure it had the power to do that. It was hard to believe that it did, because what was once just Connect Church was now two different churches, because of Robert and Rhoda Petersen's decision to start their own church. The issue had already died down, and a reluctant and heart-broken acceptance regarding the situation had come over most of the members of their church. Nova, however, still held hope in her heart that their church would one day be whole again.

With that in mind and a prayer in her heart, Nova returned to her household chores. She still had a few errands to run before she would have to pick up the twins. Something about the familiarity of just picking her kids up from the school Nova and Caleb had once attended hit Nova hard. It had been three days since Caleb had brought up the possibility of moving, and the twins were warming up to the idea. Nova, on the other hand, was still shaken by the overwhelming transition ahead of them. After all, the people they knew in Ancoria were mostly from Caleb's side of the family. His twin and his sister lived there. Would Nova be able to move away from her mother and brother? Nolan certainly wasn't going to move countries, and Ma? She was so attached to the home they had grown up in, they couldn't even get her to move to a bigger house. How much more a country?

The tug-of-war between wanting to move and wanting to stay kept going on within Nova, even if a conviction in her had already solidified. It was like she knew without a doubt they were moving. She was just in the process of accepting it and dealing with all the changes that came with it.

Caleb had promised they wouldn't move until after the play was finished, and that gave Nova some degree of comfort, because in a lot of ways, the play's ending reflected their journey off to a new adventure, a new phase of their lives as a family.

Hours later, after tossing the laundry into the dryer and turning the dryer on, a ping on her phone distracted her from the chores she was doing. Nova checked her messages as she dragged her feet toward the kitchen, her mind going through options on what they could have for dinner.

The first message was a long, gushing one from Serene.

> **Serene:** Nova! I read it the moment I got your email, and I couldn't put it down. I just finished reading, and I'm breath-taken. This is amazing. Has Nolan seen this? He's been sending me some of the music he has written for the play, and I can already imagine it with the script, and it's incredible. Nova, I can't wait to work on the set for this!

Nova didn't bother to type up an immediate reply. She never knew how to respond to people gushing about her work. Despite all these years of writing, she had never gotten used to it.

She moved on to the next message.

> **Jenna:** My mind is spinning with possibilities for how the choreography will go. This is so epic, Nova. I just might start reading

your books now. Can I share it with Max already? I can't wait to hear what he thinks!

Nova: Sure. Let him read it. If he already knows what the story is about, it'll give us an edge when we have to present it to the church board.

Jenna: Great! Thanks, Nova!

The next message was from her husband.

My Beloved: What's for dinner?

Nova: What do you want for dinner?

My Beloved: I'm craving meat.

Nova: I'll start thawing the steak then.

My Beloved: Wonderful. See you later!

There was one message left, and almost instinctively, Nova already assumed it was from Rachel. She was right.

Rachel: Hi, Nova. I just read the script. Are you free right now? Is it okay if I come over? I think I need someone to talk to.

Nova hesitated before she replied. What could Rachel possibly want to talk about? Nova scrunched her nose to give it some thought. Did she have the energy to spend the rest of her free afternoon with Rachel Petersen? Nova figured she might as well go for it, because there was a real possibility they might be moving to another country soon. Why not connect with and bless as many people as possible while they were still here? She typed up a response to Rachel.

> **Nova:** Sure, Rachel. Come over. Is everything okay?

> **Rachel:** Let's talk about it when I get there.

For some reason, that response only made Nova nervous. What did Rachel want to talk about?

There was no way to find out until Rachel arrived, so Nova headed to the kitchen and brought out the tri-tip steak out of the freezer. She thumbed online for possible new recipes for the steak and eventually settled for a good ol' grill. She could also make mashed potatoes and gravy on the side. Why not celebrate? She had just finished writing an entire play.

She had already finished mashing the potatoes when their doorbell rang. Nova quickly washed her hands and wiped them dry with a kitchen towel before heading for the front door. There, Rachel Petersen stood, with her lips trembling and tears rushing down her eyes.

"I don't think I can do this anymore, Nova," she said. "It's all too much for me."

Nova had no idea what was going on or why she was crying, so she didn't quite know what to say. Her only option was to welcome Rachel into her warm embrace. "What happened?" she asked.

"I read your play," Rachel said. "And I think it triggered something in me, Nova. It's almost like you based the entire play on me."

"Oh." Should Nova tell her that wasn't the case at all? Nova didn't know for sure, but it was clear that she would soon learn all about the orphan soul of someone whom most people at their church would easily pinpoint as the other brother rather than a prodigal daughter.

PART FOUR

The One Who
Shot Away

twenty-five

BREAKDOWN BRINKS & COFFEE COPES

When Rachel received Nova's email, she was beyond excited to read what Nova had come up with for the new play. She loved Nova's books, and she had played a key role in making Nova's first libretto come to life. This being Nova's second play, Rachel already had high expectations going in, but she didn't quite expect how Nova's characters and words would impact her. By the time she reached the ending, she was already in tears, and for some reason, her immediate impulse was to send Nova a message, asking to meet. She hadn't exactly expected to receive an immediate reply, so she took a drive in her car to distract herself with a few errands she needed to run, while thinking of the play and why it was having such a profound effect on her.

Once Upon a Prodigal was the story of two brothers at odds with each other. Most people saw her as the other brother, and her fiancé, the prodigal son. They both certainly fit the bill, with Jeremy having had a reckless youth, while Rachel had tried to follow all the rules her entire life. That wasn't what had gotten to Rachel. What she had found herself struggling with was how much she saw the other brother in her mother. It highlighted the quiet struggle she had been going through as she tried to straddle her way between their church and her parents.

How had it gotten to this point? Why did all of it leave her with this sense of hopelessness she couldn't shake? And how was it that Jeremy was so cool about all of this? Deep inside, Rachel was about to completely unravel, and she couldn't even complain about it. How could she? Everyone else around her had been going through much more difficult things. Could Rachel complain to them? About what? Her wedding? How difficult it was to plan it, given the broken relationships between her parents and most of her friends? Most people would only tell her to postpone the wedding if it was so difficult. That wasn't what Rachel wanted to do.

Desperate for a moment of normalcy, Rachel spotted her favorite coffee shop, Café Perivóli, and decided to get coffee and maybe even a sweet treat. However, just as she parked, her phone buzzed. It was a message from Nova. For some reason, receiving a message from Nova telling her to come right over shook her. She hadn't quite expected that. Nova was one of her heroes, and she had always taken care to protect her image in front of Nova. Could she really show herself vulnerable to someone like Nova, who seemed to have it all together, despite everything she had gone through in the past months?

Rachel couldn't back out, having been the one to initiate this meet-up. She gave up on getting coffee and drove on to the Grant villa, Nova's cute little neighborhood being about a half hour away.

By the time she got there, Rachel was already quivering. She couldn't understand the chaos consuming her soul, filling her chest, and clouding her mind. When Nova opened the door, tears were already falling down Rachel's cheeks. Despite her embarrassment, she blurted out the words expressing her soul. "I can't do this anymore, Nova," she said. "It's all too much for me."

Nova's confused look made her all the more embarrassed. Still, when Nova spread her arms to welcome Rachel with a hug, she was quick to get lost in Nova's embrace.

"What happened?" the older woman asked.

"I read your play," Rachel said. "And it triggered something in me, Nova. It's almost like you based the entire play on me."

"Oh," was Nova's only response as she ushered Rachel inside the house.

After they made themselves comfortable in Nova's living room, Rachel was quick to explain what she meant as she sniffled. "Don't get me wrong. I know you didn't base it off of me, but it spoke so much to my heart in multiple ways that you might as well have."

"I understand," Nova said. "I get that a lot with my books, maybe because I do base my characters off of my own experiences and encounters with people. I don't write a character based solely on a person — just bits and pieces of them. I find that there are so many truths and themes that connect all of us, and it makes stories relatable. Jesus shared *The Prodigal Son* to His disciples for a reason. He knew many of us could relate to that story, and I find it fascinating that He could tell such universal stories. I'm blessed that by God's grace, my stories resonate with readers."

They entered the kitchen, where Nova pulled up a seat for her in front of the dining table. She then handed Rachel a box of tissues. "I'm actually starting with dinner prep early, because I have to pick up the twins in an hour, and I might not have enough time to finish cooking by the time Caleb arrives."

Rachel bristled. Nova most likely had a lot going on in her life, and here Rachel was whining over getting triggered by a written piece of work. What was she doing? Rachel quickly wiped her tears away with a tissue and stood to her feet.

"Can I please help?" Rachel asked. "I know I'm intruding on your time, so I'd love to be somehow be of service while you go about your day's work."

"Oh, don't worry about it." Nova waved a dismissive hand at her as she transferred the mashed potatoes from a food processor onto a glass baking pan. With half of the food in the processor and another half in the pan, Nova paused. Her eyes cleared before she raised her gaze to meet Rachel in the eye. She nodded. "Sure. We can talk while we make the food. There's mozzarella cheese in the freezer. Do you mind grating some?"

"On it." That allowed Rachel to breathe a little better as she went about helping Nova with housework.

"I was thinking of making gravy with these, but I'll just add cheese on top and heat it up in the oven."

"Sounds delicious," Rachel said as she brought out the cheese from the freezer. "Where's the grater?"

Nova pointed to a cabinet next to the fridge. "It should be right there."

Rachel took it out, her mind reeling, as she mused over the awkwardness of this situation. She had gone here on the brink of a breakdown, and ended up making dinner with Nova. A smile appeared on her face. God had such a unique way of drawing her into unexpected situations, but Rachel wasn't sure if this was God getting her here, or if it was just her current emotional instability.

"So, what happened?" Nova asked as Rachel started grating the mozzarella. "Seems like you're going through a rough time."

Rachel braced herself for the conversation ahead as she continued to fill a plastic bowl with grated cheese, her mind drifting off elsewhere. "I don't know how to explain it, Nova. I'm kind of embarrassed that I even came here. It was an impulse move to message you more than anything, and now, I feel kind of awkward about it."

"Don't feel that way. You are welcome in our home any time you want to talk. Especially when what you're going through has something to do with my writing."

Was there an edge to Nova's tone? Rachel winced. "I hope you're not getting me wrong, Nova. It's not like I'm trying to imply that your script has impacted me in a negative way. That's not it at all. It's just that while I was reading it, I kind of saw in it so much of the kind of relationship I have with my mom."

A tense silence followed — a silence that lasted long enough for Rachel to wonder if she had said the wrong thing somehow.

"I think that's enough cheese," Nova said.

Rachel looked at the bowl in front of her and found it half full. Yes. That was definitely more than enough for the dish Nova was preparing.

"You're welcome to have dinner with us, Rachel." Nova took the bowl and sprinkled the cheese on top of the mashed potatoes while Rachel returned what was left of the mozzarella in the freezer and placed the grater in the sink. Nova pushed the platter inside the preheated oven.

"I can't have dinner," Rachel said. "Jeremy and I are having dinner with Dad and Mom tonight."

"Oh." Nova nodded. "That's good to know. Send my regards to them."

"I will."

"So, what is this about you relating the play to your mother and you?"

"Only that—" Was she saying something offensive here? That was certainly the sense Rachel was getting from this conversation. "I'm not sure how to explain." She bowed her head. "I'm sorry for wasting your time, Nova. I didn't want to—"

Nova shook her head. Her expression softened. "I asked you to come over, and it's because I want to be here for you. Do forgive me if I'm more than a little distracted. My mind is preoccupied with a lot of things. I'm transitioning to full-time writing, and our family is considering this huge move. With the play done, I have to start thinking about my next series of books, and while I am excited about it, a part of me is also a tad bit overwhelmed."

Rachel swallowed hard. Here Nova was, going through all these things, and what was Rachel about to say? That she was overwhelmed too, because of her wedding and the fact that she was struggling with her relationship with her mother and her parents' decision to leave Connect Church? Everyone at church seemed to have already moved on from her parents' choice to leave, and Rachel didn't even know what the play was for anymore. Still, she had committed to work on it, so she couldn't back out. And what was this about Nova moving? Rachel squinted her eyes at Nova. "Wait. Did you just say your family is considering a huge move?"

Nova winced. "Yes. That. Please don't tell anyone just yet. Nothing is final."

"Of course." Rachel nodded. "You can trust me."

"I'm sure I can." Nova sighed. "So, our family spent last summer in Ancoria with Caleb's family, and he's apparently been praying about it all this time. He's sure the Lord is leading us to move there. He dropped the idea on us last weekend, and the twins seem to be warming to it."

"And you?" Rachel asked, as she tried to process how huge this was. Caleb and Nova had been staples of Connect for years. To think about their family's absence was hard for Rachel to wrap her mind around.

"I think we should go for it, to be honest," Nova said. "Deep inside, I know it's the right move for us, because I really did fall in love with Ancoria, but a part of me also struggles with the idea of leaving the familiar behind." A wry scoff came out of Nova. "I want to go, but I don't, and I'm not sure any of that makes sense, but that's where I'm at."

Rachel smirked. "I'll be honest, Nova. Sometimes, it's hard for me to relate to you, because you seem to have it all together. Even after what happened to Caleb—"

"I don't think I can thank you enough for what you did to save Caleb's life, Rachel."

"Oh. Uhm. Right." Rachel lost her train of thought. "Hmm. Yeah. Anybody would have done the same thing had they been in my shoes."

"Well, they weren't in your shoes." The oven dinged. Nova went to check on her platter. "That will do." She then poked the pieces of meat by the sink. "Still hasn't thawed enough. I'll have to grill it after I pick the kids up." She cast a glance at Rachel. "I need to pick them up soon. Would you like to join me for the drive and continue the conversation there?"

Rachel had half the mind to say no, but she was still so curious about what Nova had shared, so she nodded instead and said, "Sure."

"Great. Let's go then. Maybe we can even pick up a coffee on the way."

"Oh okay." Rachel nodded and followed Nova as she headed for the door.

Once they were in the car and Nova started driving, Nova continued the conversation. "What were you saying again? You find it hard to relate to me?"

Rachel sighed. "Oh. Yeah." She tried to recall her train of thought. It was proving difficult. "I don't actually remember anymore what I was trying to say."

Nova laughed. "That happens to me a lot. It's totally fine. I just want you to know, Rachel, that whatever it is you're going through with your family, God is going to get you through. I mean, just look at what He did for Caleb and our family. We almost lost him, and that would have devastated us, but God did not allow that to happen. He preserved us. And now, we're crazy enough to think about packing up everything and moving to another country! It's overwhelming, but it's life. I'm sure it's a challenging dynamic between you and your parents right now. I totally get that, but you, Rachel. You're about to marry Jeremy, a man you love, and as overwhelming as it might feel right now, remember: life is just that way. There will always be something pressing against us, vying for our attention, and we learn to endure. We overcome."

Rachel nodded. Everything Nova said was true — inspirational, even — but part of Rachel wished that Nova could have just taken the time to listen. More and more, with what she was going through, it was becoming clear that she was on her own.

Everyone had already let go of Robert and Rhoda Petersen. No one was willing to fight for them to return.

No one but Rachel. Somehow, in a roundabout way, even if Nova had barely listened, Rachel arrived where she needed to go, realizing that some battles were solo fights. This was perhaps one battle Rachel had to face in solitude, because people around her were fighting their own battles and couldn't spare a minute to fight alongside her.

Still, Rachel hoped what Nova said was true. She would eventually overcome. She just needed to endure.

twenty—six

CRITICAL CALM & BOYFRIEND BANTER

A knock on her door sent Rachel into full panic mode as she rushed to put her pink dress on. Was that Jeremy already? It was only a few minutes past six o'clock, right? He said he would be arriving to pick her up at six-thirty. Rachel's heart stopped when she realized the clock on her wall wasn't actually moving. Adrenaline rushed through her as another knock on the door echoed across her space. She checked her phone. It was already ten minutes past six-thirty!

Barefoot, Rachel rushed to the door and pulled it open.

Jeremy had his eyes downcast, his brows furrowed, but when he fixed his eyes on her bare feet, a smirk appeared on his face. With his head still bowed, he lifted his twinkling eyes to meet hers, the lopsided smirk on his face growing.

Rachel's breath hitched. This man had been such a constant in her life, growing up. How had she only now realize how handsome she found him? She corrected the thought. Jeremy had always been handsome to her. She had just never entertained the idea that she would eventually agree to marry him.

He snickered at her.

"What?" Rachel asked.

"Nice dress." Jeremy squinted an eye at her. "I'm not sure your choice of shoes matches your outfit."

Rachel let out a huge huff as she raised her hands in the air out of frustration. "We're running late, I know, but it has been an interesting day." She rushed back to her bedroom to find shoes to wear. "Today has been an emotional roller coaster, and I don't know how to cope with it."

"Oh? What happened?" Jeremy was moving around in the kitchen, probably getting himself a glass of water.

"Nova finished writing the play." Rachel grabbed a pair of white sandals to match the pink dress. She didn't have to get all fancy. It wasn't like she was attending Sunday service.

"You're still doing the play?"

Rachel hopped on one foot, as she tried to get a sandal on the other, while exiting her room, so she could have a face-to-face conversation with her boyfriend.

He laughed when he saw her, and as expected when Jeremy was around, he whipped out his phone and pointed it at her to snap a photo. "This is interesting."

"I can't believe you're making content out of my lateness."

"It rarely happens, so I need to have it on record. I think this is the first time I've ever seen you late for anything."

"Yeah, but—" Rachel groaned when she was unable to hook the strap of her sandal around her ankle. "Why is this so difficult to put on?" She stumbled onto one of the living room chairs. "I can't believe we're going to be late. I'm already in enough hot water with Mom."

"You are?" Jeremy creased his brows as he approached her, a glass of water in hand. "I didn't notice at all. Why ever would your mom be upset with you?"

"Haha." Rachel bent over on the edge of the chair to put her sandals on properly. "I shouldn't have gone to Nova's earlier."

"Yeah. What were you doing there?" Jeremy leaned against the wall. "Also, you're still going on with this play?"

"Yeah. Didn't I tell you we were pushing through with it?"

"No." Jeremy took a sip from his water. "You haven't mentioned it in a while. I assumed you guys were dropping it because of what happened to Caleb."

"That was what?" Rachel stood up and tapped the sides of her feet together. "A month ago? We've always planned on pushing through with the play. It was just a matter of giving Nova time to finish the script while Nolan works on the music. Hasn't Serene mentioned any of these to you?"

"Nah." Jeremy shook his head. "Conversations with Serene have mostly centered around her pregnancy and Lily Red."

"How is she?" Jeremy was about to respond, but Rachel raised her forefinger in the air to get him to wait. "Let me just retouch my makeup and get my things, and then we can go."

"This is going to take a while, isn't it?"

Rachel frowned. She couldn't afford to take her time. "Yes. That. I guess we need to go now, huh?"

"Understatement of the year," Jeremy said.

"Let me just grab my things, then."

Five minutes later, they were already in Jeremy's car, driving out of Rachel's apartment complex.

"Why did you go to Nova's place again?"

Rachel gave him a recap of how she had tried to go to Nova's place to kind of work through what she was experiencing, only to feel bad about it after, because of how much Nova already had on her plate. "I felt like a nuisance."

"Nova probably wasn't thinking about it that way, though," Jeremy said. "From the little I know of Nova, she can lose herself in her own mind. Given what she had gone through as a kid, I think it was her way of coping. Now that she's an adult, I guess it carried over."

"Was it as bad as it seemed? Nova's and Nolan's childhood?"

"Most likely worse than we realize. I was so young when most of it went down. It's mostly Serene who remembers everything that happened. She doesn't talk about it much anymore. By the time I was old enough to understand how bad it was, their father had already passed away, and things were a lot more peaceful with just Nova, Nolan, and their mom. From that point on, most of the drama came from Nolan."

"I remember that time." Rachel snickered. "Mom had so much to say about Nolan's and Serene's relationship. Especially after Nolan had that reality show of his."

"Well, your mother has a lot to say about everyone's lives and relationships."

Somehow, that hit Rachel the wrong way. Her defenses shot up for her mother. "What does that mean?"

Jeremy smirked, oblivious to how his statement had affected her. "You know your own mother, Rachel. She tends to have an opinion about how everything in church should go. None of it ever matches her standards, no matter how hard we try."

"She means well, though. You know that, right? It's because she genuinely cares about the people in church that she expresses her opinions the way she does. She has good intentions."

"Sure, but you know what they say about the road to hell being paved with good intentions."

Rachel's eyes widened. Where was this coming from? She had never heard Jeremy talk about her mother this way. "So, are you saying my mother is going to hell?"

Jeremy threw his head back as he turned a corner. "What? No! That's not what I meant."

"Then what do you mean?"

Jeremy stopped the car at a red light. He turned to face Rachel in the passenger seat. The way his cheekbone twitched revealed how surprised he was that she was upset. "All I'm saying is that Mrs. P may have good intentions, but her good intentions and the way she imposes her standards on others have hurt a lot of people."

"What if they needed to get hurt? The Bible says open rebuke is better than secret love. What if her rebuke is the way for people to get to a point of self-reflection and being real before the Lord?"

"Fair." Jeremy nodded. His lip twitched as the car moved forward. He set his gaze ahead.

"Aren't you going to say anything else?"

"I'm not sure what else I can say, Rachel." Jeremy shrugged. "She's your mother. I recognize you may have a different perspective of her, but if you look at it from the perspective of someone who isn't Rhoda Petersen's daughter, and just someone who has received plenty of cutting words from her, then surely you can recognize that objectively speaking, Mrs. P is a critical person."

"It's unfair to generalize her that way, Jeremy. I would think that after all this time spent with our family, you would at least have more compassion toward her."

"I do, but most of my compassion toward her stems from hoping she would see the error of her ways, so she could get to a place of healing."

Rachel swallowed hard. Her blood was simmering, but it wasn't just because these words were coming from the man she wanted to marry. It was the knowledge that most of the people at their church saw her mother that way — that much, Rachel was sure of.

The neighborhood of Rachel's childhood came to view, and Rachel found herself bristling at the dinner to come, because though part of her knew Jeremy was telling the truth, somehow, reading Nova's play earlier had brought up this defensiveness within her toward her mother.

When Jeremy pulled over in front of the house Rachel had grown up in, he took a deep breath before looking at Rachel. "You're not mad at me, are you? Come on."

Rachel flinched when he tried to brush a finger against her cheek. She shook her head. "My mother isn't critical. She's just trying to raise a standard of righteousness for the church, because she loves the

Lord. Jeremy, if you're going to marry me, I think you should at least have less of a critical view of my mother, because by marrying me, you realize she becomes a part of your family, right? Also, how can you criticize someone for being critical without being critical yourself?"

Jeremy opened his mouth to say something, but shook his head instead. "Fine. You're right. I'm sorry." He sighed. "I didn't notice I was seeing the speck in her eye and not the plank in mine. It wasn't right of me to have been so vocal in pointing out her flaws. I will try to see her in a kinder light, okay?" His shoulders sagged. "Now, don't be mad at me. I'm sorry."

This time, she let him brush his fingers against her hair, tucking strands of it behind her ear. She took hold of his hand and kissed the back of it. "I love you," she said. "Just try not to talk about Mom that way, okay? I already hear so many people in church talking negatively about my parents, and it's getting to me."

Jeremy's fingers flinched against her hand holding his. His lip twitched, but all he said in response was, "I love you too, Rachel. Now, let's get through this dinner together."

Rachel let go of the fact that he was making it sound like they were submitting themselves to some form of torture. She would accomplish nothing by pushing an argument with him. They reached the front door with Rachel, determined to do everything possible to change Jeremy's opinion of her mother. They entered without knocking, hands clasping each other's, Rachel leading the way.

"Dad? Mom?" Rachel called out. No response. She took a peek in the living room. No one was there. A savory aroma wafted from the kitchen to the foyer. Rachel smiled. If there was one thing everyone loved about Rhoda Petersen, it was her cooking. "Something smells delicious."

Rachel tugged Jeremy toward the dining room, on the way to the kitchen, but their search for Rachel's parents stopped right there, because her father and mother were already eating in the dining room.

At the sight of them, Mom raised a brow at her. "You're late," she said. "And what are you wearing, Rachel? You couldn't even bother to make yourself look presentable."

Rachel's heart sank. So much for convincing her fiancé that her mother wasn't critical at all.

twenty-seven

FIERY FAMILIES & HIDDEN HURTS

Jeremy squeezed her hand. He was most likely trying to encourage or support her, but it only made knots form in Rachel's stomach. Her mother's cold stare was seeping under her skin and prickling her nerves. Her mother certainly wasn't going to make dinner easy for anyone. Was she surprised?

Rachel let out her best practiced smile. "It was my fault we're late, Mom. I lost track of time after spending several hours with Nova." Rachel's lower lip twitched when her mother's stern glare remained. "She finished the play. It's quite beautiful."

Mom didn't respond. Relief washed over Rachel when her dad cleared his throat.

"Go get plates for yourselves and join us," he said. "There's plenty of food to eat." He laid a hand on Mom's shoulder. "Your mother made a delicious dinner."

Mom harrumphed, but she rose from her seat, anyway. "Sit down, Jeremy. Rachel and I will get the plates and bring out more food. There isn't enough here."

Jeremy's hand flinched in Rachel's hold. "Of course, Mrs. P," he said.

For some reason, the way Jeremy still called her mother the same way he called her since childhood brought a genuine smile to Rachel's face. It was one thing remaining constant amid all the changes. Also, she was well aware of how much more comfortable Jeremy was around her father than her mother. She let go of his hand to follow her mother to the kitchen.

The tension was palpable inside her mother's state-of-the-art kitchen — a place Rachel had always kept in pristine condition as a way to escape her mother's ire.

"Everything okay, Mom?"

"What kind of question is that, Rachel?" Mom raised a brow as she brought out two of her finest plates, ones she reserved for fancier occasions.

"A genuine one." Rachel brought out place mats. "I'm sorry we're late."

"I taught you to respect other people's time and to stand by what you say you will do."

Rachel asked for a supernatural grace from Above as she tried to discern how best to respond to her mother. "You are right, Mom. I should have known better."

Mom's shoulders sagged, and her expression softened. She placed the plates on the counter and proceeded to take a baking dish from the oven containing two pieces of rosemary chicken she had kept warm for Jeremy and Rachel. Her heavy countenance moved Rachel's heart, but Rachel never quite knew how to get past her mother's tough exterior. Few people did. She had once been close to her mother, but this rift in church and Rachel's engagement to Jeremy had taken its toll on their relationship, and Rachel was more sorry over that than being late for dinner. In silence, Rachel pulled open the drawer where Mom kept the silverware and placed it over the plates.

"Thank you for all you do, Mom," she said. "I hope you know how much I appreciate it."

"Hmm," was all she got in response from her mother before they both returned to the dining table where Dad and Jeremy were engaged in what seemed to be a cordial conversation.

The moment the men became aware of their presence, however, there was a sudden shift in mood that vibrated across the entire space. Rachel and Jeremy exchanged glances as she placed the plates in their proper places. She sat next to him opposite where her mother sat, while Dad stayed in his spot at the head of the table.

"Jeremy, could you kindly say grace for your food and Rachel's?" Dad asked.

"That's unnecessary, Robert," Mom said. "We've already said a prayer for the food, and that prayer included theirs."

"There's no such thing as asking for too much grace, Rhoda. God knows we need all the grace we can get. Let the man pray for their food."

Mom opened her mouth before shooting a quick glare at Dad, but she quickly sealed her lips and got a hold of herself. Her mother's obvious distress planted a seed of desire in Rachel's heart to redeem Rhoda Petersen's name; otherwise, she might not be able to go through with the wedding — not when the church she belonged to was still holding a grudge against her family.

"Amen," Jeremy said.

"Amen," Rachel parroted the word of agreement even if she had been so lost in her own trail of thinking, she hadn't even heard a word Jeremy prayed.

"Let's eat." Dad winked at Rachel.

His joyous disposition unsettled her — only because moods like this coming from him often indicated something was wrong, and he was trying to make up for it with a jollier-than-usual mood. Rachel turned her eyes toward Jeremy, who now had a laser-focus on his food, his stare blank. This only served to trigger her suspicions further, because her fiancé was a typically easygoing man. Had something happened that she wasn't aware of? Had she been too busy crying over a written script to recognize something amiss around her?

"How are the wedding preparations going?" Mom asked. The slight edge in her voice wasn't lost on Rachel.

"It's going well." Rachel nodded before glancing at Jeremy, who was nodding, as well, as he chewed his food, but his eyes were still distant. Was he upset about their conversation earlier? He usually made an effort to be a lot more cordial whenever they came to visit her parents. This was not like him. "We've picked a venue, and—"

"Oh." Mom raised a brow and dropped her fork and knife on her plate. "Which venue did you select?"

"We reserved the venue where Max and Jenna had their wedding."

"Oh."

It astounced Rachel how that one syllable coming from her mother's lips could make her feel so inadequate. "Do you not like that venue?"

"It's your wedding. Doesn't matter what I like."

"Mom." Rachel cast a pleading glance at her father, who promptly said, "Rhoda."

"What? It's not like she consults us about anything anymore, Robert. She just does what she wants when she wants now." Mom shifted her focus from Dad to Rachel. "She has given us no say in her life, and I've come to terms with that."

Rachel flinched.

Beside her, Jeremy squared his shoulders and straightened his back, like he was bracing himself for a confrontation. Beneath the table, his palm rubbed her knee.

"What wedding venue did you have in mind, Mom?" Rachel asked, her voice coming out as a soft croak. "We didn't intend to exclude you. It's just that the place holds a special significance for Jeremy and me. As a couple, we thought it would be nice to get married at the place where we started seeing each other as possibly more than friends." Despite the tension, Rachel blushed when she glanced at Jeremy. "Well, at least, that's when he—"

"So—" Mom huffed out "—at least you're finally admitting it."

"Admitting what?"

"Rachel, I remember Max and Jenna's wedding. I remember questioning you multiple times if something was going on between you and Jeremy, and you kept saying no. Were you lying back then?"

"Nothing was going on between us at that time, Mrs. P." Jeremy was quick to come to Rachel's defense. "Rachel wasn't lying. She mentioned that's the first time we started seeing each other as possibly more than friends, because that was the day I started seeing her as my muse. We can all admit your daughter was stunning that day — more so than her usual stunning self — and a peek at my camera roll that day would tell you how enamored I was by her."

Mom cast a stern look at Jeremy. "I noticed." She shook her head. "I don't know what you fed my daughter that day, Mr. Sinclair, but since the wedding, she's drifted away from us — the people who loved and raised her long before you started noticing her. So—" her glare went Rachel's way "—forgive me if I'm less than thrilled to celebrate my daughter's wedding at the place where I feel like I lost her."

"Mom, where is all this coming from?" Rachel dropped her fork on her plate. She grabbed hold of Jeremy's wrist, practically able to sense the almost violent tension rippling from him. "You haven't lost me. I'm still your daughter, but I honestly don't understand why you're so upset about this. It's just a venue."

"We always dreamed you would get married where Knox and Hannah had their wedding."

"The house of Knox's grandfather?" Rachel furrowed her brows as she exchanged glances with her fiancé.

"I'm sure Hannah can talk to Eli and pull a few strings for us. It's a glorious place with great service, because they have trained staff to take care of everything. We've always talked about you having your wedding in the magnificent ballroom there. Now, you're getting married in some woodsy campsite by this gushing waterfall which subdues all the sound around it. I barely heard Max and Jenna say their vows to each other. Not that it mattered, because they barely knew each other when they got married, the same way you barely know each other now."

"Mrs. P, you said you were okay with us getting married," Jeremy said. "Why are you changing your tune now? Is this still about our wedding, or is it about something else?"

"Okay. Enough." Dad shook his head to intervene, his face taking on a serious expression as he dropped his silverware on his plate, the loud clink it made emphasizing the attention he wanted everyone to give him. "This dinner is so we can have a nice time together as a family, not so we can air out our grievances against each other."

"If not now, when, Robert?" Mom directed her ire toward him. "Rachel is never here anymore. When can we talk to our own daughter when she makes every excuse to avoid us?"

"Mom, I'm not avoiding you. It has been a busy time, because—"

"Don't make us out to be fools, Rachel. You have plenty of time to help your friends out, but you can't find time to talk to your own mother about your wedding?" Mom pointed a finger at her. "Let's be honest, Rachel. You picked a side, and you picked theirs."

"Rhoda, enough!"

Rachel flinched. This was one of the few instances she had ever heard her father raise his voice to her mother.

"I can't do this." Jeremy bowed and shook his head.

She grabbed hold of his hand, almost as a plea for him not to say anything or, worse, storm off. His sharp glare was directed at the table.

Tears brimmed Rachel's eyes. Her chin quivered. She had been aware of the tension brewing between her and her parents, but she had no idea that it had come to this, that her parents had actual grievances against her — ones that they might have good reason to have. She shifted in her seat, unable to look at Jeremy or her mother, because seeing the anger in their expressions would only break her heart.

Rachel swallowed back her tears. There was no point in getting too emotional about this. That had never worked with her mother. Crying would only get her sent out of the room, so she could collect herself before having a conversation about what she was going through. Rachel took advantage of the simmering silence to get a hold of herself and gather her thoughts before speaking.

"Mom, I'm sorry," she said. "I've been so wrapped up with a lot of things, and I didn't think it was affecting you this way. That was callous of me."

Jeremy's face darkened, but to Rachel's relief, he didn't say a word. From the firm set of his jaw, however, she could tell he was trying his best not to speak.

Mom shook her head before casting this woeful look at Rachel that shook Rachel to her core. She had rarely ever seen her mother cry, and seeing that one tear trickling down her mother's cheek spoke volumes about how hurt her mother was.

"This has been one of the toughest seasons of our lives, Rachel." Mom's voice had taken on a gentler tone, a lot less stern than it had been earlier. "Your father and I rarely speak to you about what we're going through, because we both want to be happy for you." She forced a big smile that looked faker the more it grew. "You're getting married, honey. We've dreamed of this since you were a little girl. But the truth is, Rachel, your father and I are both hurting, and a lot of the hurt comes from the family you're about to marry into." Her eyes traveled from Rachel to Jeremy, but this time, it wasn't just this stare of consternation or accusation. It was more like her eyes reflected the deep pain she had been keeping within her soul. "I loved my daughter from the moment I laid my eyes on her. We raised her to be a beautiful, God-fearing woman who loves the Lord and wants to follow Him. You—" Her lips quivered. "Mr. Sinclair, you laid waste of your life for years, and I praise God for how He has redeemed your story. God knows how much my husband and I have prayed for you and your sister. However, I never expected that you would just swoop in the way you did, and—" She choked as tears cascaded down her cheeks. "You stole my daughter away from me, Jeremy. And you did it with a smug smile on your face as you looked down on me and accused me of being a judgmental hypocrite. You have all turned against me, and I wasn't prepared for when my own daughter would do the same." With that last statement, she broke into a sob before completely unraveling in front of them. Her seat scraped the floor as she stood up and hurried out of the dining room, her climb up the stairs resounding around the house before fading away into dead silence.

Rendered speechless, Rachel sat there, heart-broken over the realization of just how much hurt her mother was experiencing. A tear ran down her cheek as her mind scrambled to figure out what to do. Her chair moved as she did. "I'll go check on her." She stood up, but Jeremy took hold of her wrist.

"No," Dad said. "I'll go."

"Dad—" Rachel frowned. "I need to talk to her."

"You're right. You do, but not tonight." He shook his head. "Sit down, Rachel."

Despite her hesitation and concern over her mother, Rachel quickly obeyed and sat back down.

"It won't get you anywhere to try to talk to her in the state she's in. I think you and Jeremy should go for now." Dad sighed. "I'll go check on her."

"Can we at least put the food away?" Rachel asked. "When can I come over again to iron things out with her?"

"Give her a call tomorrow and ask, but right now, it's best to give her the space she needs. I'll take care of everything." He brought out his wallet and retrieved a hundred-dollar bill. "You should have dinner out together. It can still be a lovely evening for both of you."

Jeremy shook his head in protest when Dad tried to hand him the bill. "No, sir. Please. You don't have to. I think Rachel and I need to have a talk about how we can repair things with Mrs. P."

"Dad—" Rachel winced "—do you feel the same way she does? About me staying at Connect? About me marrying Jeremy? Do you think this is me choosing sides?"

This pained expression appeared in her father's eyes, as he weighed his words carefully. As she waited for his response, it was all Rachel could do not to just break down right there. How had she hurt her parents this much without even realizing it?

"I don't think you picked sides, Rachel. I know your heart better than that, but I also understand why your mother feels the way she does." His shoulders sagged. He patted Jeremy on the back. "You're a good man, Jeremy. God has done quite a work of redemption in you, and I do believe God has brought you and my daughter together. Rhoda does too. She's just hurting right now."

The tension in Jeremy's shoulders melted away. "Thank you, sir. It means a lot to hear you say that."

"Now, go. I need to comfort my wife."

Her father ushered them all the way to Jeremy's car before returning to their house to face whatever it was Mom was going through. As they drove away, Rachel found herself between a trio of conflicting emotions: one, a strong admiration for her father; two, a deep guilt over having not noticed how much she had been neglecting her relationship with her parents; three, a nagging doubt about whether or not she should postpone her wedding to Jeremy Sinclair.

twenty-eight

ENDURING FRIENDSHIPS & FORBIDDEN ENDINGS

Rachel welcomed the silence inside Jeremy's car. It allowed her time to process through what had happened; however, the quiet didn't take too long, because not long after they had left her parents' neighborhood, Jeremy took a turn when he should have gone straight.

"Jeremy, my apartment is that way." Rachel pointed her thumb backwards.

"That's not where we're going," Jeremy said.

"I'm not up for a nice dinner out right now." She shook her head. "After all that, the last thing I want to do is to eat."

"Fair." His grip on the steering wheel tightened. The angles of his jawbone protruded against his skin as he nodded at her. "But, I know you, Rachel. If I take you home right now and leave you there, you're going to punish yourself the entire night by overthinking everything that your mother said. In fact, I wouldn't be surprised if you're currently deciding to postpone our wedding to please your mother."

How had he gotten to know her so well in such a small amount of time? "I don't think I'll be able to sleep tonight." She twisted her torso so she could face Jeremy as much as the seatbelt would allow her. "Aren't you even a little bothered by everything she said about you? About us?"

"About us? Yeah. That rubbed me the wrong way. Especially when she accused you of lying. I didn't like that one bit, because I knew it hurt you. Also, I was scared you might have second thoughts about marrying me, but I figured should you choose to do that, you must have a good reason for it. On the other hand, the things she said about me?" He smirked. "No. All of what she said was true, Rachel. I did swoop in and romance you into marrying me, pretty much out of nowhere. Even you and I are surprised."

"I wouldn't call fasting for three days before announcing to everyone that I'll become your future wife as 'romancing' me, but—" Rachel pouted "—I get what you're saying."

"We knew what we were getting into, Rachel. When we got engaged in China, we were aware this was what we were coming home to. A lot of people will question our decision to get married. They'll ask how we can plan a wedding in the midst of all this chaos. We still decided to do it."

"Yeah, but we've been home weeks ago, Jeremy. Shouldn't have things died down already? Shouldn't it be better? Why is all of this coming up now?"

"Because God is still working in our hearts. I know He's working in mine."

"How can you be so nonchalant about all that? Don't even deny it. You were about to snap back there."

"I did snap. It was taking all of my self-control to keep myself from blowing up at her. I wanted to push back and mention all the times growing up that she has been critical of me, my sister, and my parents. Rachel, you don't seem to want to accept that your mother is highly critical of others, but she is. Even towards you. I think this evening has shown us that."

"She's only critical of others, because she herself is hurt."

"I'll give you that." Jeremy shrugged. "That may be true, but why is she hurt? And why are you so affected by the things she accused you of? I can be nonchalant about it now, because I'm not in their house anymore, and I'm in the company of the woman I love. Why can't you be nonchalant about it, Rachel? Is there some truth to the things she was accusing you of? Have you been avoiding your parents?"

"No, of course not. I haven't been avoiding them. At least not intentionally. There's just been a lot. I've been helping Jenna transition into taking over *Lady Lacey League*. Serene has had me over several times to look after Lily Red. I helped Nova transition out of her job." She leaned the side of her head against her seat's headrest. "We've had dinner with them several times, and I call and text them whenever I'm able. I—" She frowned as she straightened her position in her seat, so she could set her eyes straight ahead to wherever he was driving to. "If I was actually avoiding them — without even being conscious of it — does that make me an awful daughter? My mother looked so heartbroken, Jeremy, and for a while there, she made me feel like I was consorting with the enemy or something."

"Rachel, this is what I was afraid of." Jeremy sighed. "None of us are enemies here, least of all you and me. I honestly believe your mom's outburst had more to do with what's going on at church than you or our wedding. That's why she's perceiving us — or maybe even just me — as enemies right now."

That made Rachel's skin bristle. "What do you mean? They've separated from Connect, and it's been weeks since they've had any contact with the church. It's not like there's anything new that's happened lately, right?"

"Yeah, about that..." Jeremy's brows lifted up. "It's just rumors at this point. That's why I didn't bother to mention it to you, but Anthony and Tabitha Price came to visit Dad yesterday. From what it sounded like, they're having second thoughts about their decision to leave the church with your parents and are now hoping they could come back to Connect."

Rachel closed her eyes as a wave of hurt on behalf of her mother swept over her. Mom and

Tabitha had been best friends for years. That must have felt like the ultimate betrayal. "No wonder she's hurting. I haven't been there for her, Jeremy. I had no idea she was going through all this, and I had an inkling earlier, too. After reading Nova's script, it was so strange how much it hit me, but not because of me. It was because of Mom. She needed me, and I was too caught up in helping everyone else."

Jeremy slowed the car down before coming to a full stop.

Rachel peeked outside. She creased her brows. Why had Jeremy taken her to his father's house? "What are we doing here?"

"I'm sleeping here tonight, but this isn't our ultimate destination. I thought we could order food and have it delivered to a house a few blocks from here. We can take a walk, talk about all of this — or not, which is honestly my personal preference — and maybe by the time we get there, the food will be there, too."

"Sounds intriguing." Rachel gave him a quick nod. "Where is there, exactly?"

"Our best friends are the only people who actually live nearby, so—" Jeremy raised his brow "—I figured we could just show up at their doorstep and invite them to a picnic in their front lawn."

"I would say crashing someone's house uninvited and unannounced is highly inappropriate, but knowing Max and Jenna, that might be something they would end up loving, so let's go for it." Rachel shrugged. "Why not? Of course, all of this is working under the assumption that they're even home right now."

"If they're not, we can have a picnic on their lawn until they get back home. What do you say?"

Rachel took a deep breath. "It would be a nice distraction."

Jeremy grinned. "Let's go then. What do you want to eat?" he asked before getting out of the car, circling the hood, and opening the door for her.

"My mom's food, to be honest," Rachel said as she got off the car.

"Eh, sorry, love." Jeremy scrunched his nose. "I don't think she delivers. Anything else?"

"I don't know." Rachel frowned as they started walking along the sidewalk. "I haven't had pizza in a long time."

"Wow. She's getting adventurous tonight." He browsed through a food delivery app on his phone to make an order. "Let's go for pizza and a bunch of other comfort food."

As he ordered, Rachel paid attention to the homes they were walking past. Next to Jeremy's childhood home was the house where Nova had grown up. A few blocks away, Max and Jenna had bought their first home. Rachel found herself wanting to live somewhere close to here, assuming they would even buy a house and not just fly off to some random country somewhere. Nova had mentioned they were moving to Ancoria, and Rachel wondered if that was at all in the future she wanted to build with Jeremy. Would they end up moving? It wasn't too far-fetched an idea; in fact, it had been something she had welcomed during their time spent in Asia. She had opened herself up to the possibility of living overseas, and she never would have entertained that possibility had it not been for Jeremy.

A completely different world and way of life had opened up to her when she had dared step out of her comfort zone. In a lot of ways, her comfort zone had been her family, specifically her mother. Upon returning from her trip overseas, it didn't take long until she discovered her comfort zone was no longer comfortable, so she leaned into the unknown instead. She had embraced anything that felt challenging, anything that could take her mind and attention away from her mother. She had been avoiding her parents, only because what had once been her comfort zone had somehow turned into her unknown.

"All done!" Jeremy announced before slipping his phone into his pocket.

"What did you order?" Rachel asked.

"Pizza. And a lot more." He slipped his hand into hers. "How are you feeling?"

"Like I have a lot to make up for when it comes to my parents. Like I'm failing."

At that, he chuckled. "You? Failing?" He smirked. "Nah. None of that, Rachel. It may seem like that right now, but this will all turn out fine. Trust me."

"How can you be so confident of that?"

"Look. I'll give it to you. Your mother has been getting to me. Especially whenever I think about all the negative things she's said about anyone in my family, including my mom, but—"

"What are you talking about?" Rachel frowned. "My mom has always loved Mama Aida. They used to be best friends."

Jeremy raised a brow. This patronizing smile appeared on his lips. "My point is that we shouldn't let it get to us, Rachel."

"Why not? We seem to have opposing ideas about the roles our parents played in our lives and theirs. Don't you think we should address that? Especially since we'll become family soon? We can't just ignore all these issues cropping up, Jeremy."

He winced. "Can't we though? I think we can, and tonight, we should."

Rachel stopped walking. She turned to the side to face her fiancé. As much as she loved this man, his nonchalance over this whole matter baffled her. Hadn't he been in the exact same dinner earlier? How could he just brush off the clear dissonance between them and these issues to the side? "I don't understand why you think this is something we shouldn't talk about. We're talking about our families, people who will be a part of our lives for beyond our foreseeable future. You don't think this is a subject worthy of discussion before we get married?"

Jeremy held her shoulders and gave her that grin that made her feel as if he was trying to transmit his joy to her. "Of course we should talk about it, Rachel. Just not tonight. Not now."

"Why not tonight? When then?"

"When the tensions aren't high, and we're not coming out of this intense confrontation with your mother. I need time to pray about what happened, and I think you do too, but tonight, I'd just like an opportunity for us to remember that we're in this together. We can have fun and enjoy the night and then discuss it tomorrow when we both have a clear head and have had time to seek the Lord about His thoughts on all of it." Jeremy shrugged. "That's what I want to do, but if you want to take a trip down memory lane and discuss the ups and downs of the relationship between my family and yours, then sure. Let's do it. I just doubt it will be productive, and I don't want to go to bed miserable and hurt tonight."

His words sent her soul into this conflict of wanting to be right and also acknowledging that she had many times before heard her mother speak against the Sinclairs, the family she was about to marry into. Was she willing to spend the night accounting for any past situation Jeremy might bring to memory? They were alone right now, and she was with the man she loved. Would she rather plunge into an all-out argument? Or cherish this moment he was trying to create for them? She sighed. "We'll talk about this tomorrow?"

"Let's have brunch together. Café Perivóli. We haven't been there in a while. After we talk, I can drive you to your mother's."

"I wasn't planning on—" Rachel frowned. Did she want to talk to her mother the next day? "I don't think she's ready for that."

"We'll find out tomorrow when you call your father to ask." Jeremy smirked. "I know you, Rachel. You won't have peace of mind until you're able to discuss this with your mother."

Rachel shrugged. "You're probably right, but let's see how tomorrow turns out."

Jeremy grinned. "So, you agree to make the best out of tonight for now?"

Rachel rolled her eyes. "Fine."

"Sweet!" Jeremy brought out his phone as they started walking forward again, turning at a corner, where they were only two more blocks away from Max's and Jenna's home.

Rachel frowned at the camera. "What are you doing?"

"Taking a picture of my girlfriend, so I can immortalize this night."

"Why would you want to remember this night?"

"It's the first night we almost got into a major argument as a couple, but we survived without breaking any bones."

Rachel raised a brow. "For now." She then flashed a smile. "Hopefully, we spend a lifetime with not a single broken bone between the two of us.

"Agreed." Jeremy snapped a photo. "Beautiful. By the way, you look gorgeous tonight."

"Ha!" Rachel threw her head back as she skipped ahead and started walking backwards as Jeremy filmed her. "Tell that to my mother. Apparently, I'm not presentable enough for her." She caught her own words and her eyes popped open. "This isn't live on social media, right?"

He shook his head. "I would tell you if we were live."

She blew out a sigh of relief. "Good."

For the rest of the two blocks to get from where they were to their best friends' home, they tried to get as creative as possible with the photos they were taking. Once they got to the front yard of Max's and Jenna's townhouse, Jeremy lifted his camera up, so they could take a selfie together. Somehow, Rachel's smile was genuine. It wasn't something she had to force out, and as she wrapped her arms around Jeremy's waist, smiling at his camera's screen, her heart bubbled with so much gratefulness for being a part of this man's life. She was never more sure that she wanted to be part of this man's family, but it did sting as she wondered if he wanted to become a part of hers. The realization hit her hard enough so that she backed away from Jeremy.

"Hey." Jeremy put down his phone and gripped her hand. "What's wrong?"

"I know we said we wouldn't talk about it, but I just have to leave this question out there, so you can pray about it tonight."

Jeremy nodded. "Sure. Ask."

"If you marry me, my mother will be your mother-in-law. She will probably have many more opinions about our family than you would be comfortable with, much less happy about. Are you sure you want to marry into that?"

His grip on her hand tightened as his eyes narrowed, almost as if the question physically hurt him, making his face wince in pain. "I want to marry you, Rachel," he said. "That, I don't have any doubt about, but as for having Rhoda Petersen as a constant voice in my life, telling me how inadequate I am — which is most likely how she views me — I'm not thrilled about that. That's something I need to pray about, for sure."

Just as his smile caused joy to radiate from him to her, his sadness over the situation moved her even more, and for the first time since they had said yes to marrying each other, Rachel began to have serious doubts if they had heard right from God. Was this God's will for them? Or had it all been just their emotions carrying them away, because of what a novelty their shared experiences out in the world had been for both of them?

Out of pure impulse, Rachel kissed Jeremy's cheek. "I love you," she said.

"I love you, too," he responded with a nod.

It was strange how the melancholic undertone in their words made it feel like they were saying goodbye to each other.

Right then, Jeremy's phone started buzzing at the same time a car pulled over. The first of the food Jeremy had ordered earlier arrived, with more coming.

Their third order had already arrived when the front door opened at Max's and Jenna's house. Out stepped Jenna, who gave them this dumbfounded look. "What are you two doing here?"

Jeremy grinned at her as he lifted the takeout food in his hands. "We wanted to go on a picnic, and we figured we could use your front yard."

"You two are crazy." Jenna shook her head.

"You can join us," Rachel offered with a shrug of her shoulder.

"Now, you're talking." Jenna grinned. She went back in the house. "Max! Two crazy people are in our lawn, but they brought us food, so it's okay!"

Minutes later, the couple emerged from the house with blankets and pillows. Their presence diffused the tension Jeremy and Rachel had shoved to the background when they had decided to put a pin on the issues they were facing. An hour later, the couples were lying on either side of the blanket, with empty boxes of food scattered between Rachel and Jenna. Max was on Jenna's side, and Jeremy was on Rachel's.

A hushed silence — one that was almost reverent — filled their little group as they stared up at the sky. There weren't many stars out that night, though Rachel wanted to imagine there were more of them than was visible. She missed the starlit skies from her trips out in the middle of nowhere in the Philippines or in China, where city smog hadn't yet blurred the firmament above.

This moment put some perspective back into Rachel as she realized how small she was in comparison to the vastness of God's creation and plan. When Jeremy's arm rubbed against her shoulder, and his hand clasped hers, a breath escaped Rachel. An ache in her heart emphasized the thoughts brewing in her brain. Would it come to a point where she would have to choose between him and her family? She hoped not, because she wouldn't be able to bear losing either.

"I read the play." It was Max who broke the silence.

"Good for you, man," Jeremy said. "Why is that on your mind right now?"

"I don't know," Max said. "It was just so good. Nova did a great job writing it. Also, it was an amazing reminder of how God has brought us out of the recklessness of our lives. It has been a tough year, a tough few months, but through it all, look at where we are now. Jenna and I are married. You two are engaged. Cod has brought us this far. He has been faithful to us."

As he spoke, Rachel choked up; a tear ran down her cheek. She sensed Jeremy's eyes on her, so she met his gaze, and all she could think about was how much she wanted to be his wife, but for that to happen, she needed to make things right with her mother, so she said a prayer to the God of the heavens to make all things right between her, her family, and her fiancé. After all, He was the God of the impossible, and of all the endings she could imagine for her life, she couldn't accept one that had neither Jeremy nor her mother in it.

twenty — nine

NECESSARY ARGUMENTS & NEGATIVE AVOIDANCE

Café Perivóli was already full of people when Jeremy and Rachel arrived for brunch. A gathering spot for hipsters, yuppies, and freelancers, Jeremy and Rachel had to wait a few minutes before they were given a seat. When they got to sit across the booth from each other, they made a quick order to a waiter. Once the server left, the piercing expression on Jeremy's eyes was enough to tell Rachel that it was game on.

Rachel squirmed in her seat, melting under Jeremy's stare.

"So?" Jeremy asked. "Did you pray about it?"

That was an understatement. Rachel had cried throughout the night. She had been heartbroken over the way her mind had been tormenting her, playing out scenarios that always ended up with her either losing Jeremy or her parents. "I'm not sure if I would call it praying." She scoffed. "I wrestled."

Jeremy smirked. "From the bags under your eyes, I can tell it wasn't an easy time."

"I can say the same of you, based on the bags under yours."

"Fair."

"I'm glad we spent time with Max and Jenna, though. What Max said about how Nova's play impacted him struck a cord with me, because he was right. God has been so faithful to us all the way to this point in time." Rachel sighed. "All that to say, you were right. It did help that we took a step back and let the emotions die down before having this discussion."

A lopsided grin appeared on Jeremy's face. "The truth is, Rachel, I'm not sure what we're here to discuss. I want to marry you. That hasn't changed from your side, has it?"

Rachel gulped. "Of course not. I still want to marry you. I'm just concerned about what that will entail. You obviously have a strained relationship with my mother, and I struggle to think about what the consequences would be for our marriage, if you're still holding on to resentment toward her. She is still my mother, and after reading that play and sitting through her outburst last night, I'm more than a little protective of her. She's hurting, Jeremy, and I don't think our church has ever given her a fair shot."

Jeremy clenched his jaw as he lowered his eyes. "I prayed about our conversation last night. To be honest—" He flinched as his face crumpled up into this pained expression as he looked at Rachel, almost teary-eyed. "I don't want to lose you, Rachel, but if I tell you what I really feel, I'm afraid I might."

Rachel's ears stung at what he said. All her inner defenses shot up as she squared her shoulders. For a moment, she wanted to back out of the conversation and live in denial, pretending like none of this was happening. After all, that's what they had been doing for the past few weeks since they had returned. However, it had gotten to the point where they needed to address this issue or risk making a mistake they would regret for the rest of their lives. "You'll have to tell me anyway."

"I know." A bittersweet smile appeared on his face.

They paused when the server came with their coffee and breakfast plates. Both had ordered a lot, but neither of them seemed to have any interest in eating as they just stared at their food.

"I wish I could assure you that you won't lose me, Jeremy, but I can't right now. This is something you need to say. It is something I need to hear."

Jeremy nodded. "Last night revealed to me just how much anger I have toward your mother. I wish it wasn't so, Rachel, but she was highly critical of us. Forget all the past years. Just consider last night and how critical she was of me. No matter how much I tried to change, it was as if nothing I did, nothing I could ever do, would ever be enough for her. And I don't understand it, because my family — Mama Aida, especially — has only ever tried to be kind and accommodating to your mom."

"Is that the case, though?" Rachel winced. "Because Mama Aida is almost immortalized as a saint in our church, and don't get me wrong — she was amazing — but I do feel like there's something more behind the strain in relationship between your mother and mine." Rachel bristled. "Do you know what happened between them in the past? Before your parents got married?"

Jeremy shook his head. "All I know is that they started Connect Church together — the three of them. Dad fell in love with my mother, and they naturally took over the church. Mrs. P always assured them she was fine with everything, but somewhere along the line, she started becoming more and more abrasive and critical toward my parents. Mama always just sort of brushed it off whenever we heard of your mother saying something hurtful or critical about us. It's like she and Dad somehow accepted that your mother is just that way, and there's nothing any of us could do about it. When Serene started complaining about how your mom was treating Nolan back when they were dating as teenagers, Mama Aida even defended your mother."

Rachel wanted to come up with a bunch of defenses to come to her mother's aid, but she held herself back. There was no point in doing that, because those were her boyfriend's genuine memories of her mother. Still, she refused to accept an image of Rhoda Petersen as a hyper-critical villain. "Is there any way you can get along with my mom, Jeremy?"

"I don't think I'm the problem here, Rachel. It's her who doesn't like me. Do you want me to spend the rest of my life trying to convince her to like me? Because I do get along fine with your father, but with your mom, I feel like she's mad at me over things that happened between her and my parents a long time ago. Do you think that's fair?"

"No. Of course not." Rachel sighed.

"Where does this leave us, then?"

"Jeremy, my only concern is that if I marry you, this rift between you and my mother will haunt us for the rest of our lives. It will always be a source of conflict in our marriage, and I don't want that. I want our future children to be able to get along with my parents. I long for you to have a healthy relationship with them as well."

"Plenty of people don't get along with their in-laws, Rachel."

She frowned. "Should we be one of those people? Is that the kind of family you want to build with me?"

"What should we do about it, then?"

"Would you be willing to go with me to my mom's house this afternoon? Maybe talk it out with her? Get to the bottom of it?"

Jeremy shrugged. "I'm willing to do just about anything to be with you, Rachel, so I'm not the one who should be answering that question. It's her."

Rachel bristled. He was right. "Let's see if they're even willing to have us over."

"I can ask your father," Jeremy said. "It might mean something if I'm the one who's asking."

"Good idea."

Jeremy took out his phone and gave Rachel's father a call. "Hello, sir. Yes. I'm with Rachel right now, and we were wondering if we could come over this afternoon to iron things out with Mrs. P? We're still heart-broken over how things played out last night." Jeremy paused to listen, nodding his head slowly. "I understand. Right. We'll try again tomorrow, then."

Rachel's shoulders sagged. How could she make peace with someone she loved, when that person couldn't even be bothered to see her? Mom certainly wasn't making it easy for Rachel to build a case for her.

Jeremy lifted his brow when he checked his phone. "Did you get a message from Nova?"

"No." Rachel rummaged through her purse for her phone. "I haven't checked my phone since we got here." She checked its screen, and sure enough, there was a message from Nova.

"She's inviting everyone to come over," Jeremy said, even as Rachel read the invite.

"Well, not everyone," Rachel said. "Just us ladies involved with the play and our husbands. I guess you count as my husband."

"See, Rachel?" Jeremy grinned. "No matter what happens, the wedding has to go on. We wouldn't want to make a liar out of Nova, do we?"

Rachel rolled her eyes, but there it was right before her. The easy path. The reason why she had been "avoiding" her mother. Everything else was so much easier than dealing with the pain and pressure brought about by her mother's brokenness.

And so it continued. Rachel was once again swept away by what was happening around her, as she shoved whatever was going on with her mother into the background. Making peace with Rhoda Petersen had to wait. For now, Rachel had a play to put on — a play that was ironically started, so they could make peace with her mother.

thirty

MISUNDERSTOOD HEARTS & MUTUAL HURTS

Chill acoustic music and laughter from the back yard welcomed Jeremy and Rachel when they entered Caleb and Nova's home. The aroma of chili, jalapeños, and cumin filled their nostrils — a sure sign that someone was making Mexican food. Nova's smile as she opened the door for them was warm and inviting.

Something about the festive atmosphere hugged Rachel and made her feel immediately at home — a stark contrast to the tense welcome they had received when they had gone to visit her parents the night before.

Nova shut the door behind them, rubbed Jeremy's arm to acknowledge him, and embraced Rachel. "How are you and your parents?" Nova whispered in her ear.

Rachel gave Nova a weak smile while Jeremy walked past them to bump fists with Max.

Nova nodded in understanding. "Do you want to talk about it? I'm sorry I was so distracted yesterday. So much was going on, but I have been praying about you and your family."

"Thank you, Nova," Rachel said. "I appreciate the prayers. I'm not sure there's much I can say about it right now. Everyone seems to be in a happy mood. I don't think this is the time and place to talk about my mother."

"Right. Just know that if you ever need to talk, I'm here. I felt so bad about yesterday. I should have listened more."

Where was this coming from? Nova had seemed so detached yesterday afternoon. Why the sudden care and concern? Rachel pushed away the dread consuming her. "You have a lot going on. It's fine. I'm fine."

From the backyard, Jenna walked in right as Jeremy and Max walked out. Upon seeing them, Jenna leaped up and down, linking her arms with Rachel.

"I'll be in the kitchen. We'll all be ready to eat soon," Nova said.

"Do you need any help?" Jenna asked.

"No. Everything's taken care of." Nova shook her head. "You girls can wait in the living room. Serene is there. The men have the grill going. We will eat soon."

With Nova heading off to embody the perfect host, Jenna led Rachel to the living room.

"Do you know what's going on?" Rachel asked. "I thought we were here to discuss the play. This is more like a party."

"We are, and it is." Jenna shrugged. "I think Caleb and Nova have an important announcement to make, and I'm dying to know what it is!" She skipped forward to emphasize her excitement.

Rachel knew what it was, but she had promised Nova she wouldn't tell anyone.

"Do you think she's pregnant again?" Jenna's brown eyes widened in speculation. "Wouldn't that be cool? I mean, the twins are almost teenagers now."

Rachel shrugged. "I guess we'll find out soon."

A squee came out of Jenna's lips. "I'm so excited."

In the living room, they found Serene sitting on the L sofa, with a pencil in hand and a sketch pad on her lap. Her full focus was on whatever art it was that she was creating.

Rachel and Jenna sat across from her, exchanged glances, and tried not to giggle too much at how oblivious Serene was to their presence.

"In the zone," Jenna mouthed to Rachel.

Rachel raised a brow and nodded.

It took several minutes of Serene's continuous sketching before she lifted her eyes and drew a breath, as if surprised to see them there. Her cheeks grew red, covering her splash of freckles. "How long have you two been there?"

Jenna giggled. "Not that long. A few minutes."

"Sorry." Serene cringed. "I haven't been in as creative a flow as this in a long time. So grateful that Ma is taking care of Lily Red today, because from the moment I woke up, all I wanted to do was paint."

"I'm not in any creative flow—" Nova entered the living room and sat next to Serene "—but I am also thankful Ma took the twins. A day with Grandma for all the cousins. It's good for everyone. Gives us parents a break and some time to recalibrate." She peeked over Serene's shoulder. "That's beautiful."

Serene hugged the sketch against her chest. "It's not done."

Nova shrugged. "Already beautiful as it is. Imagine how gorgeous it will be once it's complete."

"Can we see?" Rachel asked.

Serene flipped the sketch around and showed them an image of a woman embracing Jesus. The woman was an older one. It was Rachel's mom.

Rachel choked up as she blinked back the tears and tried not to cry. "Wow."

Serene smiled at Rachel. "Woke up today feeling like I wanted to draw my mother, and I did. I have quite a few sketches of her back home, but eventually, it kind of morphed into wanting to draw Mrs. P." She grinned. "I sent some of them to Nolan, and he said Mrs. P was on his mind this morning as well. He even rewrote one of the songs in the play, and it's with her in mind."

Rachel narrowed her eyes. "Really? Have you heard the song?"

"I wish! He's not done with it yet, but he did tell me the working title of the song is *Misunderstood.*"

That made Rachel bristle, as she gave Serene a quizzical look. "Did your brother tell you what happened last night?"

"No." Serene shook her head. "I haven't spoken to him since a couple of days ago. Is Jeremy here? He's so wrapped up in his own world, he didn't even bother to look for me once he got here."

"He's with Max," Nova said. "I tasked them to take care of the barbecue while we wait for Caleb to arrive from work."

"Nolan might be able to catch up as well." Serene flicked her brows up and down. "He has a few nights off from the tour, so he's flying here to spend time with us, then he flies back again to join the tour in a few days."

"That's awesome." Nova grinned. "It would be nice to have him here." There was a hint of melancholy in her voice that made Rachel wonder if anyone else knew about their plans to move to another country. "Anyway, most of the food is already prepared. We're just waiting for Caleb and Nolan to get here, so we have time to talk." She then leaned over so that she was sitting on the edge of the sofa before sending Rachel this apologetic look. "Before that, I did wake up this morning praying for Miss Rhoda, as well. I even got a message from Hannah all the way from Ancoria asking about your mother. Sorry about yesterday, Rachel. I should have paid more attention, but I did pray for her this morning, because God reminded me of why we started this play to begin with."

Rachel's lips quivered. Why was everyone suddenly showing concern for her mother? Had something happened? Had they found out what had happened at her mother's house the night before?

Jenna held her hand. "How is Mrs. P? You and Jeremy didn't mention anything last night, but things seemed a little tense between you and Jeremy, so we prayed for both of you."

Rachel gasped for breath as she tried to push a sob back. There was no way they were going to make her cry over this. "Is this what you called us to meet here for? To discuss my mom?" She was finding it hard to believe Jeremy hadn't mentioned anything.

Nova shook her head. "No. Not at all. Caleb and I have wanted to do this for a while now — gather everyone together for this big announcement of ours." Nova gave Rachel a wink. "But, I also wanted to discuss the play with all the men here, so we can figure out how to move forward, and it just so happens the play makes us all think of Miss Rhoda, because—" she shrugged "—she's one of the main reasons we wanted to do this play in the first place."

Rachel wanted to keep a smile plastered to her face, but Nova's words were making her flinch and twitch like her programming had somehow caught a bunch of glitches. "It's been hard." Right after she sputtered out those words, a sob followed. Try as hard as she could to hold it back, the tears kept coming.

Serene rushed toward her and wrapped her in an embrace. "I'm sorry," she whispered in Rachel's ear. "You're about to marry my brother, and all this time, I've been oblivious to how all of this has been affecting you. It's a tough spot that you are in, and we want you to know that we love you and we do love your parents too. We wish this split had never happened."

Nova and Jenna laid their hands on Rachel's back and both started praying in whispers Rachel could no longer decipher as she sobbed on Serene's shoulder.

It was Serene's prayer she could hear. "God, thank You for Rachel. Thank You for her faithfulness to You and all the ways she has served and inspired so many of us to follow hard after You. She has been faithful to You throughout her life, and this is an exciting time for her as she plans her wedding to Jeremy. Don't let the enemy steal that joy from her. Let there be peace even as they prepare for this wedding. And we believe that You are the God of the impossible, and You are even able to reconcile and restore the relationship between many of us and Rachel's mother. Thank You that You have used her as an agent of peace throughout everything that has been going on. We honor You for her life, and we pray that You will make a way for relationships to be restored between Mrs. P, ourselves, and our church. Thank You, God. This we pray in the Name of Jesus, Amen."

"Amen," Nova said, but continued on with her own prayer. "I also ask, Lord, that You restore the heart behind why we produced this play. It is not only to entertain, but to remind us of Your great work of redemption and reconciliation. We don't know how You will do it, but we believe You can still repair the rifts between us. Whatever is going on between Rachel and her parents, let there be peace. Let there be joy in all the days leading to her wedding. We pray this in Your Name, Amen."

"Amen," Jenna agreed, but then continued praying still. "Lord, I also want to thank You for Rachel. She has served so many of us and just as Serene said, her walk with You has challenged us to walk in Your ways, as well. Whatever difficult time she's going through, remind her of all the good she has done. I am following You today because of our friendship and all the prayers she has said on my behalf."

"My brother is following You today because of her," Serene added.

"My husband is alive because of her," Nova said.

"Remind her of all the ways she has been a blessing," Jenna finished. "You are a Rewarder. Reward her for her faithfulness and her righteous influence on so many. Thank You, God, for Rachel. This I pray, in Christ's Name."

All of them said, "Amen," while Rachel continued to sob, but this time, not out of pain or hurt over her mother, but out of gratefulness to the Lord for these people whom He used to remind her of Who He was and what He was capable of.

All the ladies embraced her, and somehow, this gesture healed her, because if they could welcome her into their fold, surely they could also welcome her mother.

thirty — one

DIVINE HEALING & DARING HICCUPS

The moment Caleb and Nolan arrived, all the couples gathered on the rooftop of the Spanish villa that had been Nova's and Caleb's home for years. Fairy lights and garden lamps lit their surroundings as they shared a generous feast together.

Beside Rachel, Jeremy laughed at some joke Max was telling him. The general feeling around them was that of happiness and contentment, security in knowing that each of them belonged there, loved and accepted. Surrounded by all this, Rachel couldn't help but say a prayer on behalf of her mother, as she recalled all the prayers her sisters in Christ had spoken earlier. Surely, God would listen. Surely, God had her mother in mind, considering the ways He had spoken to Nova, Serene, Jenna, and others about that day.

"Hey, everyone!" Caleb walked to the rooftop with his phone screen facing them. "Knox and Hannah say hi!"

Rachel's ears perked up at the name of her mentor, as everyone waved and greeted the couple with a hello. When Jeremy handed the phone to Rachel, she got a chance to speak to Hannah.

"How is everything?" Hannah asked.

Rachel winced. "It could be better, but I'm trying to focus on the positive side of things."

"That's the only way to go, sometimes." Hannah gave her a reserved smile. "I gave your mother a call this morning."

"How did that go?" Rachel grimaced as she prepared herself for whatever Hannah had to say.

"She's fine, Rachel. She's struggling, given everything that's happening, but give her some space and time and she should be okay."

"At least she's talking to you."

"Is she not talking to you right now?"

Rachel shook her head. "We had a confrontation last night, and issues that have been simmering between us just kind of boiled over."

"Sorry you're going through this." Hannah nodded. "For what it's worth, I don't think she's upset with you as much as she's upset with the situation she's in right now. I'd like to believe she's seeing the error of her ways and is now praying to God for what to do next. We're praying with her, as well. Me and Knox."

"It helps to know that so many are praying for her."

"Of course!" Hannah's eyes widened. "Your mother is one of the main reasons I love the Lord so much, and she may have had her missteps these past months — or years — but it's only because she loves the Lord, and she loves Truth. I believe God has His hand in all that's been happening right now."

"Thank You, Hannah. That's encouraging. We miss you."

"We miss you, too. You and Jeremy might want to consider having your honeymoon here in our island kingdom."

Rachel grinned. "We'll talk about it."

Knox showed up on the screen. "What did I miss? Oh, hey, Rachel! We're excited to attend your wedding!"

"You'll fly all the way over here for it, right?" Jeremy butted in.

"Of course!" Knox exclaimed. "We wouldn't miss it for the world."

Caleb cleared his throat. He and Nova were standing at the head of the table.

Rachel grinned. "I think they're making their announcement."

"Rachel," Caleb said. "Do you mind flipping the camera phone so Hannah and Knox can hear our announcement?" He then nodded toward Max. "Can you please do the same, so Josh and Vienna can listen in?"

"Right." Rachel looked at the screen. "You heard the man."

The couple nodded. Rachel turned the camera and tried to put Caleb and Nova within view of Knox and Hannah. Max was doing the same with his phone.

"We were going to wait until later to make this announcement," Caleb said, "but after discussing it with Nova, we do feel an urgency to make this happen right after the twins' school year, and we will need the support of everyone if we're going to make it happen. You guys are people we'll be working closely with in the next few months, so you'll most likely find out one way or another, so we figured we could make it official and announce this to you guys first."

"Caleb, bro, I love you and all—" Nolan brushed his hands against Serene's hair, while she leaned her back on him "—but come out with it already. What's the announcement? You're killing me with suspense over here."

Caleb grinned. "I love you too, bro, but you better brace yourself for this one." He exchanged glances with Nova. "We've been praying about this for a while now."

Nova's eyes widened. "You've been praying about this for a while. I only found out about this recently."

"True." Caleb nodded. "But collectively, if you add all the time I've been praying about this, it's been a while."

"What's the announcement?!" several of them, including Rachel, asked.

"Our whole family is moving to Ancoria next year," Nova blurted out.

A moment of stunned silence filled the place.

The ladies in the live calls — Hannah and Vienna — squealed at the news.

"What?" Nolan asked. "Nova! Does Ma know?"

"I told her this morning when I dropped off the twins." Nova nodded.

"And she's okay with it?"

Nova shrugged. "You know Ma. She says she'll pray about it, but she'll support me and Caleb, whatever we decide."

"We think it's what's best for the twins," Caleb said, "and after a lot of prayer, we believe it's where God is leading us."

"I'm shocked, but I'm glad I was here for the announcement," Nolan said. "Hey. You're giving me a great reason to pack up and go visit once this tour is over." He exchanged glances with Serene. "What do you say, love? We can spend a few months there? Maybe after the baby is born?"

"That sounds lovely," Serene said.

"Wow. I don't know what to say," Max said as he stood up and hugged Caleb. "We trust God is leading you in this."

"Hey," a muffled voice — Josh's — came from the phone Max was clutching in his palm as he embraced the older man. "Vienna and I are still here."

"Oops." Max winced. "Sorry about that." He sat back down and pointed the camera back at Caleb.

"We are so stoked that you're doing this! It'll be great!" Josh exclaimed.

Caleb grinned. "We are too. We have a lot to do before we go, but we're excited and ready for it." He then cleared his throat. "There is another announcement — I'm guessing it's an announcement — but it's not coming from us. It's coming from Jeremy, so I would like to give the floor to Mr. Sinclair over here." Caleb gestured toward Jeremy, who rose to his feet.

Rachel creased her brows when he winked at her. What was he up to?

Caleb and Nova took their seats by the table so Jeremy could take the floor.

"As you all already know, when we were in China, I asked this lovely young woman—" he pointed at Rachel "—to marry me, and she said yes."

Rachel's cheeks warmed.

"Now, we have been going through quite a bit of a struggle when we got here. Especially because of what happened to our church. You all know what I'm talking about."

Rachel bristled. Why was he saying this in front of everyone?

Jeremy took a deep breath before laying his hand over his heart. "Rachel, I've dropped the ball on this, and I'm sorry. I should've realized how important your family is to you, and I just want you to know that I will fight for you by fighting for the peace between me and your parents. Scripture encourages us to be peacemakers, and that's what I want to be in this situation. I love you, Rachel, and I do believe you deserve more than what I've been giving. If I am doing right by you, there should be no doubt in your mind that I care about not only you but also your family."

Where was he going with this?

"That being said—" he went down on one knee in front of her and pulled something out of his pocket "—I just want to assure you I'm all in when it comes to this. I am still so determined to marry you no matter what happens." He revealed what was in his hand. It was a diamond ring. "This was my mother's," he said. "She wasn't able to give it to me personally, but Dad had kept it all these years. He gave it to me this morning before I came to see you at the coffee shop. You don't have to wear it now, Rachel. You can wear it once I have your mother's blessing, but keep it until I've earned your trust. It's just a symbol of me being confident in what we heard from the Lord when we said yes to marrying each other."

Rachel didn't even hesitate, because of the confidence brought to her by the prayers the ladies had uttered earlier. "I'll wear it, Jeremy. I believe God can work through us to make our family whole."

The smile on his face made up for whatever conflict had been going on in the past months. When he slipped the engagement ring on her finger, he had this grin on his face and this twinkle in his eyes. Once the ring was on, he narrowed his eyes at her and said, "There's one more thing." He reached for his back pocket and handed her a small note. "This came with the box. It's in my mother's handwriting."

Curiosity flooded over Rachel, and it seemed it did the same to the other ladies, because they crowded around her. Rachel opened the note and gasped upon reading what it said.

Dear Jeremy, I have been reserving this ring for the woman you will someday marry. I'm praying that whomever you've chosen to give this to is a beautiful, God-fearing woman, but deep inside my heart, I'm sure you are already aware that a large part of me is still hoping you will someday marry Rachel Petersen. I believe there's something about the two of you together that can display God's ability to make the broken whole. If she's not the woman you're marrying, however, then laugh at your old mother's winsome musings and know that I bless whomever it is you have decided to marry. I'm sure you have chosen a lovely woman who will be the right help mate for you. If it is Rachel, though, my heart is delighted that you have made such a wonderful choice in the woman you are about to marry. I love you, Son. Love, Mama Aida

Someone sniffled behind her before Rachel could hold back the tear streaming down her face.

"Mama has always loved you, Rachel," Jeremy said.

She could barely make out Jeremy's face through the blurriness of her tears. "I have always loved her too."

He cupped her face in his hand. "She would be so happy right now."

"Like I am!" Serene exclaimed, tears already running down her face as she hugged her brother and then Rachel. Once that happened, the rest of the night turned into a hug fest, and as cheesy as it all seemed after, Rachel couldn't remember a time when she had felt as loved and accepted as she did then.

Now, all she had to do was to find a way to get her mother to experience love and acceptance the same way.

thirty-two

UPENDED TODAYS & UNKNOWN TOMORROWS

bead of sweat formed on Jeremy's brow. Rachel scrunched her nose at it, because it was winter time, and it was a particularly chilly day. Was he as nervous as she was? Did they not have a good reason to be? Seated in the living room of Rachel's childhood home, they were waiting for her mother to show up. Jeremy's grip on her hand tightened. Rachel flinched at the ache in her knuckles as his hold squeezed her fingers together.

"Jeremy," Rachel said.

He flinched and cast a glance her way. "What?"

She stared at his hand on hers.

"Too tight?"

She nodded.

He winced. "Sorry." He loosened his grip and rubbed the back of his neck with his free hand. "A little nervous," he admitted.

"I am, too." She bowed her head as she brushed her thumb against his skin.

"This feels like a make-or-break moment."

"It does," she said, "but we've been praying about this. God is with us tonight. He won't let this go sideways." She wished she was as confident inside as her words made her sound.

Jeremy didn't get the chance to respond, because Rachel's mother and father showed up beneath the arch leading to the living room. Both Jeremy and Rachel stood upon their arrival. Rachel and her mother caught each other's eyes. Their stare lingered before Rachel rushed forward to hug her mother.

"I'm sorry, Mom," she whispered.

Her mother stood stiff within her embrace. "We don't need to make this a dramatic scene."

Rachel's resolve floundered, but she squeezed her mother tight before letting go. Jeremy then took his turn, hugging her mom.

The way her mother's eyes widened made it clear this gesture from Jeremy surprised her. Rachel kept her smile toward her mother before giving her father a hug. The bags under his eyes betrayed how tired he was. Mom must have been putting him through the ringer. Rachel cringed. Was there more she could do for them? Why did she feel so helpless?

They all took their seats in the living room, with Rachel and Jeremy on the loveseat and Dad and Mom in two chairs separated by a end table of dark mahogany. Their hands held each other's as they laid it on the table between them. Rachel's heart warmed at her parents' clasped hands.

Mom was the first to speak after everyone had settled down. "I would like to apologize to all of you for my conduct the other night." It sounded like she was forcing the apology out of herself. "It was unbecoming of me to act the way I did, and I am not proud of how I handled my frustration that day. I was wrong taking that frustration out on you both." She directed her eyes at Jeremy. "I'm sorry, Mr. Sinclair. I shouldn't have said the things I said about you, but I hope you understand where I am coming from."

Rachel shifted in her seat, inching closer to her fiancé to show him her support, but also as a way for her to feel more protected through this confrontation.

Jeremy nodded. "Yes, Ma'am. I understand."

"Thank you. I'm grateful you still have space in your heart to hear me out." She then turned her focus on Rachel. The way she looked at her daughter, like she was so overcome with disappointment, shook Rachel. Her eyes dropped toward the ring on Rachel's finger, and her face crumpled in grief. "That ring was Aida's, wasn't it?"

Jeremy and Rachel exchanged glances before she nodded. "It is. How can you tell, Mom?"

At that, Mom scoffed. "I would recognize it anywhere. Things were never the same between the three of us — Sam, Aida, and me — since they got engaged. That ring changed everything."

Jeremy cleared his throat. "If you don't mind my asking, Mrs. P, what happened between you and my parents? Growing up, it was hard not to notice the rift between the three of you. More and more, it felt as if it was beyond repair, but none of you ever addressed the issue, and I've never understood it. Through all of it, though, I can assure you my mother loved you to her very last breath. Of that, I am confident."

"That is true, perhaps." Mom's gaze was distant, her eyes moist, her expression tender. "Believe it or not, Jeremy, I loved her, too. I was instrumental in leading your mother to Christ. Did she ever tell you that?"

Jeremy threw his head back in surprise. "Whenever we asked her about who had introduced her to God, she had always spoken of this old Samoan mama."

"Yes, that's right." Mom nodded. "Mama Vida led her to Christ in terms of sharing the Gospel to her and discipling her. She was the one who discipled Sam, Aida, and me. She taught us everything after we came to know Christ back in high school. It was me, however, who brought Aida there. She was my classmate. Your father, on the other hand, was Mama Vida's neighbor. She took all three of us under her wing."

Why had no one ever told her this story before? "And Dad?" Rachel asked.

"I didn't come along until after your mother was in college," Dad said.

Rachel creased her brows. "What happened?"

Mom smiled, her eyes glazing over, as if she was taking a trip down memory lane. "We were all in love with the Lord, and Mama Vida always showed impartiality to all three of us. She loved us all equally, and she taught us everything she knew about God. That was precious to us, because we all came from broken families. Sam, Aida, and I were only children coming from painful backgrounds, so we cherished all the love Mama Vida poured on us." Mom's shoulders hunched over as she fidgeted with her fingers, her gaze still distant as she continued her story.

"It was hard for us to go to college, because it meant leaving Mama Vida behind, but it never felt like she was too far away, because we kept writing letters to her, and she never failed to write back. At university, the three of us helped each other out as much as we could to get us through university. We shared rent, we worked odd jobs, and we shared the Gospel to whomever would listen to us. Sam and Aida were the closest thing I had to a brother and sister. We did almost everything together, as a team."

At that, Rachel and Jeremy exchanged glances. Through all the years they had seen their parents interact, they had seen nothing of the dynamic Mom was talking about.

"It was in our sophomore year that things changed," Mom continued. "We began a campus ministry almost on a whim. Just a few gatherings at first, but every week, more and more people came to know Christ. We always believed it was the fruit of Mama Vida's prayers, and we were more than eager to bring the harvest in. By the time we were seniors, we already had a team of leaders. Marcus and Naomi Grant were among them, and so was your father." She nodded at Rachel. "Mama Vida came to visit one of our gatherings once. I could never forget that particular visit, because that's when Sam proposed to Aida. We all expressed concern over how fast they were going, but they were both so sure that God wanted them to be together. Eventually, Mama Vida blessed their engagement. After their wedding, she ordained Sam as the pastor of Connect Church, while still recognizing that it was Sam, Aida, and me who pioneered the church."

"Sam and Aida took the lead," Dad said. "Most of us were for it. Sam and Aida had such love for people and the church. They made excellent pastors, and we were all willing to submit to their authority, but as time passed on, there was no denying how they pushed your mother to the side. None of us saw it as intentional on Sam and Aida's part. It happened naturally. Over time, Rhoda got edged out of the decision-making. It's like she was once part of leadership, one of the founders of Connect, and then she wasn't anymore."

"We were already finished with college when we bought the property you now know as Connect Church. It was nothing back then. Just an abandoned lot that used to be a skating rink or something like that. Do you remember, Robert?"

Dad nodded. "It was a mess. The structure was close to being condemned, but we rescued it and built it back up."

"Were you already married, then?" Rachel asked.

Mom shook her head. "Marcus and Naomi already had all six of their children when we were married."

"I didn't pursue your mother until much later in life, when I was already more stable in my finances, and I could offer her a secure life. Rhoda had such high standards, and I wanted to live up to it before pursuing her. Your mother was a stunner, but not many of the men in church pursued her. Too intimidated."

Despite the sadness in Mom's eyes, her smile widened as she looked lovingly at Rachel's father. "Not you."

"Not me."

Rachel had to smile at the love that still existed between her parents. Through thick and thin, they had stood by each other, and it warmed her heart to see them still able to look at each other in such a loving way after all these years.

"What happened to Mama Vida?" Jeremy asked.

Mom's face fell. She let go of Dad's hand and pushed her palms against her lap, as if to straighten her skirt. "The last time Mama Vida visited was the time she spoke blessing over Sam and Aida, as well as Connect Church. She said that many of the children of this church will grow up to be a blessing to the nations."

Rachel's breath hitched. Hadn't that come to pass? So many of the families in Connect were spread all across the globe, sharing the Gospel of the kingdom to all willing to listen. Even she and Jeremy intended to eventually travel overseas after getting married. A sense of loss came over Rachel. Why hadn't she known about Mama Vida until that day?

"Mama Vida said that Sam and Aida would father and mother many," Mom continued. "She spoke specifically to Aida and blessed her with the same anointing that God had given Mama Vida when she was still a little girl. A mother's heart. Since then, people have started calling Aida what you call her now. Mama Aida. After that visit, Mama Vida returned to Samoa to be with her family. Next time we heard of her, it was from her daughter informing us that she had gone on to heaven." A bitter smile formed on Mom's lips. "She was the only mother I've ever known, and before she passed away, she chose Aida over me." Tears threatened to fall from Mom's eyes, but she quickly wiped it away. She squared her shoulders as a way to fight back against the tears threatening to reveal her weakness and pain. "My father was a hard man, and he was the only family I had, because my mother died when I was still a little girl. He came to know Jesus later in life soon before he died, but he was an alcoholic for most of my life."

Rachel had never heard her mother speak of her grandfather before. The only thing she had ever heard about her grandfather was that he had been so happy when he had first met her as a two-year-old.

He had forgotten everyone because of his dementia — even Mom — but he had never forgotten Rachel. "Did Mama Vida never say anything to you about losing your standing as a leader in the church? Did she just brush you off like everyone else?" Rachel asked. "No word of comfort or encouragement at all?"

"Mama Vida was loving, but she was also tough and straightforward. A no-nonsense type of person." Mom sighed. "She taught us to be strong in the faith and to be resilient, so it wasn't like I could go to her and start whining over how Sam and Aida were running the church. She wouldn't have just rebuked me and told me to submit. I certainly didn't want to do anything to jeopardize my relationship with her, because we were still close. We talked. We still exchanged letters. She still loved me, but I was never able to shake the feeling that after Sam and Aida became a couple, she began favoring them over me. The last thing she ever said to me before she passed away was to guard my heart toward what I deem as unfair." This time, a tear escaped her left eye before she could wipe it away. It trickled down her cheek as she spoke, unaware of it. "Time and time again, your church—" she cast a glare at Jeremy "—has rejected, shunned, and abandoned me, and I would always remember what Mama Vida told me. To honor her, I tried to guard my heart from all the things that I saw as unfair about the way the church was treating me, but when Sam passed up Robert as the lead pastor of Connect Church, even after all the years we have served the ministry, I couldn't take it anymore. Max is a wonderful young man." She gave Rachel a stern look. "You know I believe this to be true."

"I know, Mom." Rachel nodded.

"But how is he more qualified than your father? I couldn't believe my ears when Sam announced it. I couldn't believe he was doing this to me all over again."

Rachel bristled at the way her mother kept emphasizing this injustice done against her. By trying to honor Mama Vida's final admonition to her, had Mom spent decades piling up all the hurt and bitterness within her? Unsure of how to respond to her mother, she addressed her father instead. "Dad, do you really want to pastor Connect Church? Can you not lead without being the lead pastor?"

Dad sighed. "I don't know if it's something I would say I want, but it's certainly something I expected. I understand where your mother is coming from. It did hurt when Sam announced that they were opting for Max to take over leadership of the church. Sam made it sound like he didn't even consider us. Your mother and I were hoping that he would have the grace to recognize our faithfulness throughout the years, because for decades, we have served Connect without asking for anything in return. Surely, you can recognize that."

Jeremy nodded. "I can definitely attest to that. I have seen it growing up. You've both been selfless in serving the church."

Rachel grabbed Jeremy's arm, grateful that he was quick to assure her parents.

"All of that didn't seem to matter." Mom's voice broke. "It was all so unfair. As if that wasn't difficult enough, my own daughter, whom I love with all my heart, decided to abandon me as well. It was more than I could take, Rachel."

Rachel's stomach flipped. "Mom—" What was she to say that could give her mother comfort? Unsure of what to say or do, Rachel let go of Jeremy and moved across the room so she could kneel in front of her mother. She laid her hands over Mom's knees and looked into her mother's eyes. "Sorry. I never meant to abandon you, though I understand now why you perceived it that way." Rachel buried her face in her mother's lap. "I should've been around to support you and listen to you. Instead, I went my own way and failed to honor you. You've always been so strong and so capable, Mom. I guess I can thank Mama Vida for toughening you up in a way, but it might have also contributed to why you've felt abandoned or neglected by others. You didn't seem to need me to be there for you, so I focused my energies on all the other people who were struggling and actively seeking my help. As for our wedding, of course I want you to be a part of it, Mom, but I don't know even know how to talk to you about it without fearing the possibility of hurting you simply because I'm marrying Jeremy."

As if to prove her point, Mom's countenance darkened at the mention of her marriage to Sam and Aida Sinclair's son. She averted her gaze from Rachel to Jeremy, her posture and expression stoic and tense. Her stare lingered on Jeremy before the contours of her face softened. She began brushing Rachel's hair. "No matter who you choose to marry, Rachel, it will be hard for me to deal with the idea of you getting married, because it's hard for me to let you go. I kind of wished you would marry someone who will keep you close to me, not someone who will most likely take you to the ends of the earth with him, but I see the way you two look at each other. You love this man. I can see it."

Rachel nodded. "Yes, Mom. I do, but I also love you. It would mean so much to both of us, if you were on board with this, but Jeremy and I have been talking, and we've both agreed. Until we have your complete blessing, we won't push through with this wedding."

Her mother's dim expression lit up and caused fear to grip Rachel's chest. Would Mom actually ask her not to marry Jeremy?

The moment lasted for an eternity before Mom shook her head. "I don't want to be the one to stand in the way of the love you've found in each other. All I'm asking is that you let me into your life once again. You're my only child, Rachel. I've prayed to God about your wedding and the man you will marry since you were born. Is it so hard to believe that I would want to be more involved in planning such a momentous day in your life?"

A weight rolled off of Rachel's chest, lightening her spirit and freeing her soul. "I hear you, Mom. To be honest, I'm so excited to show you my plans.

There are so many things about it I'm sure you'll love."

Mom grasped her hand. "A time for everything, Rachel. We'll catch up soon." She moved her head as a gesture for Rachel to return to her seat.

Once Rachel was sitting next to Jeremy, her mother shifted focus toward her fiancé.

Jeremy gulped.

Rachel patted his knee as a show of support, but her mother's glare was making even her squeamish.

"What to do with you, Mr. Sinclair?" Mom sighed. Her usual sharp and stern demeanor when addressing Jeremy disappeared into this softened expression that relieved Rachel. "I have wronged you, Son. It embarrasses me to say that throughout the years, I can think of multiple occasions when you have caught me speak critically about you, and not once have I ever apologized. God has done a wonderful work in your life, and far be it from me to deny His goodness by pretending that I don't see what a changed man you are. I'm glad it's you who will marry my daughter, if only because you are fully aware of how precious she is. I trust you won't take her for granted."

"Never." Jeremy spoke the word with so much conviction, one would need to have a targeted vendetta on him to not believe it. Rachel held her breath as he spoke out the next words. "Mrs. P, I love Rachel, and I have you and Mr. P to thank for the wonderful woman she has become. I admit I have held resentment against you over the years, and I apologize for that. I realize now that I cannot claim to love Rachel if I have no intention of honoring you both. Sir—" Jeremy nodded at Dad, then at Mom "—Ma'am, on behalf of Connect, I apologize for all the ways we've neglected you or pushed you to the sidelines. We have failed in so many ways to recognize your contribution to our community, and in so doing, we have failed to love you like God asks us to. I'm not speaking just for myself when I say we wish you would return. Rest assured that we will welcome you with open arms."

A long silence followed — long enough for Rachel to fear that Jeremy might have said the wrong thing. Dad rubbed Mom's shoulder. Their eyes locked and lingered in each other's gazes, like they were communicating solely through eye contact.

Mom bit her lip before addressing Jeremy. "I can't blame you for holding resentment against me. I hope you can forgive me for the ways I have wronged you and your family."

"Forgiven," Jeremy said.

"As for the apology on behalf of the church," Dad said, "we appreciate the gesture, and we thank you for the assurance of an open-arm welcome. However, this is a time for Rhoda and me to get on our knees, humble ourselves, and seek God. We both are in a broken place and are willing to acquiesce to whatever God leads us to do. If you both can pray for us at this time, we would appreciate it."

"Of course. Our hearts and prayers are with you," Jeremy assured. "If there's any way I can serve you both in this season, please let me know."

"That's a kind offer." Dad smiled. "We will keep that in mind, Jeremy. Thank you."

An awkward silence followed, none of them sure how to proceed with this new atmosphere of forgiveness and reconciliation now permeating the room.

Jeremy mouthed at Rachel, "What now?"

She shrugged.

To her surprise, her mother laughed. "Enough of the tears and the melancholy now. How about you tell me about your wedding and about that play you've been working on?"

Rachel almost cried upon seeing the genuine smile on her mother's lips. Rhoda Petersen's countenance now held so much light, like a veil had been lifted, revealing once again her joy, her peace, and her beauty. For the first time since she had returned from overseas, Rachel felt free to gush about her wedding and express excitement over her future. She spent the rest of the afternoon with her mother, while her father and Jeremy took time to get to know each other one-on-one.

And so, that afternoon, Rachel's family — past and future — merged into one, and together, they walked along life's road to wholeness and healing.

Unfortunately, the road was longer than Rachel had hoped it would be, because in the weeks to come, her parents still refused to lay down their arms and return to Connect Church.

thirty-three

REDEEMING PLAYS & REVERENT PRAISE

A cacophony of voices rang through the earpiece in Rachel's ear as she rushed to the entrance of the theater they had hired for the three-day run of *Once Upon a Prodigal*. She checked off several items on the to-do list on her clipboard and tapped the butt of her pen on her chin. She needed to check in with Serene to find out if she had already gotten the supplies she needed to fix the broken set piece. Was Jenna still in her dressing room, hanging from a hoop like a sleeping bat? Rachel would have to check, because two of the dancers were arguing over whether or not they were practicing the latest choreography.

All of that would have to wait until later, though. Rachel checked her watch as she passed the lobby to get to the theater entrance. Her parents would be here any moment now.

"How is my stunning girlfriend tonight?" Jeremy shoved a camera in her face as he walked in step with her.

"Busy!" she exclaimed, the smile on her face never wavering. "Mom and Dad are almost here."

"Wonderful," he said, though his eyes widened at her in mock panic. "Allow me to join you as you fetch Father and Mother dearest. Is everything working according to plan? Would you like to share with the audience what it is like to produce something like this, Miss Executive Producer?" he asked as they hurried toward the main entrance, where her parents would soon arrive.

"I think we'll have a full house tonight. Good job on promotions." She patted him on the shoulder.

"Thank you." He bowed his head. "And everyone else? Everything in order?"

"Jenna, our choreographer, is reprising her role as the angel suspended mid-air, but she's hanging on her hoop like a meditating bat while two of her dancers are trying to figure out the latest choreography. Serene, our set designer, is on her pregnancy's third term, and she's waddling about with a paintbrush, adding finishing touches to her magnificent set pieces and repairing the one that broke during final rehearsals yesterday. Nova, our script writer, is cool as a cucumber as she sits in the front row with Nolan, who wrote all the songs. Brother and sister hoarded some major artistic talent, I tell you. Max, our technical director, is freaking out somewhere over something related to technology. I didn't understand most of what he said. Caleb, our lead actor, is memorizing his lines, while babysitting his niece and his teenage twins, who all have roles in the play tonight. Good recap for you?"

"Perfect." Jeremy then pointed the camera at the entrance. "Now, for the most important part of this event. The arrival of the couple who could star in a play called *Never Once a Prodigal*!"

Just as he finished saying the words, Rachel's parents arrived in their car. While Dad tossed the keys to the valet, Rachel hugged her mother.

"There are so many people here, Rachel!" Mom exclaimed. There was something about her that was softer around the edges compared to before. She even waved at the crowd waiting to enter the theater.

"Hello, Son." Dad hugged Jeremy, who had enough good sense to drop the camera for a few minutes to give her parents a proper welcome, before embracing Rachel.

"I have to take you guys to your seats right now." Rachel ushered her parents into the building. "They're going to start admitting people in soon, and it'll be chaos when that happens, so it's best you get comfortable now. You're in the front row with Pastor Sam and all the other parents. I hope you don't mind?"

Mom took a deep breath. "Will Tabitha be there?"

Rachel nodded. "I made it a point to sit you next to her."

Mom squeezed her hand and smiled. "Thank you."

"Honey, we have our tickets. Our seat numbers are there. I'm sure we can figure things out from here," Dad said. "You seem to have a lot on your plate right now, so go and take care of whatever's next on your list." He gave her clipboard a pointed look.

"You sure?" Rachel asked.

"We're sure." Dad laid his hand on the small of Mom's back. "Now, go. We're excited to see what you've been working on."

Rachel pressed her palms together in prayer, her clipboard secured under her armpit. "Please pray that everything will go well."

"We will!"

Her father and mother proceeded across the lobby and to the main theater while Rachel hurried off backstage with Jeremy, following her with his camera still pointed at her.

"What are you? Paparazzi?" Rachel made a face at Jeremy.

"This is footage for our documentary," he said. "Besides, my followers can't get enough of you."

Rachel smiled and waved at the camera before addressing his audience. "It's crazy back here, and I wish Jeremy would take footage of someone else. Anyone else other than me."

Jeremy laughed before pointing the camera towards himself. "Can you blame me? I can't help it. She looks amazing, even in all the madness of opening night. It's crazy in here!"

As Jeremy addressed his social media following, Rachel hurried on from task to task, all the while saying a prayer on behalf of the play and her parents, hoping that a spirit of reconciliation would touch their hearts, and any rift in their relationships would reach full restoration.

Despite how preoccupied she was with making sure everything was going according to plan, Rachel carried that prayer in her heart for the rest of the night. To her relief, apart from a few mishaps that they easily fixed, the play flowed smoothly, with every song and every scene going on as wonderfully as they had hoped it would. When the cast delivered their final lines, the lights opened, and the curtains closed. A hush swept across the theater before wild applause filled it. When the curtains re-opened, Rachel stood backstage, stunned at the sight of all the people standing on their feet.

The actors bowed on stage. Once all the cast and crew had finished curtsying, Caleb pointed at Rachel, while Nova dragged Jeremy to the stage. This was it. The moment they had been praying and preparing for. This was the real measure of whether or not this play would be a success. Rachel had tears in her eyes when she stood next to Jeremy on stage. The cast and crew left, and the crowd stayed seated, most of them probably wondering who Rachel and Jeremy were.

Jeremy spoke through the microphone. "Hello. I'm Jeremy Sinclair, and this is my soon-to-be-wife, Rachel Petersen. You might know me from my Podcast and my videos promoting this play, and Rachel is one of the executive producers of this show."

Someone in the crowd started clapping loudly. "You both did a great job!" someone yelled. Applause followed.

Once it died down, Jeremy grinned at the crowd they could barely see because of the spotlight glaring at them. "Thanks for that," he said. "There are a lot of people who made this play possible, and we would like to thank everyone who worked with us to make tonight happen, but this play goes back several generations. Rachel and I are here to share a little about how this play came to be."

He handed the microphone to Rachel.

Her heart was pounding against her chest. She was shaking so hard, mostly because of her awareness of the significance of the play and how she hoped it would impact her parents. She smiled at the audience before speaking into the microphone. "Many of the talented people who are part of this play come from our church, and it is a church that isn't perfect, but it is a church that we love. A lot of us grew up at Connect Church, which I'd like to believe has also been growing in its maturity and love for Jesus, as we ourselves did. We've been going through a rough time these months, but the cast and crew of this play would like to take this opportunity to remind everyone of how faithful God has been to this church over the almost four decades of its existence. There are several generations of Connect Church that are represented here, and we would like to show you this video to remind you of the roots of this family of believers."

Behind them, the LCD screen started playing a video that Jeremy and Rachel had been working on together, a project triggered by the conversation they had shared with Rachel's parents months before. The video showed old pictures they had dug up of Mama Vida, Jeremy's parents, and Rachel's mom. On screen, flashed images and videos of campus gatherings, the first few meetings of Connect Church in the dilapidated property that had now become their beautiful church building. Finally, the video showed a group picture of the families of Connect Church from a summer camp they held a year ago. Everyone was together, with big smiles on their faces.

When the video ended, and Jeremy and Rachel walked out on stage, the first thing they saw was Rachel's father and mother hugging Pastor Sam. All three of them were in tears.

It was only when Rachel saw that scene that she could say *Once Upon a Prodigal* was indeed a success.

On the Sunday after the limited run of *Once Upon a Prodigal*, gratefulness stemmed out of Rachel's heart when she entered the lobby to find her father and mother there. They were having a conversation with Pastor Sam, laughing over something. It was as if they had never left to begin with.

The gratitude turned into reverence toward a God Who was in control of their situation, but something told Rachel that God was far from finished just yet. He still had more in store for them.

After all, that week, she was finally going to marry the love of her life.

Worship gushed out of her as she lifted her heart and soul to a God Who, no doubt, cared. So caught up in the glory, Rachel didn't notice when the worship team started winding down the music until Mom took hold of her hand.

An unusual sign of affection, Mom kissed her on the cheek. "I don't say this enough, Rachel, but I love you."

"You don't need to say it, Mom. You've shown me your love many times over."

They sat down as Pastor Sam took his place on stage. "I'm not sharing the Word today, but I wanted to get up here to give the Sunday announcements and take the opportunity to acknowledge the hard work so many of you did to produce and pull off *Once Upon a Prodigal*. Can everyone with any involvement in putting this play together stand up, please?"

Rachel stood along with almost half of the congregation. The rest who remained seated clapped to acknowledge them. From the front row, Jeremy turned to lock eyes with her. He pointed at her before clapping. She did the same for him.

"Thank you for all the hard work you guys did. The play was such a testament of God's love and ability to restore the relationships of prodigal sons and daughters not only to Him but also to their fellow Christians. Many lives were touched by the performance." Pastor Sam laid his palm over his heart. "Mine certainly was. From the bottom of our hearts, thank you. Your hard work, talent, and passion haven't gone unnoticed, and surely, God has recorded the service you have given out of love for Him in His book of remembrance. Let's give them all another round of applause, shall we?"

Claps and cheers echoed throughout their church hall as Pastor Sam gestured for them to sit down.

"As great as the artistry was behind the play," Pastor Sam continued, "I admit that what touched my heart the most was the video my son, Jeremy, and his fiancée, Rachel, showed at the end of each run of the play." Pastor Sam's voice cracked as he finished the sentence. "It was such a reminder of God's faithfulness toward our church, as well as all the people who have helped make it what it is right now. I'm glad to have Rhoda and Robert back here this morning. They are pillars of this church, and I apologize for having overlooked their contribution to this congregation for years." Pastor Sam bowed his head at Rachel's parents. "Robert, Rhoda, please forgive me. You are valued here, and we thank you for the many ways you have served this community."

Mom's hold on Rachel tightened. Rachel rubbed her mother's shoulder with her free hand. Both her parents nodded at Pastor Sam to acknowledge the apology.

"This is a season of transition for our church. There are a lot of changes ahead, and you will hear more on this in the coming weeks, but for now, I'd like to call our very own Jenna Owens, wife of our future pastor. Max will share the Word later this morning, but before he takes the stage, Jenna has something in her heart that she'd like to share with us. As a little background, Jenna has taken over

Lady Lacey League, an organization started by Max's mother, Annette. It is an organization that promotes Godly purity. A good chunk of the profits of the play will go to support this organization, but Jenna is about to tell us how God has been leading her to steer the organization forward."

Jenna jogged up the stairs and took the microphone from Pastor Sam, who returned to his seat.

Seeing her best friend on stage made Rachel smile. She couldn't be more proud of Jenna.

Jenna wrung her hands before taking the microphone and sharing about how *Lady Lacey League* would now become a part of a broader organization called *Prodigals Once*. The aim was to seek out unchurched youth who want help to get out of reckless living and back to the arms of their Savior. As Jenna spoke, it was almost impossible for Rachel to believe that Jenna herself had once been a prodigal.

"I believe this is high time for the prodigals to return to the Father, and for us to start living out His kingdom life, displaying what it is like to be part of a kingdom family," Jenna said. "My own family is a testimony of what God can do to restore families back to Himself." Jenna waved at her mother, Eden, who was sitting next to Max's mother, Annette.

Jenna had just begun introducing another aspect of her organization, seeking to help connect foster kids to Godly homes, when Nova came up to Rachel and whispered in her ear, "Do you have plans for after the service?"

Rachel nodded. "I have lunch with Jeremy and my parents."

"Never mind that." Nova shook her head. "Come join us for lunch. You and your mom. Caleb plans to invite several men out, including your father and Jeremy."

"Oh." Rachel creased her brows. "Sure."

Nova squeezed her arm. "See you later," she said, before returning to her seat.

Curiosity got to Rachel, but the rest of the service edged out her inquisitiveness over what Nova had planned.

Max shared about God's plan to reconcile His people — Jews and Gentiles — together to form one family in Him. Rachel hung on every word, even as her heart ached for unity in the Body of Christ. So captured by what Max was sharing, she barely noticed how time zoomed by, until Max asked everyone to rise for a time of activation and reflection.

As Rachel focused on the Lord, faith continued to blossom within her as she believed for God to finish what He had started in uniting their church family. Her heart full at the end of the service, Rachel walked into the lobby with a huge smile on her face.

Jeremy squeezed through the gathering of various groups of people in the lobby to get to her. "Caleb invited your dad and me to lunch fellowship with some of the other men."

"Yeah." Rachel nodded at him. "Nova told me. She has plans for Mom and me."

Jeremy's eyes narrowed. "Interesting. What are those two cooking up? Any ideas?"

"Beats me."

"Well, we're about to find out. We need to leave soon. You and Mrs. P are good?"

"We'll survive."

"Perfect." Jeremy kissed her on the cheek. "Have a great time." He winked at her.

Her brows flicked up in surprise. Did he know something about these impromptu gatherings that she didn't?

With a big grin, Jeremy strode toward Max, who was standing by the door with Jenna, shaking hands with people, who were giving him encouragement over the Word he had shared.

Behind Rachel, someone harrumphed. When she turned around, she found her mother there, a brow lifted at Max. "He has a long way to go, before he can match Sam."

Rachel chuckled. She linked arms with her mother. "Since when was matching Pastor Sam the goal? Besides, Max isn't even thirty. You're right about him not being ready, but that's why he has you and Dad and all these men and women who love God backing him up, interceding for him, and counseling him."

Mom sighed. "You're right, of course. He's certainly better than Sam was at that age. Anyway, has Nova told you about this plan of hers?"

"She did." Rachel scanned the crowd surrounding her. "Have you seen her? I'm not sure where to go." She stood on her tiptoes and stretched her neck to look over the multiple little huddles congregating in the lobby. She couldn't find either Nova or Serene. Standing back on her feet, Rachel sighed. "We can just wait until they show up, I guess."

Mom pointed behind Rachel, and almost immediately, Jenna appeared beside Rachel. She placed her arm around Rachel's waist and pulled her in for a quick side hug. "This is going to be amazing," she said.

"What's going to be amazing?" Rachel asked.

"Come with me and find out." Jenna grinned. "Hi, Mrs. P." Without hesitation, Jenna pulled Mom in for a hug as well.

At first, Mom was stiff against Jenna's embrace, but she eventually eased into it. "Hello, Jenna."

"It's good to see you here." Jenna placed her palm over her chest.

"It was good to hear you talk so passionately about your non-profit. It's a good cause that we would love to fully support. We need more Christian organizations helping foster kids find good homes and a healthy environment where they can flourish."

Jenna leaped to her feet with excitement over the work she was doing. "That is the heart behind the organization, for sure."

"It's nice to see you so eager to take this on, Jenna." Mom took hold of Jenna's hand. "You have blossomed over the years, and it's been a pleasure to witness God's hand throughout your life, forming you into the woman you are now."

"Thank you, Mrs. P. That means a lot coming from you." Jenna smiled. "But!" She lifted a forefinger. "We need to go." She winked at Rachel. They followed her past the lobby to the hallway leading to the Sunday School area. "We've all been so busy with the play, but since I'm still the matron-of-honor for your wedding—" Jenna curtsied "—I didn't want you to think that I was shirking my duties." Jenna stopped in front of the Sunday School room.

"Jenna, what did you do?" Rachel asked.

Her best friend winked in response before pushing the door open to reveal the room completely transformed. Shiny streamers hung from the ceiling. Fairy lights twisted around twine, going from ceiling to floor. Clipped to the twine by tiny decorative wooden clothes-hangers were pictures of Rachel from her childhood to her adult years.

"So, this was what you were asking Rachel's childhood photos for," Mom told Jenna.

"Serene, Nova, and I — Hannah, also — have been planning this for weeks," Jenna said. "There were many willing to contribute."

Mom stopped in front of one photo that Jeremy had taken of Rachel. "You're so lovely here."

Beside the image was a note from Jeremy: *Couldn't stop staring at this photo long after I shot it. One of my growing list of favorites when it comes to shots of Rachel. She is undoubtedly my muse.*

Rachel didn't think she was capable of loving someone this much. Once they passed through the photo exhibit, behind it was a feast surrounded by the ladies of Connect Church. All around, square banners of different colors — mimicking sticky notes — hung from the ceiling with short, jotted notes on it of how Rachel had been a blessing in their lives.

Before they shared a meal together, one by one, the women of Connect Church shared memories of Rachel and how she had, in one way or another, served them, prayed for them, and been a blessing to them.

Finally, it was Serene's turn to speak. This time, however, it wasn't Rachel whom she appreciated.

"I believe Rachel already knows how much I adore her, how much my family adores her, and it's an understatement for me to express how thrilled I am that she will soon be my sister-in-law. Believe it or not, I still keep reminding my brother how blessed he is to end up with someone like you, Rachel—" Serene chuckled "—and he should never take that for granted." A thoughtful smile appeared on her face before she lowered her green eyes. "This afternoon, however, the woman I'd like to acknowledge is Mrs. P." She gave Mom a nod. "We've had our ups and downs through the years, Mrs. P, but I think we've all fallen short of giving you the recognition and understanding you deserve. You have been so passionate about setting a righteous standard for many of us, and that is reflected even in the way you raised Rachel. She is the lovely, amazing woman she is now, because you and Mr. P raised her this way, and all our lives have been subsequently blessed by hers. But more than just being Rachel's mother, you have been passionate about challenging us to walk in God's ways. You have been constantly reminding us that our loyalty must belong to God, so even when we have to make difficult decisions, we stand by those choices to honor Him. Thank you, Mrs. P. In a lot of ways, you raised not only Rachel, but us, too. You have truly been a mother to this church."

"Amen!" Nova raised a cup to that.

When Rachel turned to thank her mother, she found Rhoda Petersen in tears, and somehow, it felt to Rachel like finally, "the other brother" just realized she had been loved all along.

PART FIVE

The Other Brother and the Prodigal Son

RHODA & JEREMY

RHODA
& THE
RUINED

When the daughter of Aida Sinclair called her a mother to Connect Church, a dam broke within Rhoda, like a release of decades' worth of pent-up frustration over being constantly painted as some sort of villain reprimanding everyone for their wayward ways. She had come to realize through the experiences of the past months that she had gone about all of it in the wrong way and had wrestled with God many times regarding this issue. Still, it was her heart's passion for God's truth and holiness driving her to those measures. In her core, she did love all these women and only wanted God's best for them. That had been her heartbeat since coming to know Jesus, but tainted by her bitterness and own self-righteousness, she had only pushed people away and hurt them.

With Serene now addressing her contribution to Connect Church and recognizing the heart behind it, Rhoda's heart twisted with longing for Aida's presence. How she missed Aida! How she wished she could take everything back — all the criticism and resentment she had thrown Sam and Aida's way. As Serene spoke, Rhoda faltered next to her daughter, who quickly wrapped her in a warm embrace.

Right then, the older women of Connect — some of which had been Rhoda's friends for decades —

started taking their turns to appreciate her. Rhoda held herself together as she listened to them speak and give her appreciation.

Finally, the time came when they gave her space to address everyone. Rhoda cleared her throat and nodded. "These months have shown me how rough I am around the edges and how so many of you have adjusted to me and tried to accept me, as I am. I come off as abrasive and tactless, and I've never apologized for it. I shudder at the thought that, in my zealousness, I might have been a stumbling block to many. It took these past weeks for me to realize just how much bitterness and resentment I've been holding onto in my heart and how I weaponized my pain to justify my lack of grace, mercy, and love." She swallowed hard. "I apologize. There are many of you I hurt through the years, and I ask for your forgiveness. The Lord is still teaching me to discern His heart and will and not just act out of how I believe things ought to be. In that regard, I am definitely still a work in progress. I am learning to speak truth in love, and I thank you for those of you who have shown me kindness throughout these years." Rhoda caught Nova's eyes and nodded toward her. Nova wiped away a tear.

In that moment, it was as if God opened her eyes to what He had given her all along. Even through seasons when she hadn't realized it, God had given her a family who had been there for her, even when she wasn't aware of their presence and support.

She shouldn't focus on the things she deemed unfair, because God's grace had never been fair, and therein lay the beauty of His magnificent grace.

Rhoda shifted in the passenger seat as her husband drove through the neighborhood she had once always dreaded visiting — the one where Sam and Aida had built a home and raised a family together.

"You all right?" Robert asked.

She nodded. "Better than I ever have been before."

"Then why all the fidgeting?"

"I don't know." Rhoda shrugged. Even she could tell there was less of an edge in her tone. "It's still strange to spend time with Sam, especially now that everyone knows the root of why I've been so critical of them all these years."

"Fair." Robert slowed their car down in front of the house. "All this time, were you aware of this resentment, Rhoda?"

"I was," Rhoda admitted. The memory of an emotionally tumultuous afternoon that led her to the driveway of Serene Stone flashed through her mind. "There was even this one time when I felt like having a discussion with Serene about all the hurt her mother had caused me. I was already on their driveway, but I caught myself, and backed out when I saw Nova approaching the Stone mansion with her children."

"How have I not heard of this?" Robert asked.

"I didn't feel the need to inform you of actions I myself could not understand, much less explain. All these years, I found it difficult to admit to myself that was the reason I was acting out. The undercurrent of bitterness and self-pity has always been there, and I've tried to bury it in layers of what I thought was the kind of forgiveness God wanted me to exhibit, but all I really did was deny myself healing."

"And now?"

Rhoda smiled at her husband. "I see you, Robert, and I see how good God has been to me. I've been so focused on the things that have been taken away from me, I didn't fully appreciate the things God has given me. I love you so much."

"I love you too, Rhoda. God allowed all of this for our good. I believe it."

"So do I."

Robert parked the car before turning to her. "Ready?"

She nodded. They headed on to the Sinclair residence to fellowship with Rachel's future in-laws, as they all prepared for the upcoming wedding of their children. That day, a sense of family and togetherness permeated the atmosphere, and for the first time in her life, Rhoda felt loved enough to have confidence that she no longer needed to keep proving herself worthy.

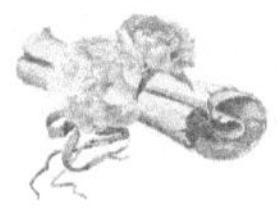

Jeremy and Rachel had been so right. The waterfall provided a stunning backdrop to their garden wedding, and in the wee hours of dawn, Rhoda discovered a strange hankering to slip out of the hotel room and spend her morning devotions by the lake and the gushing waterfalls.

Her toes dipped in the cool water with the sun's rays slowly spreading over her surroundings. Rhoda sat on a smooth, large rock, dangling her legs over it. She wrote quietly in her journal as a way to process one of the most important days of her life: her daughter's wedding.

I remember the morning of my wedding and how full my heart was when it came to marrying Robert. It was one of the few days I wasn't thinking about all the things in life that were unfair, and what a bad hand life had dealt me. Today should be one of those days, where I'm just so full of joy and happiness over how precious this day is for my beloved Rachel, but I can't help it. Aida is on my mind today. We always joked that she was the prodigal son, and I was the other brother, because I have always been a straight arrow, and she has always been more on the reckless side when I first met her. Now, as if to prove the existence of God's sense of humor, my precious Rachel — straight arrow, that she is — is about to marry Aida's reckless Jeremy.

And I couldn't be happier for them, because if I set aside my filters and see them for what they are, I can understand why God brought them together. They complement each other the way Aida and I once did, the way Robert and I do now. He is the calm to my chaos, and I thank God for bringing him to me at just the right time.

I pray for today's wedding. I can scarcely believe that my Rachel will become one of the Sinclairs, and by association, so will I. It's ironic, but I'm sure God is smiling about it. He's just interesting that way. Thank You, God, for bringing Jeremy and Rachel together. Whatever Your plans are, I am certain it will be the best for both of them. Bless this day. Bless my daughter, and yes, bless my son.

Right after she put a period on that last sentence, a flash of a camera jolted her out of her reverie. She turned her head to the source of the clicking sound and found Jeremy pointing his camera at her.

He looked up from the camera and smiled. He still wasn't dressed for the wedding and was walking around in a white polo, khaki shorts, and brown leather sandals. "Rachel takes after her mother when it comes to beauty," he said.

"You already have my approval to marry Rachel, Mr. Sinclair. No need for the flattery." Rhoda reserved her smile for later, when her soon-to-be son-in-law could figure out a way to deserve it. "Besides, I wouldn't say Rachel takes after me completely. She also has a lot of Robert's features."

"True." Jeremy nodded. "You both gave her great genes." He approached her, kicked off his sandals toward the grass, and sat next to her on the rock. "I hope you don't mind me disturbing your peace."

"The deed is done. You might as well stay."

He chuckled and said, "Thank you," before opening the screen of his camera.

Rhoda set her eyes on the rippling waters beneath her bare feet, now right next to Jeremy's.

He showed her the image he had just snapped. It was of her writing in her journal, this distant, pensive look on her face, but a smile was on her lips, with her blonde hair — already streaked with silver — brushed to the side.

"See?" Jeremy smiled. "Beautiful."

"You take great shots. Nova told me you shot some of my favorite images of my daughter."

"As I said—" Jeremy shrugged one shoulder "—she's my muse."

Silence followed as the waterfalls continued to gush into the river lake. It reminded Rhoda of how the deep called out to deep, as mentioned in Scripture.

"Thank you, Mrs. P," Jeremy said.

"For what?"

"For giving this wedding your blessing. It means the world to Rachel to have you on board, and I don't say it enough, but it means the world to me as well."

"Take care of her, okay?" The words came out of Rhoda's lips with more force than she had intended. "She's so precious to me."

"I will cherish her my entire life." Jeremy's lip twitched. "I'm aware I'm not what you had in mind when you foresaw who she might marry, and I can't promise we'll stay put in here and give her the house with the white picket fence and all that. The American dream, after all, was never mine."

"I am aware. The moment I started seeing sparks of interest between you and Rachel, I began to accept the possibility in my heart that you might whisk her away to one country after another."

Jeremy narrowed his eyes at her. "When exactly did you start seeing those sparks of interest, Mrs. P?"

"Long before either of you recognized it. With you, I've seen it since you were a young man. You've always cherished and looked after Rachel, even when you were in your wild, juvenile years."

Jeremy smirked. "That was how you saw me? A wild juvenile?"

"If the shoe fits. You fought your way out of it, and you're now at least a lot more decent than you were back then. Just don't fall into old patterns."

"With you as my mother-in-law, I doubt it could even be possible. We would, for sure, receive your much needed intervention, should I be foolish enough to revert to old ways."

"Oh, I will intervene—" Rhoda caught herself as a sigh escaped her. "At least I will want to, but I also know that the moment your marriage to my daughter becomes official, I am no longer the authority over her life. You are. It scares me to think of that."

"To be honest, it scares me, too," Jeremy said. "I don't want to mess this up."

"My Rachel has proved herself stronger and more capable than we've ever given her credit for. I doubt she'll allow you to mess up."

"Heh." Jeremy nodded. "I'm counting on that."

Another period of silence followed as both of them stared at their feet wading in the river. And it was as if God's depth was calling out to theirs to plunge into the rivers of his grace.

"Jeremy," Rhoda said.

"Yes?"

"I think it's high time you stop calling me Mrs. P."

"What would you rather I call you?"

"You can call me Mom, if you'd like."

The grin on his face showed his delight over what she said. "I would love that. Mom, it is then."

At that point, the sun was already steadily climbing toward its peak. The comfortable silence between them continued as they headed toward the breakfast buffet, ready to face the day that would eventually end with Jeremy Sinclair and Rachel Petersen becoming husband and wife.

thirty-five

JEREMY
& THE
JOYOUS

An intoxicating mixture of peace, joy, and gratitude filled Jeremy as he and "Mom" returned to the log cabin where a breakfast buffet was already waiting. Before they reached the dining area, however, soft hands held his elbow and made him stop.

The blue eyes that mirrored that of the woman he was about to marry looked up at him as a soft smile appeared on Rhoda Petersen's face. "Before we go, I just remembered something Aida used to pray for when we were still in high school. We often prayed about the men we would someday marry and the children we would have with them. Your mother always prayed to have a son someday. Even back then, she insisted she would someday name her son Jeremy, after the prophet, Jeremiah, because she longed for a son who would learn to serve the Lord even as a young person."

Jeremy choked at the words his soon-to-be mother-in-law was telling him. Why was she bringing up all of this now? His heart ached over how much he missed his own mother, and how much he wished Mama Aida could be here for this day.

"Jeremy means 'lifted up or exalted by God'. I believe in God's power to lift us up from wherever we are, in his perfect time, and I release that blessing over you and Rachel right now, Jeremy. He will guide you according to His plans. I trust you will have a marriage where you will both lift each other up and encourage each other so that God may be exalted in your lives. Finally—" she smiled "—though we did drift apart during the later years of our lives, I still do know Aida and her heart in a unique way, because I'm the only one who witnessed who she was before she came to Christ. Jeremy, you're so much like her, it astounds me. Serene takes more after your father in how reserved and balanced she is, but you— You're the one who takes after Aida, and if she can see you right now and the man you have become, mark my words, Son. She would be so proud of you."

The tears brimmed Jeremy's eyes, and he quickly wiped away a tear that trickled down his cheek before it could reach his chin. "Thank you, Mom," he said. "You can't imagine how much those words mean to me. I miss her so much."

His new mother smiled and nodded, and Jeremy knew she meant it with all her heart when she responded, "So do I."

After finishing a cup of brewed coffee, Jeremy retreated from everyone and went to the bedroom where the groom's clothes had already been laid out on the bed. In less than an hour, the camera crew would arrive to photograph and film him for the video to be shown later.

In the solitude, Jeremy put up his camera on the stand, connected it to his laptop, and pointed it to himself. He then started recording while streaming live to his social media network. "Hello, everyone!" He nodded his head at the camera and made a face. "I can't believe it. Today is the day. I am about to marry the love of my life, and the great thing about it is I started the day with her mother. That's right. I'm already pals with my mother-in-law. To be honest, I wasn't sure that would be possible, but here we are now. Nothing is impossible if we have faith in God coming through for us. He has definitely been coming through for Rachel and me. I can't wait to marry her!"

A knock on the door interrupted his live broadcast. Instead of ending the recording, Jeremy hurried to the door and let Max in. "You know my man, Maximus," he said to the camera. "He's been my best friend since childhood and has saved my life more times than I can count. Say hi, Max."

Max gave him a funny look before waving at the camera. "You're not going to film the whole wedding, are you?" Max asked.

Jeremy grinned. "Should I?"

Max laughed. "You tell me."

Jeremy focused on the camera and gave his audience a huge smile. "You all have been part of our love story — Rachel and me — and we're grateful for you. However, the reason I wanted to drop by your screens this morning is to let everyone know that as grateful as we are for all you guys have contributed to our lives in terms of your support and encouragement, this is a day I would love to keep intimate, a day I want to record and cherish in my heart without worrying about how to frame a perfect shot. Until our wedding update, dear friends, I have to disconnect." Jeremy kissed his two fingers before saying, "Love you! Peace out!" He turned the camera off and gave himself fully to this day, because he refused to miss a single minute of it.

The rest of the morning flew by quickly, and shots of adrenaline carried Jeremy through it until finally, he was standing at the end of the aisle, watching his bride approach him. As she walked, it struck him how so like the Bride of Christ Rachel was. Imperfect, but made pure and holy by the sacrifice of Christ. As the Bride needed to submit to the will of God to refine her into becoming more like the ready bride she needed to be, so Rachel needed to submit to the will of God, time and time again, throughout her life. The mere knowledge of how much Rachel wanted to serve and obey God was enough to challenge Jeremy to become the best man he could be for her and their future family. The one prayer circling his mind was that he would be able to honor her and love her the same way God loved the church.

When Rachel finally reached him, and he took her hand from her father to lead her to the altar, there was a sacred reverence filling him. He was often the kind of person who tried to keep things light and easy. Most of the people in his life would describe him as carefree or free-spirited. But that ceremony carried a weight about it that Jeremy couldn't take lightly. He had never been responsible for any other life, besides his own, for so long, and now, this incredible woman was about to become his wife — someone he was committing to love, protect, and cherish for the rest of his life.

Even as he said his vows to her, Jeremy felt the weight of each word he was speaking.

"Rachel," he said. "The more I think about it, the more I wonder if I've always been in love with you, I just didn't have the courage to call it love. You make me want to become a better man. You make me want to become a better follower of Christ, and I stand here today, dumbfounded, and so deeply grateful that God would entrust a woman like you to me. Thank you for being willing to follow me as I follow Christ. Before all our loved ones, our family and friends, today, I pledge myself to you as I take you to be my wedded wife, and in doing so, before the Lord, I commit to honor you, love you, and protect you. I will be the kind of husband worthy of your respect. I love you, Rachel, and I want to honor you not only with my words, but with the way I live my life."

Rachel smiled. "Jeremy, I didn't think you would be the kind of man I would willingly follow everywhere, but somehow, God brought us together, and by doing so, He also managed to bring our families and communities together. You know things about me that most don't know, and you loved me anyway, and I believe that is why our union can bring healing to others, because we ourselves have experienced healing. I am honored to be your wife, to be the one who will serve you and love you and be the mother of your children. Thank you for loving me, not only for what you see, but because of — and sometimes, despite of — everything that makes me who I am. I love you, Jeremy."

There was a surreal nature to everything that followed, mostly because Jeremy felt like he was floating as they put the rings on each other's fingers. Finally, Pastor Sam instructed him to kiss the bride.

Jeremy lifted the veil and smiled at his beautiful bride before gently holding her chin between his fingers and pressing his lips against hers for the very first time. As their kiss deepened, her lips trembling against his, Jeremy still couldn't believe that God had taken him this far.

Only then, when they finally declared Rachel to be his lawfully wedded wife, did Jeremy feel like he was no longer a prodigal son. No. At that moment, he became one among those who were prodigals once, never again.

The One Who Tripped Away

HANNAH CARTIER

THE
PRODIGAL
COUPLE

giant striped umbrella shielded them from the fierce sun as their children's laughter resounded with the crash of the waves against the sand. Their coastal getaway had been the perfect retreat to let the kids have some fun outside, distracted by the ocean, while Hannah and Knox stole time to catch up on what was going on back home.

Sitting under the dry grass roof of a wooden cabana, Hannah relaxed on the soft, colorful cushions of the large, round, rattan chair she had snuggled herself in. Her phone screen displayed a crisp image of Serene, showing her newborn baby boy, Shiloh, in her arms. Nolan sat next to her on the hospital bed, kissing her temple, while Lily Red snuggled next to her, cooing at her little brother. It was one of the rare public images Nolan ever shared of his family on social media. Love and support from his fans flooded the comments — a lot of which expressed admiration not only for Nolan but also for Serene.

Nolan's caption said it all: *My inspiration. We're far from perfect, sure, but stop and take this image in. It's beauty in exchange for our life's ashes. They're so beautiful. This moment is beautiful. My Serene is beautiful, brave, talented, and strong. My music and life would be nowhere without moments like these and without a woman like her.*

Hannah's heart lifted even as she jotted down a comment of her own: *Congratulations! We can't wait to meet him once you guys decide to visit us here!*

Nolan and Serene had been through so much after that stupid article written about Serene, and it was great to see them come out of it thriving as a family unit, stronger than ever.

Hannah sent a quick message to Serene to express her love for them. Serene responded with photos of little Shiloh.

"Why the smile?" Knox arrived, his stride confident. He was feeling the aviator sunglasses he had on a little too much, but Hannah wasn't complaining, because it suited him well. He handed her the drink she had requested — a cold root beer float, perfect for the bright summer day.

Hannah handed him her phone so he could browse through the images Serene had sent over.

"Wow. What did they name him?" Knox asked.

"Shiloh. It means *tranquil*." Hannah took a long sip from her refreshing drink.

"Tranquil, the son of Serene." Knox grinned. "How appropriate. I'm glad they're getting peace after all the upheaval they went through."

"I'm glad Nolan's tour is over. He needs to be with his family right now," Hannah reiterated.

"Nova sent you a message." Knox returned her phone to her.

Hannah checked what Nova sent and found a link to the video of *Once Upon a Prodigal*. "Finally! They sent us the play!"

Knox squeezed himself into the chair next to her, a glass of soursop shake in his hand. "Let's watch it."

"Like now?"

"Why not? We'll have a few breaks to check on the kids, but Flair is with them. They'll be fine."

Hannah checked on Jaxon and Eliana burying their older brother, Cameron, in a pile of sand. Their family friend, Flair, was playing along with them, shoveling sand onto the pile.

She grinned and nodded. "Let's watch."

An hour and a half later, Hannah snuggled against Knox's embrace as the final song of the play reached its climax on the laptop Knox had over his lap. She sniffled as she shed a tear at the remembrance of her own prodigal son story. "It's so good," she said.

"Right? They definitely outdid themselves. This is an excellent production."

"And a great story. Especially knowing what a challenge it is for many of us — the prodigals and the other brothers of the church — to get along sometimes."

"The righteous and the reckless." Knox grinned. "Which one were you again? I remember how my righteousness struggled with how reckless you were."

"Oh, please." Hannah rolled her eyes. "I was a good girl through and through."

"We're like the walking cliché of the good guy falling in love with the bad girl." Knox nodded.

"That's not how it went, for sure."

"Yeah? Bad girl falling in love with the bad guy?"

"Pfft." Hannah grinned as she playfully smacked his cheek. "Fine. I'll give that to you, since we're all sinners in different ways."

He closed the laptop and set it aside before reclining on the wooden lounge chair he was on. Their focus was fixed on Cameron and Jaxon watching Flair braid their little sister's hair. "Which one do you think Cam and Jax will be? The prodigal son or the other brother?"

Hannah shrugged. "I'd like to say neither, but they would most likely end up being a bit of both. I really don't care as long as they find their way to the Father's embrace."

"They will. We won't stop fighting for them until they do."

There was a fierceness to the way Knox said that statement that made Hannah believe it to be true, and that was all she could ask for in the family that God had given them. That all five of them would become a kingdom family — part of a glorious whole — who would never stop contending for God's promises over their lives until God's kingdom would come and His would be done for their family, their loved ones, their cities, and their nations — on earth as it is in heaven.

- THE END -

THE ONE
WHO WROTE YOU
A NOTE

Thank you for reading *Prodigals Once*!

I almost didn't write this novel. At some point after writing *The One Who Wrote Away*, I wondered if there was more story to tell for this collection of books. I honestly just wanted to move on with a new series I've been excited to write, but as I continued writing the stories of the characters of Connect Church, the conviction grew in me that this book needed to be written. I needed to follow through with the vision God had placed in my heart for this set of books.

Mainly because *The Prodigal Ones Collection* is not just the story of imperfect, but saved, individuals finding the people they love. It's the story of a church, and I'd like to think it's not just the story of this one fictional church, but the story of my church and maybe even yours.

As someone who grew up in church, a lot of the themes explored in this book rings true to me. Throughout the writing of this collection of books, I often got messages from people telling me that they had their own "Mrs. P" in their churches. I would laugh and say I did too, but even through the writing of this novel, I saw so much of Rhoda Petersen in myself. The need to be understood, the feeling of being rejected because of not fitting a certain mold expected from people at church, being critical of others because of my own pain — those were themes I definitely resonated with, and I hope you were able to, as well.

I hope that even as you read about the stories of these characters and how God brought them to a point of healing and reconciliation, your heart has expanded towards people in your own church — both the prodigals and the other brothers. We all are in need of love and the church is a wonderful way for us to find the Father's love together, even as we ourselves may find it difficult to be brothers and sisters in Christ, even when we don't see eye to eye.

After all, whatever our upbringing, we were all prodigals once, and it is only by the Father's grace, love, and mercy that we are able to stand accepted among the beloved today. May we all learn to love more within the church as the day of our Lord's return draws near!

Shalom and Mabuhay!

joanna alonzo

THE **O**NE
WHO WROTE
THIS BOOK

Joanna Alonzo is an author of Christian fiction novels with grit, grace, and wonder. She has a Bachelor's Degree in Information Technology from St. Louis University, but her creative leanings drew her away from software development to a career in faith and uncertainty. Her homebase is La Trinidad Valley in the Philippines, but she wanders around too much to have a permanent residence. She is a fascinated apprentice to the Greatest Storyteller of all and loves to highlight His supernatural grace in her stories. She loves having coffee chats with people, but isn't a fan of them hugging her too much. Find out more about her and her work at **www.joannatheparadox.com**.